— WARRIOR PRINCESS BOOK TWO —

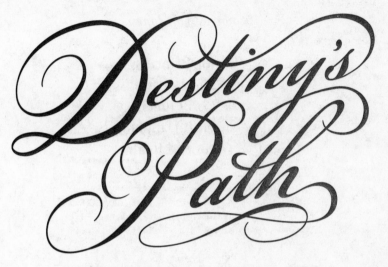

Destiny's Path

—— WARRIOR PRINCESS BOOK TWO ——

Frewin Jones

HARPER TEEN

An Imprint of HarperCollinsPublishers

HarperTeen is an imprint of HarperCollins Publishers.

Warrior Princess, Book Two: Destiny's Path
Copyright © 2009 by Working Partners Limited
Series created by Working Partners Limited
www.harperteen.com

Library of Congress Cataloging-in-Publication Data
Jones, Frewin.
     Destiny's path / Frewin Jones.
          p.   cm. — (Warrior princess ; bk. 2)
     Summary: When fifteen-year-old Princess Branwen
tries to turn away from her destiny as the one who will save
Wales from the Saxons, the Shining Ones send an owl in
the form of a young girl called Blodwedd to guide her and
Rhodri on the right path.
     ISBN 978-0-06-087146-8 (trade bdg.)
     [1. Fate and fatalism—Fiction. 2. Princesses—Fiction.
3. War—Fiction. 4. Magic—Fiction. 5. Saxons—Fiction.
6. Wales—History—To 1063—Fiction.] I. Title.
PZ7.J71Des   2009   2009014587
[Fic]—dc22   CIP
                                                              AC

Typography by Ray Shappell
09 10 11 12 13   CG/RRDB   10 9 8 7 6 5 4 3 2 1
❖
First Edition

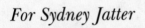

For Sydney Jatter

1

BRANWEN AP GRIFFITH pulled back on the reins and her weary horse gradually came to a halt, snorting softly and shaking its mane. She swayed in the saddle, her long black hair cascading down the sides of her face. Her limbs trembled with fatigue, and her whole body ached. Rhodri's horse went clopping on for another few paces through the trees before it, too, halted. The half-Saxon runaway looked back at her, his brow furrowed, his bright brown eyes sunken in his ashen face.

They had traveled far together, following the magical path of glittering light that had drawn Branwen from her home and all that she held dear, leading her toward the destiny prophesied for her by Rhiannon of the Spring, the ancient earth spirit.

Rhiannon of the Shining Ones.

Branwen had fought long and fiercely against the ominous visions of the woman in white, struggling to free herself of the destiny that gaped like a dragon's maw in front of her, a destiny that threatened to swallow her entire life.

But the foretelling would not be denied. What was it the bard had sung to Branwen—to her alone—in Prince Llew's Great Hall?

The Old Gods are sleepless this night
They watch and they wait
For the land is in peril once more
And the Shining Ones gather
To choose a weapon, to save the land
The Warrior
The Sword of Destiny
A worthy human to be their tool
Child of the far-seeing eye
Child of the strong limb
Child of the fleet foot
Child of the keen ear

Such a weight for a girl who had seen only fifteen summers. To be the savior of her land and of her people. To drive back the rising tide of bloodied Saxon iron. To be a warrior—a leader.

But Branwen had taken up the fearful burden and followed Rhiannon's path. And for friendship's sake, Rhodri had come with her.

She was clad in the chain-mail jerkin and the dark green cloak once worn by her brother Geraint. He no longer needed them—he'd been murdered by Saxons, his ashes blown away on the wind. His sword was at her hip now, and his round wooden shield, white with a rampant red dragon, hung from the saddle. The jerkin and cloak were flecked and stained with dried blood; the shield was notched and dented from the blows of swords and axes. These marks were the result of Branwen's fighting, not Geraint's. Dead too young, her brother had never met the Saxons in battle—had never grown to be the warrior he should have been.

Branwen and Rhodri had ridden through the starless gulf of the night, following the flickering silver path through dense forests and over ridge and bluff, spine and spur of the high hills. With the passing of time, as the mystical moonshine path had waned and its light had bled away into the ground, Branwen's hope and faith had faded with it, replaced by frustration and growing anger.

She turned and gazed back the way they had come.

The distant ridges of the hills were now showing sharp and black against a streak of dreary gray light.

Dawn was coming.

A dawn empty of all magic.

Where was Rhiannon?

Branwen gritted her teeth, a cold fire burning in her heart at the capricious nature of the Old Gods. If the Shining Ones offered her no guidance, no clear path to her destiny, then why should she not simply turn back and fight the Saxons in her own way—on the familiar ground of Cyffin Tir?

Back there, her home was burning. Her father lay dead on the battlefield. An image of the battle-weary, grieving face of her mother, Lady Alis, forced its way into Branwen's mind. She could almost hear the words her mother had spoken as Rhiannon's path had unreeled itself into the night.

This is the Old Magic, Branwen. It is wild and pitiless. Do not follow this path, Branwen. It will devour you!

And she remembered her own reply.

It won't, because I'm part of it. The Shining Ones have chosen me. They brought me here. They helped save us. Let me go to them, Mama. I'm doing this of my own free will.

A fresh wave of anger and disillusionment broke over Branwen as she thought of all she had left behind.

"Who am I, Rhodri?" she demanded as he dismounted and led his horse back to her. "Who do the Shining Ones *think* I am?"

"You are Princess Branwen, daughter of Prince Griffith and Lady Alis of Cyffin Tir," he replied, his face full of compassion as he gazed up at her. "And you're exhausted and ready to drop. We should rest now. For a while at least." He gave a faded smile. "Can your destiny wait a little while longer, Branwen?"

"What destiny?" hissed Branwen, her head swimming. "*Whose* destiny?" She struggled to remain upright in the saddle as she threw back her head, using the last of her energy to shout into the night. "Rhiannon! Where are you? What do you want of me?"

But the rugged hills and the shadowed forests made no reply.

"I will not go purposelessly into the west," said Branwen. "The shining path has vanished and Rhiannon hides herself from me!" Red anger flooded her mind. "Even her winged messenger has left us. Where is Fain? I will not follow blindly," she continued bitterly. "If this is all the Shining Ones offer, then I will turn my back on them!" A wave of absolute exhaustion struck her, and she lurched in the saddle. "I'm going back, Rhodri," she murmured. "Back to my own people. That way lies the hope for the future. That is the true path to my destiny. . . ." A black fist closed around her mind and Branwen felt herself falling.

She was vaguely aware of strong arms around her and Rhodri's friendly voice in her ear.

"Let destiny go for now," he said. "You need rest and you need food inside you. Just put your arm around my neck. Let's find a soft spot for you to lie down on."

She allowed herself to be carried, one muscular

arm under her knees and another behind her back. Her head lolled on Rhodri's shoulder. She could hear his rasping breath as he lowered her to the ground.

She opened her eyes and found herself half lying under a massive old oak tree, its gnarled and twisted roots rising on either side of her like knuckled fingers. Her nostrils were filled with the smell of damp earth and rich mold.

"You wait here," Rhodri said. "I have something we both need." Branwen watched him walk to where the two horses were standing. He led them to a tree and tethered their reins loosely to a low branch. He ungirdled the horses' saddles and drew them off, laying one on top of the other under the tree, then unwound a small sack from his saddle and came back with it hanging from his fist.

"What is it?" Branwen asked tiredly as he crouched at her side.

"Not much, but hopefully enough for our present needs," replied Rhodri. "A hunk of bread and some cheese and a small flask of milk that I managed to purloin from the stores before the battle started. A wise precaution against hunger, if I do say so myself. Providing for an empty belly was a lesson hard-learned on the lean and hungry roads of Brython."

Branwen smiled grimly. "This is more than Rhiannon has given us," she said.

"Ahhh, well . . . *Rhiannon*," murmured Rhodri, sitting cross-legged at her side and handing her a chunk of bread and a piece of ripe yellow cheese. He looked sideways at her. "You aren't really turning back, are you?"

She shook her head. "I don't know," she said. "But this is not what I expected when we began to follow the shining path. I imagined it would take us . . . I'm not sure . . . somewhere . . . *special*. A place where everything would be explained." She narrowed her eyes. "I should have known better. Rhiannon seems to delight in confusing me, in tormenting me with her riddles. . . ." She dug the heels of her hands into her eyes, trying to shake off the lethargy that dragged at her limbs and clouded her mind.

She looked at Rhodri, sitting quietly at her side, chewing the bread, his tawny hair hanging in his eyes.

"If you were me," she asked, "what would you do?"

"I would eat and drink and sleep," Rhodri replied. "Maybe things would seem clearer then. Who knows?" He looked at her with deep sympathy in his eyes. "I've never met anyone with a destiny before, Branwen. What do you think Rhiannon is playing at? Is this some kind of test?"

"Haven't I passed enough tests?" Branwen asked.

Surely she *had* done enough? She had heeded Rhiannon's terrible warning.

Your enemy comes creeping over the eastern hills even as we speak, cloaked in deception. Speed is your only ally now, Branwen. Fly as fast as you can, and you may still save many lives.

She had galloped her horse down the mountain like the west wind, desperate to thwart the Saxons' plans to kill her mother and father and to burn the hill-fort of Garth Milain. She had taken part in the battle that raged at the foot of the ancient mound. She had killed men. And then, despite her efforts, she had seen her father cut down and her home burned. The battle had been won—but at what cost!

Heed me, child: When the battle is done, for good or ill, you must make your choice: to follow your destiny, or to turn forever from it. But choose wisely, for your decision will seal the fate of thousands. This is my final foretelling.

And Branwen had made that decision. She had left her grieving warrior mother standing proud but haggard on the charnel house of the battlefield—had left her home, Garth Milain, in flames.

"Sleep," Rhodri said gently, his hand on her shoulder.

She slid sideways and rested her head in his lap, feeling the soft touch of his hand on her hair as the dead weight of her fatigue finally dragged her into slumber.

2

BLOOD. FLAMES. DARKNESS. Screaming chaos.
Savage voices shouting in an unknown
tongue.

Hel! Gastcwalu Hel!

Hetende Wotan!

Gehata! Tiw! Tiw!

Branwen's sword clashed against a thrusting spear
point, knocking it aside. The whirl and *thunk* of axes
rang in her ears. Around her, arrows fell, thudding
into flesh. There was the hideous, tearing crack of
iron cleaving bone. A sword slashed down toward
her neck, the agonizing impact knocking her to the
ground as her blood spurted hot and high.

Branwen awoke with a jolt into a pale dawn. She
knew she could not have been asleep for very long. It
was that mysterious time halfway between night and

day, with the sun still hidden under the horizon.

She sat up, unwilling to fall back into her gruesome dreams. Rhodri was leaning against the trunk of the old tree, his head drooping, his eyes closed. She hoped his dreams were sweeter than hers. She looked fondly at him, remembering their first meeting. She had been lost and alone in the fog-bound mountains. She had thought him a Saxon marauder and clouted him with a stick, only learning her mistake afterward. He wasn't an enemy, but he had spent most of his life in Saxon captivity.

Branwen learned much later that Rhiannon of the Spring had engineered their meeting, and they met again, in the forest outside Doeth Palas, the fortress village of Prince Llew of Bras Mynydd. For some unexplained reason, their fates were intertwined.

By all the saints, that seemed a whole lifetime away! But it was not—she and Rhodri had fled Doeth Palas only two nights past.

She rested against the tree once again, gazing up into the branches, watching the shifting patterns of the leaves in the breeze, oil-black against the cloudy sky.

A small, almost inaudible scuttering caught her attention. Then she felt the kiss of a tiny motion on her hand, which was lying in the brown leaf mold that gathered in heaps and drifts under the tree. Soft feet had pattered over her fingers. She tilted her head a little, trying to see.

It was a mouse—a small gray mouse. Branwen smiled, her heart lifted by the sight of the little beast as it nosed and plowed its way through the rot and debris between her hand and her leg, its whiskers twitching, its eyes bright and black and shining.

The mouse scampered around her hand and dived under a gnarled root, vanishing with a whisk of its tail. Branwen lifted her hand—slowly, slowly— and took a piece of bread, crumbling it in her palm. She rested her hand, palm upward, close to the root.

"Come on, little one," she whispered. "Come and feed."

She waited, listening to Rhodri's slow, deep breathing, her eyes on the dark gap under the root.

A pink nose appeared. Whiskers quivered. The mouse emerged, rising onto its haunches, sniffing the air. Could it smell the bread?

It moved closer, its body trembling. It lifted its forepaws onto her hand, sniffing the breadcrumbs.

That's it. Eat your fill, my friend. Have no fear.

But to her disappointment, the mouse turned and slipped away under the root again without eating.

You can trust me, little one. I won't harm you.

She heard furtive movements from beneath the root—more movement than could be explained by a single mouse. A family of mice, perhaps?

She smiled with joy to see the mouse appear again. And to her delight, the mouse was followed by five others, perfect little mice children, scuttling

11

and tumbling over the rotting leaves as they followed their mother's lead.

Biting her lip, Branwen hardly dared to breathe as the mother sprang onto her hand, leading the children to the food. Their feet tickled Branwen's skin as they gathered and fed in her bounteous palm.

Suddenly, a shape came sweeping down from the sky. Branwen's heart jumped. It was a grayish-brown shape, gliding phantom-soft on widespread wings. She gasped and jerked her head back as it pounced. Then it was gone again—a mouse clutched in either claw.

The other mice fled.

"No!" Branwen howled in distress, her whole body contracting in a spasm of horror, her hands beating the ground as the owl glided away into the trees.

Rhodri woke with a start. "Branwen? What?"

Branwen scrambled to her feet, running in pursuit of the gray predator.

She heard Rhodri chasing after her. He caught her arm and brought her to a halt.

"Branwen? What is it?" he asked.

"An owl took the baby mice," Branwen cried. "I gave them bread. They were on my hand."

Rhodri stared at her. His voice was low and calm. "Owls eat mice, Branwen," he told her. "It's what they do."

She turned on him, angry for a moment. "I know that," she said. "I'm not a fool!"

He paused before speaking. "So why has it upset you so much?"

She held her palm out toward his face. "They came because I offered them bread," she said. "They trusted me and the owl took them. It was my *fault*."

His brows knitted. "It's your fault that owls eat mice?" he said.

She glowered at him. "No. But I tempted the mice into the open," she said slowly. "If I hadn't been there, they would still be alive." She walked back to the tree, but couldn't bring herself to sit again beside that root.

She pointed down to where it lifted from the leaf mold. "Keep away from me, if you wish to live," she called.

"Branwen, stop," said Rhodri. "Try to sleep some more. Things will seem less bleak when the sun is up, I promise you."

"I can't sleep," said Branwen. She looked solemnly at him. "Rhiannon told me I was the Sword of Destiny—the Emerald Flame—the Bright Blade who would save the people of Brython from the Saxons." Her voice rose. "And yet I cannot keep even a handful of mice safe!"

Rhodri bit his lip, looking anxiously at her but not speaking.

Branwen's shoulders slumped. "Rhiannon was wrong," she said. "The Shining Ones chose badly." She took a deep breath. "Do you hear me, Rhiannon?

You chose the wrong person! Choose again. Choose better next time!"

She turned and walked toward the horses. Rhodri snatched up the bag that still held the remnants of their food and drink.

"You want to ride on?" he asked. "Without any real rest?"

"Ride, yes," said Branwen. "On? No!" She picked up her saddle and threw it over the horse's broad back.

Rhodri frowned at her. "You're going back?"

"I am." She stooped and fastened the saddle girth. "Back home where I belong." She stood up. "I'm not the great leader the Shining Ones need," she said. She pointed into the east. "We took the Saxons unawares and threw them back for a time. But you know the truth better than I do. You were Ironfist's servant. How big is the Saxon army that is encamped outside Chester?"

"At least ten times the number that came against Garth Milain," Rhodri said, his voice subdued. "Maybe more."

General Herewulf Ironfist was the strong right hand of the king of Northumbria—the hammer with which the Saxons intended to smash Brython. Shortly before Rhodri had escaped his long captivity, he had learned of Ironfist's plan to take Garth Milain by treachery. It was Rhodri's warning that had prevented a massacre. But even forewarned, the House

of Rhys had found the battle to be closely fought—
and dearly won.

"And what will be your ex-master's response to
the defeat of the host he sent against us?" Branwen
asked.

"He will be angry," Rhodri said. "He may decide
to send five times that number against Cyffin Tir to
make sure of a swift and complete victory."

Branwen nodded as she climbed into the saddle. Her weariness was gone now—she felt renewed
energy flowing through her, a new certainty. "And
if he comes, I will be where I *should* be—at my
mother's side. Shoulder to shoulder. Blade by blade.
Let Rhiannon find someone else to be Savior of
Brython."

Rhodri picked up his own saddle. "Then I will
come with you," he said. "Let the wrath of the Shining
Ones fall upon both our heads, if it must be so."

"No," said Branwen. "Your home lies in the west.
You have no mission in the east and I won't let you
put yourself in danger because of me."

"You rescued me from torture and certain death
in Doeth Palas," said Rhodri. "And I should repay
you by scurrying off into the west while you ride eastward? I think not!"

"You're a fool, then."

"Perhaps," said Rhodri. "But a grateful and faithful fool, I hope, and one who will never desert you."
He bent to tie the saddle girth under his horse. "And I

ride with you knowing that we will probably be killed at journey's end. Killed quickly if I'm lucky, because if Ironfist captures me alive . . ." He left the sentence unfinished. Then his face appeared over his horse's back. "Escaped servants are dealt with most harshly if recaptured," he said. "I have seen it once and have no wish to see it again—especially not if I am to be the victim. The Saxons have cruel and slow ways of punishing those who seek to defy them."

"Then you're twice the fool," Branwen said with a wry smile. "Come—saddle up. I would be home again as soon as possible." She looked around, feeling as though inhuman eyes might be watching her from the shadows under the trees. Had Rhiannon really departed, or was she merely standing back, watching with those terrible ice blue eyes—waiting, catlike, for Branwen to make a wrong move?

Rhodri had once said, *How do you run away from a goddess? Where can you hide?* Branwen had no answer to those questions, but the sooner she was down off the mountains and out of the forest, the safer she would feel. The thought of being once more with her mother was like a guiding light in the front of her mind. To the east, then—to Garth Milain and whatever else fate and the Saxon menace had in store for her.

Branwen watched as Rhodri clambered awkwardly into the saddle, then they both turned toward the brightening dawn. The light was gray and grainy still, but it was slowly climbing the sky and snuffing out the stars, and a hint of dusky green had begun to color the forested hills that tumbled before them.

Branwen clicked her tongue and nudged her heels into her horse's flanks. Rhodri followed dutifully behind as they rode into a wide clearing.

They had not gone more than a few paces across the open ground when a sudden gust of wind came swirling out of the west, lifting Branwen's hair and whipping it about her face.

She turned, her eyes narrowed against the wind as it came hissing through the trees, fluttering the leaves, bending the branches.

"It seems the very air is intent on helping us along our way," said Rhodri, his hair flying and his clothes flapping about him. "A good omen, perhaps?"

"But do you feel it?" Branwen called to him. "It's strange. It isn't cold."

It was not. Instead it came dashing through the trees as warm as blood and as relentless as a racing tide. The wind grew in intensity, filling the forest with creaking and rustling and groaning as the boughs of the trees were twisted and wrenched, their leaves quivering with a shrill sound like the swarming of bees.

It flung itself in among the rusted leaves of the past autumn, sending the debris of the forest floor whirling into the air so that Branwen and Rhodri had to cover their faces with their arms for fear of being blinded.

The horses snorted and whickered, their manes and tails torn by the wind, their eyes rolling in fear. It was all Branwen could do to keep her seat as the wind—scorching now—buffeted her and slapped her face with its hot hands. Her shield was torn from the saddle and went bowling across the forest floor.

Above her, shredded clouds flew across the sky; below her, the ground seethed in racing turmoil. Suddenly the forest vibrated to a deep, reverberating howl.

Branwen clung on grimly as the wind sought to tear her from her horse's back. She knew now that this was nothing natural. This was no wind of the world—this was something *other*. A warning—a lesson—a punishment! Beside her, Rhodri was hunched over in his saddle, his horse staggering.

Blindly, Branwen reached for her sword, drawing it and brandishing it defiantly in the air.

"I . . . do . . . not . . . fear . . . you!" she shouted, the wind throwing her words back into her throat. "Do . . . your . . . worst! I . . . *will* . . . go . . . home!" The maniacal wind dropped as suddenly as it had risen. The swirl and storm of dead leaves ebbed and fell away around them, and all became silent.

It was as if the forest and the mountains and the sky and the very ground beneath her feet were suddenly poised and listening.

Waiting.

Rhodri lifted his head, his mouth open, gasping.

"Is that all you have?" shouted Branwen, turning in the saddle, staring defiantly into the west and waving her sword above her head. "Is this what I should fear?"

"Branwen!" Rhodri's voice was urgent, ringing with alarm.

She turned to follow the line of his eyes.

The rushing air was thronged with owls on the attack.

3

B EFORE BRANWEN COULD react, the leading bird struck her, its brown wings wider than the span of her arms, its golden eyes circular and luminous and deadly. A tawny wing hit her hard in the face. Claws raked at her sword hand, drawing blood. She snatched her arm away, and her sword fell from her fingers.

She reeled in the saddle, aware of Rhodri shouting behind her. A second owl came at her, its sharp beak open, its talons stretching forward.

The other owls descended on them, twenty or more in number, enough to overwhelm them. Great owls were all around Branwen, circling, swooping, floating on the air, silent as ghosts. Wings struck her from all sides. Claws tore at her clothes and tangled in her hair.

Her horse reared up, neighing in fear and pawing at the air. She tumbled backward out of the saddle, striking the ground with such bone-jarring force that the breath was beaten out of her.

As she struggled to rise, she saw Rhodri vanish in a maelstrom of battering wings. Still the owls came plunging and plummeting down upon her, grabbing at her clothes and ripping her hair with their deadly claws and knife-sharp beaks, giving her no chance to get to her feet.

"Stop! Stop!" Branwen cried, striking out with her fists. But there were too many of them for her to fight. She huddled on the ground with her arms held up, trying to protect her face. The world was all owls, silent and terrible and huge. She was completely blinded by the bodies and wings of the mobbing birds.

Through the clamor of the attack, though, she heard hoofbeats fading rapidly away. Her horse, fleeing in fear. Next she heard Rhodri's horse—also galloping away! Was Rhodri leaving her, escaping from the talons and the ripping beaks? If only she could *see!* If only the birds would give her a moment's respite!

She was startled by the feel of a hand on her arm. Rhodri! He was on hands and knees, his head down to protect his eyes from the chaos of the wheeling birds.

And then, quite suddenly, the owls drew off,

leaving Branwen and Rhodri huddled together on the ground, gasping for breath.

The owls rose into the sky, their eyes glowing as they circled the small clearing, as though they were confident in the weakness of their prey and content now simply to patrol—to keep Branwen and Rhodri pinned down in the clearing.

Gathering her wits, Branwen moved her hand cautiously toward her slingshot. Her sword had fallen out of reach, and she was sure the birds would not allow her to make a grab for it. Perhaps if she let off a stone to show at least that she was capable of fighting back, they might hold back long enough for her and Rhodri to run for shelter under the trees.

She ducked as an owl swept close over her head.

Branwen loosened the pouch from her belt and picked out a stone. She kept low, bent over to hide her movements, bobbing her head every time one of the birds plunged toward her.

"Are you hurt?" Rhodri gasped, crouching low to the ground.

"No. Just a scratch on my hand."

"I'm not hurt either, but they could have caused much harm. Branwen—why are they doing this to us?"

"I don't know. I'm going to sling a stone at the largest one—I think it may be their leader. When I hit it, run to the trees if you can."

"Aim well, Branwen," warned Rhodri. "If you

anger them, you had better prove you can hurt them—otherwise I don't hold out much hope for our survival!"

"I won't miss!" Branwen said confidently. She was ready. The knuckle of stone was nestling in the fold of the slingshot.

A wing grazed her shoulder.

Now!

She rose, whirling the slingshot around her head. An owl flew at her face. She flipped her fingers open, and the stone sped straight and true at the owl that had first attacked her.

The stone struck the bird high on the wing. It gave a fearsome screech as it faltered in the air, then spiraled downward. Branwen dived to the ground, enclosing her face in her interlaced hands, as several owls came for her. Through the cage of her fingers, she saw the wounded owl tumble heavily down through the trees and into a dense pile of leaves. Its wings flapped, and then the bird became still.

Branwen lay facedown on the ground, hoping she had given Rhodri time to escape. She was certain the owls would not let her go—not after she had injured their leader.

Strangely, though, the flurry of wings was all around her but still she felt neither claw nor beak. Why were the owls not ripping at her?

And then, mere moments after the fallen owl stopped moving, the rest of the flock drew off, rising into the air and speeding away over the trees. Branwen heard their faint, eerie hooting as they departed.

Gasping, she pulled herself to her knees and dragged a hank of hair from her face, staring all around. The owls were gone.

She got to her feet. Rhodri had stopped halfway to the trees. He walked back to her, gazing around them uncomprehendingly.

"You did it," he said, his eyes wide. "You drove them off."

"I think I killed their leader," said Branwen, pointing to the heap of leaves that lay at the foot of an ancient, wrinkled oak tree. "I wish I had not needed to do that. It was a magnificent creature, and it did me little harm."

"Magnificent, maybe," Rhodri pointed out. "But did you see the size of those claws?"

"I did," said Branwen, sucking at her bloodied hand. The wounds were not deep or very painful—she had suffered worse injury in her childhood adventures in the forests. "But they only cut me once—to force me to drop my sword. It is very strange. I don't understand it." She looked into the sky. "And why did the others fly away like that?"

"I have no idea," said Rhodri. "And there is something else I do not understand." He pointed under the trees. Their two horses were standing in the shadows, calmly waiting as though the owl attack had never happened.

"This is not natural," Branwen said. "None of this is natural—but I do not know what it means." A movement caught her attention—the slightest of tremors in the pile of leaves where the owl lay hidden.

Could it be alive?

"Rhodri, you have some healing powers," Branwen said. "I think the owl may not be dead."

They ran across the clearing.

Rhodri reached the mound of dead leaves first and stooped over, carefully sifting through it with his fingers.

"It must be buried deeply," he murmured, raking more leaves aside.

"Be careful!"

A sudden burst of movement erupted from beneath the leaves, as though the injured bird was thrashing about in agony. Rhodri jerked back, startled.

"I cannot see it!" he gasped. He reached down again.

Suddenly, a slender human arm shot up out of the leaves, and a narrow, long-nailed hand caught his wrist in a fierce grip. Rhodri gave a shout of shock and alarm as he struggled to free himself, digging in with his heels and heaving backward.

A form rose out of the leafy mound—not a bird, but a slim-bodied girl about Branwen's age.

With a yelp, Rhodri finally managed to yank his arm free. He fell back, hands and feet scrabbling on the ground to get away. Branwen, too, took a step back, her fingers groping for a stone to fit into her slingshot, her eyes fixed on the girl.

She was shorter than Branwen by a full head, and her thin body was clad in a dappled brown garment that left her arms and legs bare. Her skin was the color of toasted wheat, and the long, curved nails of her hands were as white as stone. But it was her face that held Branwen's attention. Round and wide-cheeked, it was framed by a feathered fall of dark brown hair. In the center were two huge amber eyes, lustrous and deep, under sweeping brows. Although beautiful, it was a face filled with fury and pain.

One of the girl's hands came up to touch a small wound on her upper arm. An impossible suspicion dawned in Branwen's mind. The owl that she had hit with the stone was nowhere to be seen—and in its place was this strange girl—a girl with an injury on her arm! Could it be . . . ?

The girl's blood threaded down to the pile of leaves, dark as pitch. Her wide mouth opened and she let out a piercing, inhuman scream.

Rhodri scrambled to his feet, moving well away from the strange girl and closer to Branwen. The girl's mouth snapped closed. She lowered her head and stared balefully at them, her eyes burning like molten gold. Her whole body trembled.

Branwen's mouth was dry. She swallowed hard. There was something frightful about the glaring girl—something feral. But she had confronted the supernatural before, and she was resolved to show no fear before this uncanny stranger.

"I am Branwen ap Griffith," she said. "My companion's name is Rhodri. Will you give us your name?"

The girl's throat moved, and she opened her mouth as if she was trying to speak. But for a few moments only harsh, croaking sounds came from her.

"Don't be afraid," said Branwen. "We mean you no harm."

The girl coughed and put her hand to her throat.

"You're hurt," Rhodri said. "I can tend your wound if you will let me."

He took a tentative step toward the girl. She fixed her huge, owl's eyes on him, and her lips drew back in a snarl. One hand still rested at her wounded shoulder, but she raised the other like a claw.

Branwen watched her closely, seeing the blood that spun down from her injury, seeing the dangerous, predatory shine of her golden eyes.

"Rhodri, be wary," she said quietly. "Don't you see what she is?"

Rhodri glanced back at her. "What do you mean?"

"She is the owl I hit with my slingshot," said Branwen, hardly able to believe what she was saying—but knowing that it was true.

Rhodri halted in his tracks, staring at Branwen. "What . . . what do you mean? She can't be. Look at her—she's human."

The girl finally found her voice. "Not . . .

human . . . ," she croaked in a strange, throaty tone. "Not human . . . but cursed to appear so." She coughed again. "My name . . . is Blodwedd." Her uncanny gaze switched to Branwen. "You have injured me," she cried, stepping forward with the claw of her hand still lifted—toward Branwen's face. Branwen took an involuntary step backward. "You shall pay dearly for causing harm to the messenger of the Shining Ones!"

4

"STOP THAT NOW!" shouted Rhodri, stepping between Branwen and the enraged girl. "Enough violence!"

Blodwedd halted, trembling and glowering. She was so small—the top of her head hardly came as high as Rhodri's shoulder—but Branwen sensed a strength in her.

"Were you sent by Rhiannon?" asked Branwen, moving to one side, her slingshot ready.

"Not by her," said Blodwedd, her voice less ragged now, its tone lower and deeper. "Brother to her— brother of the woods. My Lord Govannon."

Govannon of the Wood. Branwen remembered the bard's song:

> *I sing of Rhiannon of the Spring*
> *The ageless water goddess, earth mother,*

> storm-calmer
> Of Govannon of the Wood
> He of the twelve points
> Stag-man of the deep forest, wise and
>   deadly
> Of Merion of the Stones
> Mountain crone, cave dweller, oracle, and
>   deceiver
> And of Caradoc of the North Wind
> Wild and free and dangerous and full of
>   treachery

Branwen's eyes narrowed. "What do you want of me?" she asked.

"I was sent to be your eyes and ears on your long journey," said the girl.

"But . . . you were one of the owls that attacked us!" Branwen said. "Are you a sorceress—able to change at will into the form of an owl?"

The pain of loss and grief filled Blodwedd's face. "Govannon called me to him," she said, almost as if speaking to herself. "He said, 'I have a great duty for you to perform, Blodwedd of the Far-seeing Eye. You must find the Warrior-Child. You must speak with her, guide her—she is lost and wandering in mind, spirit, and body.'" She flashed Branwen an angry look. "'She will not understand your speech,' he said to me. 'She has not the skill. You must shed your coat of downy feathers. You must forfeit the wide fields of the evening sky. You must become . . . like *her*.'"

"Govannon made you into a human?" gasped Rhodri.

The golden eyes fixed on him. "No," Blodwedd replied. "Lord Govannon gave me the ugly, spindly, naked body of a human to wear *for a time*—he did not make me human. This form is but a temporary cage." She gazed up over the treetops. "When my duty is done, my wings will be returned to me."

Branwen eyed her uneasily. "So I didn't . . . When I shot you, I didn't . . . turn you human somehow?"

"Dullard!" hissed Blodwedd. "What power do you have over such things?" She winced and clutched her arm. "I am in pain."

"You attacked us!" said Branwen. "I was defending myself."

"You were riding east," said Blodwedd. "You have no business in the east. I gathered my brothers and sisters to stop you." She looked past Branwen to where the sword still lay on the ground. "I tore your skin only to rid you of your weapon," she continued. "What other injury did I do you that you should set sharp stone to my flesh?"

"I thought you were going to kill us," said Branwen.

"No, not kill. Awaken!" said Blodwedd. "Lord Govannon said to me, 'The Warrior-Child is willful and wayward—stubborn as tree roots, fickle as thistledown on the wind. She must be taught to follow the straight path and to heed the call of her destiny.'"

Branwen trembled with anger, her fists clenching and the muscles in her chest tightening. "Go back to your master and tell him he can send all the winds of the world down on me—he can set wolves on me if he wishes—I will not do what he wants me to do. Let him kill me if he can—but I will die on the home-ward path."

Blodwedd frowned. "Stubborn as tree roots indeed!" she said. "You do not listen! I cannot give your message to Lord Govannon. I cannot return to the Great One until my duty is done, Warrior-Child. Until your destiny is fulfilled. That is *my* doom!"

"Then I pity you," said Branwen. "You had best learn to love your human shape, Blodwedd—because your master has given you a task that you will never fulfill." She turned and walked away, stooping to pick up her sword and heading to retrieve the two horses. She would continue her journey east.

"Rhodri?" she called back. "Are you coming?"

"Wait," called Rhodri.

Branwen paused, turning to look at him.

"She's hurt," Rhodri said mildly. "Let me tend her wound. It could fester and go bad. It won't take long."

"As you please," Branwen said grudgingly.

Rhodri turned to Blodwedd. "Will you let me help you?" he asked. "I can take the pain away."

Blodwedd stared at him for a long while, her inhuman eyes round and full of light. She nodded.

"Stay there, please," Rhodri urged her. "I won't be long."

He walked quickly to where Branwen was standing. He stood in front of her, looking unspeakingly into her face.

"What?" she snapped, irked by his silence.

"It seems it is *my* destiny to be forever tending the wounds that you cause," he said without reproach.

He didn't need to explain further. She knew what he meant. First it was his own leg, cut open in the fall she had caused by hitting him with a tree branch. Then the falcon Fain, injured by a stone in the forest outside Doeth Palas. And now this owl-girl.

"Will you fetch herbs for me to make a poultice?" Rhodri asked.

"I will," Branwen said. "Watch the horses while I am gone." She glanced at Blodwedd. "Don't let her scare them away. And don't trust her."

"Look for comfrey and wormwood," said Rhodri. "Lobelia is also good, if you can find it. Oh, and mullein. Do you know it?"

Branwen nodded. "A tall-stemmed herb with leaves covered in hairs," she said. "It has yellow flowers with five petals."

Rhodri smiled. "You make a fine herbalist's assistant," he said.

"My brother taught me much woodcraft before . . ."

33

She set her jaw. "I will not be long," she said. "Watch her!"

Branwen headed into the trees. The sooner she returned with the things Rhodri needed, the sooner he could deal with Govannon's messenger—and the sooner they could be on their way again.

It took Branwen longer than she'd hoped to gather the plants Rhodri had asked for, and the sun was two handbreadths above the eastern horizon when she finally came running back to the clearing with her hands full of leaves and flowers.

She had half feared to find Rhodri sprawled on the ground with his face raked by claws, and the owl-girl and the horses gone.

Instead, Blodwedd sat cross-legged in the middle of the clearing, gazing up wide-eyed and smiling at Rhodri, who was leaping around in front of her, waving his arms and clearly telling an exciting tale.

"A Saxon warrior was coming at us, bellowing like an angry bear," Rhodri was saying with high animation. "'*Gehata! Bana Hel!*' he shouted, which more or less means 'You're my enemy, and I will kill you and send you to the kingdom of the dead!' He had a sword as long as a roof beam, and I didn't have so much as a stick to defend myself with! 'Get behind me,' Branwen shouted, and I can tell you, I did just that! Then Branwen and Lady Alis stood side by side on the hill. And Lady Alis called out, 'Death to the

Saxons! Let us strike as one, my daughter!'" Rhodri slapped his hands together. "And in the blink of an eye, that Saxon devil's head was rolling down the hillside like an apple from the branch!"

Blodwedd laughed. "Ha! That is a good tale! And did you feast on his flesh thereafter?"

For a moment, Rhodri stared at her with his mouth half open. Then he blinked at her, swallowing hard. "Uh . . . *no* . . . ," he replied, his forehead wrinkling in distaste. "We don't do that."

"The Saxon had an ax, not a sword," said Branwen flatly, finding herself rather disturbed by Rhodri's friendly behavior toward the owl-girl. She walked up to him and thrust the leaves and flowers into his hands. "And my mother said, 'Strike as one! The throat! Strike as one!'" She glanced at Blodwedd, whose smile had vanished. "The rest is as Rhodri told you." She looked at him. "Where are the horses?"

"Perfectly safe and very close by," said Rhodri, his face a little red, although Branwen could not tell whether the coloring was from the exertions of his recent playacting or from embarrassment at being caught entertaining the strange owl-girl. "I found a small stream with fresh grass growing beside it. They will be comfortable there . . . till we are ready to leave."

"And how soon will that be?" Branwen asked.

"Soon," said Rhodri, giving her a slightly uneasy smile. "You did well," he said, looking at the spoils of her long search. "You even found lobelia. Splendid. All I need now is water and a couple of flat pounding stones." He looked at Branwen. "I have been telling Blodwedd about the battle at Garth Milain."

"So I heard," Branwen said dryly. She pointed at Blodwedd, keenly aware of the poisonous looks the owl-girl was giving her. "You know what she is!" she said to Rhodri, not caring that the girl could hear her. "You know why she was sent here! Tend her wound, by all means—but then we're going to leave her here and go to my mother—whether her *master* likes it or not."

Blodwedd got to her feet. "You must not go east," she said. "Your destiny lies elsewhere—in the place where the Saxon hawks circle above the house of the singing gulls."

"My destiny lies where I choose," snapped Branwen. "Come, Rhodri. Lead me to the stream. You may work your skills on her—then we two shall return to Cyffin Tir." She looked at Blodwedd. "And you will not follow us!"

"I must," said Blodwedd.

"Try and you will regret it," said Branwen, her hand moving to the hilt of her sword.

"What will you do?" Rhodri asked gently. "Kill her? This is not her fault, Branwen—you heard what she said. Blame Govannon if you need to blame anyone."

"Where is the stream?" Branwen asked dismissively.

"This way," Rhodri said, his voice subdued. "Blodwedd, come with us. I want to wash the wound first."

The stream was not far away. It ran through a narrow stone gully, splashing cold over boulders and mossy ridges. As Rhodri had said, the two horses were close by, their reins held under a large stone and their heads down as they grazed.

Rhodri got the owl-girl to squat at the side of the tumbling stream while he soaked some of the broad comfrey leaves and gently dabbed with them at the small wound in her shoulder.

"Good, good," he murmured, wiping the dried blood from her dark skin. "It's not as bad as I feared— and the wound is clean." He began to shred the plants, wetting them in the stream and laying them on a flat gray stone. "This is wormwood," he told her, holding up the fernlike leaves with their haze of fine white hair. "It will prevent the wound from becoming inflamed. And this," he said, showing her the spiral leaves on the long stem, "this is mullein, for the pain."

Branwen stood behind him, prepared to help if asked, but unwilling to volunteer. A strange anger, like a fist tightening, grew in her stomach as she listened to Rhodri explaining the uses of the herbs to the owl-girl. Why was Rhodri speaking to her as if she was a chance companion met upon the way? She was no such thing. She was a creature of the Old Gods.

She wasn't even human!

I have half a mind to draw my sword and swipe her head off as a warning to the Shining Ones to leave me be!

She eyed Blodwedd uncertainly. The owl-girl looked smaller than ever now, her slim legs folded up under her as she watched Rhodri pound the herbs and grind them to paste.

She looks more like a frog than an owl! A scrawny little frog squatting on a rock. Why is Rhodri taking so long?

"I need something to bind the poultice to your arm," Rhodri said. "I would rip a length of cloth from my clothes, but they're so ragged I'd be concerned they'd fall to pieces." Branwen felt a pang—he had said something very similar to her on their first meeting. She had torn the hem of her riding gown for him to bind the wound in his leg.

Not this time. Not for her!

Rhodri's head turned toward her. "Branwen? Do we have anything that we could use as a bandage?"

You're not getting a piece of my clothing!

"The bag you brought the food in, perhaps," she said aloud. "Do you want me to tear a length off?"

"Please."

Branwen stepped over the stones to the grassy place where the horses were grazing. Retrieving the bag, she ripped a length from the mouth and brought it back.

"Perfect," said Rhodri, taking it from her. He smiled at Blodwedd, his voice soft and coaxing. "It will feel cold and a little strange, but the pain will soon fade. I shall try not to bind it too tightly. You must tell me if it feels uncomfortable. Hold your arm out now."

Looking straight into his face, Blodwedd stretched out her arm. He leaned close to her. Scooping up the green paste in his fingers, he began very gently to press it against the wound. Spirals of green water ran down under her arm.

"It is cold," she murmured.

"I told you it would be. Now I'll tie the cloth around it. If it's too tight, say so."

A hot anger erupted in Branwen.

"Are you finished?" she snarled. "I'm leaving now—the day is wasting away while we linger here."

"Almost done," Rhodri answered patiently.

Blodwedd turned her uncanny eyes to Branwen. "You must continue west. Your home is safe, Warrior-Child."

"How do you know that?" Branwen spat.

"Lord Govannon has seen it," Blodwedd replied. "The Saxons will not ride upon the hill of fierce warriors—their wrath will fall elsewhere."

"I do not believe you," Branwen said. "You would say anything to make me do what you wish."

"I have no wishes," said Blodwedd. "And I cannot speak falsehoods. Lord Govannon sent me to tell only truths."

"And I am to trust these 'truths' you tell?" asked

Branwen angrily. "No! Say nothing more to me—I will not listen. Rhodri, I'm going to ready the horses." She looked hard at Blodwedd. "Can you run as fast as you once flew?" she asked. "Because if not, you will have a hard time keeping up with us."

She turned and walked up the rocky hill, heading back toward the horses. "Do as you please—follow or not. I do not care. I am done with you!"

There was a soft sound behind her—or rather, two sounds: a thud followed closely by a dull groan.

Branwen spun around. Blodwedd was running fast up the hill toward her, a rock clasped in one hand, her face ferocious, her eyes ablaze. Behind her, Rhodri was slumped on his side by the stream.

Branwen's fingers went instinctively to her slingshot, but Blodwedd was too swift for her. The owl-girl pounced on Branwen, the rock raised in her fist and ready to beat down on Branwen's head. Stumbling backward over the uneven terrain, Branwen grabbed at Blodwedd's raised arm, gripping her wrist.

She was so strong! It was all Branwen could do to hold her off.

They fell with Blodwedd on top, her lips drawn back in a fierce snarl, her teeth sharp and white.

Using all her strength, Branwen forced Blodwedd's arm sideways, jerking it down so that the back of her hand cracked against a rock.

Blodwedd hissed with pain as the stone was knocked from her fingers. Branwen lurched, trying

40

to throw the owl-girl off. But Blodwedd wrested her arm free, forcing her legs up so that she was sitting astride Branwen's chest, her knees pinning Branwen's arms with a strength that seemed almost impossible in so slight a frame.

Blodwedd's claw-thin hands gripped either side of Branwen's head, holding her in an unbreakable grip. The owl-girl reared up over her, bringing her head down, their faces so close that their noses almost touched.

"Stubborn and willful, indeed!" Blodwedd hissed. "But you *will* listen! You *will* look!"

Branwen fought desperately to get free, wrenching her head from side to side in the viselike grip of the owl-girl's hands. But she could not loose herself.

"Look into my eyes!" shouted Blodwedd, her breath hot on Branwen's face. "See! See what is to come!"

Against her will, Branwen found herself staring into those two radiant eyes, and as she looked, the unearthly eyes grew and deepened until the whole world was drawn into them and Branwen lost herself in a blazing golden light.

5

B RANWEN WAS FLYING. Above her, the wide sky went on forever. Below her, dark and forested mountains wheeled slowly away, cut by canyons and chasms, threaded by racing rivers and falls, punctuated by jutting peaks and crests and pinnacles of stone.

She turned toward the rising sun. Instinctively, she tried to draw her gaze away from that shimmering white light, but could not. Then she found she could look into the sun—into its very burning heart—and be neither dazzled nor blinded.

The mountains fell away beneath her, descending into foothills cloaked in oak and ash and elm. She swooped down, following the plunge of the land. Ahead, a rugged, wild countryside stretched away in heaths and moorlands into a distant landscape of cliffs and bluffs and hazy blue distances.

She knew what she was seeing. She was flying over her homeland—over the long, narrow cantref of Cyffin Tir. There, in the east where the horizon blurred, lay the Saxon stronghold of Chester—no more than a dark smudge on the very edge of sight.

Herewulf Ironfist was camped there with his army—a Saxon serpent preparing to uncoil and fall upon the ancient kingdom of Powys, its iron fangs filled with venom.

The ground rushed up. Smoke was rising, thin and pale in the morning light. A tumulus thrust up out of the flat grasslands—a lone hump of hill with a blackened crown burning on its brow.

Centuries upon centuries ago—so long ago that Branwen could not hold the span of years in her mind—ancient peoples had labored to build that lonely mound. The ground occasionally offered up curious treasures: flints cut into arrowheads, delicate as dragonfly wings, sharp as thorns. Rounded stones etched with strange markings. Beads of green or blue or yellow. Puzzling glimpses of a people who had lived once on this land, who had built the hill that later became the fortified village of Garth Milain.

But the lofty citadel was no more. Its tall fence of wooden stakes was burned and broken, its huts and houses were destroyed—even the Great Hall with its high walls of seasoned timber and its long, thatched roof was now no more than a smoldering, broken-backed hulk.

People were coming and going along the steep ramp that led to the hilltop, salvaging what goods they could from the ruin, bringing down the bodies of the dead. And even from such a height, Branwen could see her mother striding through the mayhem of the battle's aftermath—striving to bring order to the chaos, marshaling her warriors, and organizing the burial of the dead. It was clear that she was preparing what defenses she could against further attack.

Tears fell from Branwen's eyes, spinning and shining like jewels in the treacherous sunlight.

But she was not allowed to linger over her heartbreak. She flew onward into the east, passing beyond the bounds of her homeland, winging into the dark land of Mercia where the Saxons held sway.

And here she saw wonders . . . and horrors.

The town of Chester sprawled beneath her, teeming with people, far more people than lived in Garth Milain, more even than dwelt in the great hill-fort of Doeth Palas, largest of the fortified villages in the kingdom of Powys. The people swarmed like ants among the houses, forging iron for swords and axes, training horses for battle, baking bread to fill the bellies of their savage warriors.

There, like a black stain on the land, she saw the great encampment of Horsa Herewulf Ironfist, the bane of Brython, the hammer of the east.

She dreaded seeing Saxon warriors pouring

westward from the palisaded camp—new forces sent to annihilate what was left of the army of Cyffin Tir. But the way west was clear of movement. Branwen gave a gasp of relief—Ironfist was not sending a second force to crush her homeland. Instead, a long line of soldiers and horsemen were wending their way northwest, their spearheads and axes and helmets glinting cold in the morning light.

You see? A low, husky voice whispered close to her ear. The owl-girl's voice. *They come not to grind Garth Milain under their heel. They have other purposes. And see now what they intend! See what fate awaits those upon whom you would turn your back. . . .*

The world spun like a golden wheel, and Branwen found herself standing on a rocky seashore, a shrill north wind smarting in her eyes and a sickly, horrible smell in her nostrils. She stood among a host of fallen warriors. She winced at the sight of bloodied faces and hewn limbs, of butchered men and horses, of cracked shields and dented helmets and shattered swords. A young man stared unseeing into the sky, eyes wide and empty, blood matted thick in his hair.

A slaughter had taken place here—and she could see from the emblems on the shields and the tattered remnants of once-proud banners that these were—that they *had been*—men of Powys.

She smelled smoke and turned. A fortress lay on a cliff overlooking the pounding sea, its high wall of drystone washed to ash-gray in the pitiless sunlight.

Its gates were broken apart. Fire raged in the open heart of the fortress, consuming the thatched roofs of hut and hall, blackening the timbers and flooding the sky with thick dark smoke. Saxon pennants flew in the wind. Saxon ships clove the sea.

A black-bearded Saxon chieftain sat in the saddle of a great black stallion, his arm raised, a grisly trophy hanging from his fingers.

A severed head.

The Saxon fist clutched the head by its light brown hair, which was clotted with blood. Branwen tried to look away, wanting rid of this abominable vision. But against her will she was drawn closer, and she found that her eyes would not close.

Her mind fought to deny what she was seeing—to break the dreadful power of the images searing her mind.

She knew that face—those blank, dead eyes had once flashed with wit and intelligence. The slender, handsome face, now bruised and beaten. The hanging jaw where a knowing smile had once played.

It was Iwan ap Madoc, from the court of Prince Llew—a charming, intriguing, but untrustworthy young man whom Branwen had met in Doeth Palas.

Iwan's lifeless eyes turned to her, and an eerie light came into them.

The dead lips moved. "So, here you are at last, Branwen." The voice was Iwan's, but it was toneless, hollow, dead. "You have arrived too late, as you can see—the west is lost. You cheated your destiny well, my friend—the war is played out and the Saxons are in the ascendancy. All is done." The voice sighed like the sea. "All . . . is . . . done. . . ."

"No!" Branwen shouted. "I never wanted this! I didn't know! Forgive me, Iwan—I didn't know!"

But Iwan's face was lost in a vortex of golden light.

6

THE WHEEL OF burning light divided and pulled back, and suddenly Branwen was staring up into Blodwedd's two golden eyes. She felt the owl-girl's weight on her chest, stifling her breath—the sharp points of Blodwedd's knees on her arms, the cruel grip on either side of her face.

"Get off me!" Branwen heaved, and Blodwedd sprang away, bounding feather-light onto a boulder. She crouched there, watching Branwen through the curtain of her hair, her fingers gripping the boulder's edge like claws.

Branwen struggled to stand. She managed to get to her knees, but a wave of dizziness pinned her there. She knelt, panting, and waited for her head to stop spinning.

"What did you do to me?" she shouted as the

world slithered and writhed around her.

"I showed you the future that will be forged if you forswear your true calling," said Blodwedd. She angled her mouth in a sharp grin. "Did you like what you saw?"

"Lies!" shouted Branwen, pulling herself upright again. "It was all lies!"

A look of disdain crossed Blodwedd's face. "I do not lie," she said. "I fly. I hunt. I eat. I watch. I sleep. I do not lie."

Suddenly Branwen remembered Rhodri. She stared down toward the stream. He was sitting up, leaning heavily on one arm, rubbing his head with his other hand.

"Why did you hit him?" raged Branwen. "He was trying to *help* you!"

"I like him. He has an open and kindly heart," Blodwedd said, looking down at Rhodri. "That is why I hit him only gently."

"You didn't need to hit him at all!"

"He would have tried to stop me," Blodwedd said with a shrug of her thin shoulders. "You needed to see what a threadbare cloth your selfishness would weave. Warp and weft—blood and death." She cocked her head, her eyes on Branwen again. "If you go to the east, you will shape for yourself a necklace of corpses that will bow your head down to the bowels of Annwn!"

"Be silent!" Branwen shouted. "I won't listen to

you anymore." She ran unsteadily down the hill. "Rhodri? Rhodri, are you all right?"

He was on his feet now, grimacing and holding his head. "She hit me!" he gasped. "I turned away for a moment and she hit me."

Blodwedd came racing down the hill, her feet as light as a breeze as she leaped from rock to rock. "Rhodri, forgive me," she called. "I did not mean you harm. I had business with the Warrior-Child. I could not let you stop me with your great heart and your strong muscles."

Rhodri winced and frowned at her.

"I shall make amends," said Blodwedd. "I shall gather wildflowers and roots and herbs for you to make a soothing mash as you did for my arm. Tell me what you need to ease your pain."

"There's no need," said Rhodri, the anger draining from his voice. "It's not that bad. The skin's not even broken. But please don't do it again!" He looked at Branwen. "What business did she have with you?"

"She wanted to show me phantoms," said Branwen. "Ghosts of the pretended future to make me change my mind about going home."

"Ghosts, you say? What kind of ghosts?"

"A Saxon army heading away north," Branwen said sullenly. "A battlefield strewn with the dead of Brython. A citadel broken and burning." She narrowed her eyes, the memory still too fresh in her mind. "Iwan ap Madoc's severed head—speaking to me from beyond death."

"And what did he have to say?" Rhodri asked quietly.

"Yes," murmured Blodwedd, her eyes filled with a knowing light. "Tell him the words of the dead."

"He . . . he told me his death was . . . was my fault," said Branwen haltingly. "But what does it matter what he said? It was not Iwan—it was just a trick."

"Are you sure?" murmured Rhodri. "In your heart—are you sure it was a trick?"

"Yes!" Branwen glared at him. "*Yes!*"

His eyes were troubled. "But, what if . . ."

"No!" Branwen shouted, uncertainty and anger boiling up in her. "Leave me alone. Just leave me alone! It's too much. I cannot bear it!"

She turned frantically and ran off into the trees, desperate to escape the confusion that was threatening to overwhelm her.

She had not gone far when she heard behind her a flutter of wings and a familiar "*caw!*"

She stumbled to a halt, holding her breath, her heart thumping, her ears straining.

"*Caw!*"

She turned. "Fain!"

The falcon was perched on a rock among the trees, watching her intently, his clever eyes bright and black. Something shone between his claws, flashing with reflected sunlight.

"*Caw!*"

"Why did you leave me?" Branwen asked. "I thought you would guide me, but you flew away, and the shining path disappeared and I was lost in the forest. *Why*?"

She walked slowly toward him.

The thing at the falcon's feet was a knife—a hunting knife with a riveted handle of brown bone, worn smooth by generations of use.

It was the knife Branwen had held when she had stood vigil over Geraint's dead body in Bevan's field. The knife she had taken from among his belongings when she left Garth Milain. The knife that she had thrown in her anger and frustration at Rhiannon of the Spring. The knife the Shining One had turned to a hail of silver drops. But how . . . ?

Fain bobbed his head and stepped aside. Branwen picked up the knife. Oh, but the worn handle felt so familiar in her hand! Geraint's knife—made whole again and returned to her.

She took a deep breath. "Rhiannon!" she shouted.

The ghost of a voice was carried to her like a scent on the breeze.

My part is done, Warrior-Child. Let others now light your path. Have faith. The stronger the tree, the fiercer the storm it can withstand. The brighter the flame, the darker the night. The truer the sword, the stronger the foe. Fare you well, child of the far-seeing eye, child of the strong limb, child of the fleet foot, child of the keen ear. . . . Fare you well. . . .

Branwen stood still for a long time, her arms hanging heavy at her sides. She held Geraint's knife loosely in her fingers. Her heart ached and her throat was so tight that she could hardly swallow.

"Caw!"

Fain's voice was sharp and insistent.

She looked down at the bird. He was watching her with an impatient glint in his eye. "The vision was true," she said. "If I go home, terrible things will happen in Powys. The Saxons will come to spread death and destruction among my people." She frowned at the bird. "I must fight my doubt as though it were a Saxon enemy. In many ways, it is. . . ."

Her destiny towered ahead of her like a mountain impossible to climb, its lofty peak soaring far beyond the extent of her vision. In her thoughts were the words she dared not speak aloud.

I shall follow their path, although I cannot see what end it leads toward. Even if I arrive at this end only to discover that I am destiny's fool.

She slipped Geraint's knife into her belt and began to walk back to the clearing. Rhodri and the owl-girl would be waiting for her.

7

BRANWEN FOUND RHODRI and Blodwedd together by the stream. He was kneeling while the owl-girl dabbed at his bowed head with wetted mullein leaves. *Making amends for hitting him,* Branwen thought. *And knowing Rhodri's good heart, it will probably be enough.*

As she approached them, Fain cut through the air and swooped down in a long curve, his wings cupping his frame as he came to rest in the grass slightly behind her. The falcon stared hard at Blodwedd, moving uneasily from foot to foot and ruffling his feathers.

"Where would you have me go?" Branwen asked, her eyes on Blodwedd.

They looked up at her as she spoke.

Rhodri glanced from Branwen to the falcon. He

smiled but did not speak.

Blodwedd glowered at her. "The Saxon hawks circle above the place of singing gulls," she said. "There you must go, and there you must tear them from the sky before their feasting begins."

"I don't know what you mean," said Branwen. "Where is the place of singing gulls?" She recalled the burning fortress of her vision. "Is it on the coast? Is it north of here?"

"Singing gulls," said Rhodri. "That would be *Gwylan Canu* in the old language." He looked at Branwen. "Do you know of such a place?"

"I do," said Branwen in surprise. "It is upon the north coast of Powys—it is the citadel of the House of Puw. Its lord is Madoc ap Rhain—Iwan's father."

Rhodri gave a low whistle. "Well, now—that would explain why Iwan spoke to you in your vision. It was *his* home that you saw in flames, and his people who were slaughtered."

"It would be a tempting prize for the Saxons," said Branwen. "Gwylan Canu stands in the gap between the mountains and the sea. If the citadel of the House of Puw could be taken, there would be nothing to stop the Saxons from sweeping west into the cantref of Prince Llew. And if that happened, what hope would there be for Powys or Gwynedd or all the north of Brython?"

"And once the Saxon cock sits crowing his triumph in the north, what will prevent him from gathering his armies and strutting southward?" said Rhodri. "Ironfist has an insatiable appetite for war, Branwen, and King Oswald will not sleep easy until all Brython is under his thumb."

Branwen glared at Blodwedd. "You said Govannon sent you to be my eyes and ears. So, do what you were sent to do—show me the way and tell me what I should do when I get there."

Blodwedd's large eyes blinked as she looked into Branwen's face, puzzled. "I have told you where to go and what you must do," she said. "I do not know *how* you are to travel to meet your destiny, nor how you should fulfill it when you reach journey's end."

"Then go back to your master and tell him to send me a guide who *does* know," Branwen snapped. She turned about, staring into the trees. "Govannon? Do you hear me? I will do as you ask—but I don't know *how*!"

She waited, peering under the branches, listening for a voice from the forest gloaming. The wind sighed. The stream chimed and sang. The sun continued to rise in a clear blue sky. No voice came from the woods.

"I think he has sent you all the help you are going to get, Branwen," Rhodri said. "The rest is up to you." He gazed northward. "How far is it to the sea?"

As though in response, Fain let out a series of shrill, carping calls.

Blodwedd watched him with her head cocked

to one side. "Not far, as the falcon's wing makes it," she said. "But there are no roads northward over the mountains. You must make your way down to the western lowlands and follow clearer paths."

"You understand his speech?" Rhodri asked in amazement.

"I do," Blodwedd replied.

Branwen turned to Rhodri. "So, we should go down into Bras Mynydd and then head north." She frowned. "A curious troop we'll look, too—you in your beggar's rags and I in my brother's battle-gear." She glanced at Blodwedd. "And *her*."

"What if we meet the prince's search parties on the road?" asked Rhodri. "They will not have stopped looking for us yet, and I've no wish to be dragged, bound and gagged, back to a certain death in Doeth Palas."

"We will be wary," Branwen assured him.

But Rhodri had good cause for his fear. Only a brief time had passed since he had been captured in the woods outside Prince Llew's citadel and condemned as a Saxon spy. Had Branwen not rescued him, his broken body would be hanging from the gallows by now. But Branwen's actions had made them fugitives, and capture by Prince Llew's soldiers would be the end of them both.

Branwen mounted up and flicked the horse's reins to get it moving. Rhodri's horse followed, with Rhodri as awkward as ever in the saddle. The owl-girl was seated at his back, her arms around his waist and her eyes uneasy.

Rhodri's words ran through Branwen's mind as they rode, sounding more and more ominous as they moved through the mountain forest and drew ever nearer to the cantref of Brys Mynydd.

What if we meet the prince's search parties on the road?

Rhiannon's sparkling path had led them into the mountains and left them in the wild, deep in an unknown forest, far from hearth and home and the well-trodden roadways of man. Even if she could have found the usual route down into the west, Branwen knew she could not risk taking it. If Prince Llew's soldiers came over the mountains, they would surely choose High Saddle Way, and at all costs she wanted to avoid meeting armed men on the high passes. She knew of no other safe pathways through the rearing peaks, but a way off these mountains had to be found, perilous as that venture might prove to be.

The whole day was spent seeking a safe corridor between crags and pinnacles of naked rock. Fain flew on ahead, never straying far out of sight and often returning to guide them away from precipitous falls—crumbling slopes where a single misplaced hoof could set the whole hillside moving in a deadly river of rubble and scree.

At last they came over the highmost ridges. As the

afternoon bled away, they began to make their way down the forested slopes to the less perilous foothills and valleys.

They made camp in a narrow defile cut by a racing river of white water. Alder trees reached out overhead, and the air was filled with the soft drone of bees. With tinder and flint, Branwen kindled a small fire; the midsummer evening was not cold, but the dancing flames were cheering in the wilderness, and the crackling, leaping fire would warn preda-tory animals to stay clear. The mountains were full of wolves, and although they seldom attacked people in the food-rich summer months, it was wise to take precautions.

Fain perched on a low branch close by. He sat silently, only half seen, a shadow among the leaves. His head was tucked into his feathers, and his black eyes were unblinking. Branwen was oddly comforted by his presence. Although he, too, was a messenger from the Shining Ones, he did not disturb her half so much as did the owl-girl.

There she was—Blodwedd the owl-girl, squat-ting huddled at the fire by Rhodri's side as he went through their meager provisions. Her arms were wrapped around her shins, her chin resting on her pointed knees, and the flames reflected in her wary eyes. There was something unnatural in her pose, as though she did not entirely know how to use her human body.

"Not much to fill our bellies after such a hard day," Rhodri observed with a sigh, laying out a small remnant of cheese and a piece of bread no bigger than a clenched fist. He upended the earthenware flask. "No milk, either."

"We have water enough to hand," said Branwen, nodding toward the gushing stream. "Give me a few moments to rest, and then I will see if I can bring down something for us to eat." She had in mind hunting with her slingshot for a hare or a small wild boar—or even a young deer, if luck was with her.

"There is no need," said Blodwedd. "I will find food for us." Her eyes shone in the firelight. "Fresh meat. A shrew, perhaps, or a plump mole." Her lips curled in a pointed smile. "They make good eating while the blood runs warm."

Branwen looked at her in revulsion.

"We can't eat raw meat, Blodwedd," Rhodri said gently. "And I'm not sure we'd like the taste of moles and shrews even if we could."

Blodwedd's eyebrows knitted. "Would a young hare be to your liking?" she asked him.

She follows him around like a newborn puppy. Things were better when it was just the two of us. Look at those big eyes of hers, gazing up at him as if the sun rose in his face!

"A young hare would suit us very well," said Rhodri. "The last hot meal we ate was roast hare. Branwen killed it with her slingshot."

"The Warrior-Child hunts with stones and

leather," Blodwedd said, getting to her feet. "I need only my hands and my teeth. I shall not be long."

"Be careful," Rhodri said. "Your wound is still fresh."

"Have no fear," said Blodwedd, resting her hand for a moment on the bandage. "We heal swiftly or not at all." So saying, she bounded off into the trees, her footfalls silent as the night breeze.

Rhodri glanced sideways at Branwen. "Roast hare, eh?" he said. "I can almost taste the juice on my fingers already."

Branwen turned away from him and stared into the fire without speaking.

"Why do you dislike her so much?" Rhodri asked.

"I don't want to talk about her," Branwen replied. "We need to discuss what we are to do next. Besides go north and tear the 'Saxon hawks' out of the sky."

"If the lord of Gwylan Canu is given warning of the Saxon attack, he will be able to close the gates and defend his citadel," said Rhodri. "Perhaps that is all Govannon wants you to do—warn them of the coming danger."

"I have already learned how little weight people give to my words," said Branwen. "When I tried to tell Prince Llew about the attack that was coming to Garth Milain, he ignored me." Bitterness laced her voice. She looked at Rhodri as a new thought came to her. "And what if Prince Llew's soldiers have already been to Gwylan Canu to warn them about *us*?" she continued. "What if we are thrown into chains the moment we show ourselves? What if their only response is to send us to Doeth Palas to be hanged?"

Rhodri raised an eyebrow. "Do you think it is your ultimate destiny to swing alongside me on Prince Llew's gallows pole?" he asked. "I doubt that very much! But you may be right—the straight road to Gwylan Canu may not be our best hope." He shot her a sudden glance. "What was the last thing that Iwan ap Madoc said to you before you gagged him?"

"I don't remember exactly—he asked me to leave his sword. He said it had been passed down from his great-grandfather, or something of that sort. What does that matter?"

"I heard something else that he said," Rhodri murmured. "He said—'You're going to have an interesting life, Branwen! I wish I could have shared it.' Do you remember that?"

"Yes. I remember."

"I think perhaps you have still one friend in Doeth Palas."

Branwen gave a harsh laugh. "Iwan ap Madoc was never my friend. If I had a friend at all, it was Gavan ap Huw—but he will think, as everyone else does, that I betrayed him when I set you free." She narrowed her eyes as she thought of the grizzled old warrior who had briefly been her confederate and her tutor in the ways of warfare. It pained her to know that he must hate her now, but there was nothing to be done about it.

"I disagree. I think we should not go to Gwylan Canu," Rhodri replied. "I think we should make our way with all the stealth we can across Bras Mynydd and tell our tale to Iwan ap Madoc."

"Go to Doeth Palas?" exclaimed Branwen. "Are you moonstruck?"

"If Iwan can be convinced that you're telling the truth, he will surely go to Prince Llew and have him send reinforcements to Gwylan Canu," said Rhodri. "A fast rider could be sent ahead to warn the lord of the citadel to bolt his gates and hold fast till the prince's warriors arrive. Ironfist will be thwarted—where he hoped to fall upon an unprepared foe, he will find all in readiness for his coming. The citadel will be saved, and you will have fulfilled the task Govannon has given you."

Branwen looked at him. "And if the saints watched over us and we made our way to Doeth Palas without being hunted down, what then?" she asked. "Our faces are known there, Rhodri. We would not get past the gates without being recognized. We'll need disguises."

"Yes! Good thinking," said Rhodri. "A dress and wimple for you, so that your hunting leathers are hidden and you can cover your head. And a cloak and cowl for me—and perhaps mud rubbed into my hair to darken it. That way we could slip in among the everyday market crowd and go unnoticed."

"And your new friend?" asked Branwen. "Have you looked closely into her eyes, Rhodri? Govannon may have given her a human shape, but there are no *whites* to her eyes. She will be spotted immediately." She shook her head. "And even if I agreed with your plan, where are we to find these clothes? We have nothing to trade for them, even if we dared show ourselves."

Rhodri stared pensively into the flames but did not reply.

Branwen sighed. "I am not even convinced that Iwan would . . ."

Her words were broken by the sudden sound of choking and gagging. A slender figure came stumbling out into the firelight. It was Blodwedd, but her face was a deep red and her strange eyes were bulging. She took a few staggering steps forward and then fell to her knees, her hands clutching at her throat.

8

BLODWEDD TUMBLED TO the ground and rolled onto her side, her knees up to her chest, her hands clawing at her neck. Hideous strangling noises came from her throat. It sounded as if she were choking to death.

Rhodri sprang up and ran to her side.

"What is it?" gasped Branwen, scrambling up in Rhodri's wake. "What's happening to her?"

"I don't know!"

Rhodri dropped to his knees, leaning close over the stricken owl-girl, trying to hold her steady as her bare feet kicked in the dirt.

"Does she need water?" cried Branwen.

"Wait!" he said. "I think I have it!"

Branwen saw his hand move to Blodwedd's mouth, but his shoulder covered what he did next. After a moment or two, Rhodri pulled his hand away and Branwen saw him throw something small and dark into the grass.

Blodwedd let out a scream then sat up, coughing and gasping for breath.

"It's all right," Rhodri said gently, holding her shaking shoulders between his hands. "You're safe now."

Blodwedd looked up at him, her face still ruddy, her eyes streaming tears.

"I could not . . . swallow . . . ," she panted. "Could not . . . breathe. . . ."

"What did you do?" Branwen asked Rhodri. "What was that thing you took out of her mouth?"

"I'm not sure," Rhodri responded. "A small animal of some kind. A vole, maybe."

Branwen stared at him in disgust. *What?*

Rhodri looked up at her. "She was trying to swallow it whole," he said. "Her throat wasn't wide enough. It got stuck. She's fine now."

"Swallow it whole?" she asked, revolted.

"Up until today she was an owl!" he snapped. "Owls swallow their food whole, then later cough up the parts they don't want, as pellets. Skin and fur and bones. She doesn't know how else to eat."

Blodwedd began to breathe more easily, her cheeks returning to their usual color, her brittle body relaxing a little.

"I shall starve!" she gasped, pulling away from

Rhodri. She turned her face to the sky, her voice rising to a howl. "Lord Govannon! Release me from this bondage! I cannot eat! I cannot fly! It is too cruel!"

She began to sob and put her hands over her eyes, her shoulders jerking. Rhodri put an arm around her and held her against him.

"It will be all right," he said to her. "I will teach you to eat as humans do. You won't starve. I won't let you starve."

There was a rustle in the leaves. Fain came swooping down on slate gray wings. He snatched up the small, dead animal from the grass and went winging back into the trees with it dangling from his claws. Blodwedd would not benefit from her kill, but the morsel would not be wasted.

Branwen turned away and walked back to the fire. She was torn between being sickened by Blodwedd and feeling the first inklings of pity for the poor creature. If only she had remained an owl, she would not be so difficult to come to terms with. Branwen knew that at this very moment Fain's curved beak would be pecking and ripping at warm flesh—she had no problem with that. That was nature. But Blodwedd? There was something demonic about her. She was not to blame, however—neither for Branwen's problems nor for what Govannon of the Wood had done to her. She was as much a cat's-paw as Branwen was herself. But all the same . . .

Branwen picked up the jug that had held the

milk—it was now half full of fresh, cool river water. She walked back to where Blodwedd sat huddled in Rhodri's arms.

"Here," she said. "Water. It will soothe your throat."

Blodwedd took the jug from her. She drank in an odd, jerky way, filling her mouth then throwing her head back to swallow.

"Is that better?" Branwen asked.

Blodwedd nodded, water trickling down her chin.

"And now come back to the fire," Rhodri said to her. "There's a little bread and cheese left." He looked up briefly at Branwen, before turning back to the owl-girl. "I will teach you how to chew food and swallow it without choking. And I'll check your wound. And while I am doing that, Branwen will go and hunt for our supper."

Branwen slipped her slingshot from her belt and headed into the woods, turning over this new development in her mind. Whatever happened to them on their journey, Blodwedd's presence would surely have a profound effect—but whether it would be for good or for bad, she was not yet sure.

Branwen could not help feeling a little pleased with herself as she threw the small wild pig down by the fireside. She had come stealthily upon it in the forest as it rooted under an oak tree, quite oblivious to her presence as she crept close enough to use her sling-shot. She had stunned it with a single deadly accurate blow to the side of the head and then quickly finished it off with a neat cut of Geraint's knife across its throat.

Blodwedd was huddled by the fire. She seemed to have fully recovered now, and Branwen noticed that all the bread and cheese was gone.

"Get some sticks for a roasting frame," she told Rhodri. "I'll prepare the meat for the spit." She crouched down, taking the pig by a hind leg and turning it over to begin dressing it. She was aware of Blodwedd's eyes on her as she worked.

"Do you want your meat raw or cooked?" she asked without looking at her.

"I do not know," Blodwedd said quietly.

Branwen grimaced. "I ate raw meat once, when I was a child," she said, still concentrating on her delicate knife work. "Afterward, I was very sick. I think human stomachs cannot cope with raw meat." She glanced at last at Blodwedd. "Try it roasted," she said. "I think you'll like it better that way."

Blodwedd nodded. "I shall try," she said.

Branwen looked across the flames at Rhodri. Blodwedd was still at his side, sitting up awkwardly on her thin haunches, holding a bone in both hands and snapping at it with her teeth. Watching her eat was not pleasant—she chewed like a dog, loudly and openly, with her lips drawn back and the juices dripping down her chin and onto her dress. The intent look of pleasure on her face showed she was clearly relishing the taste of roasted pig, so at least Branwen wouldn't have to suffer the sight of her trying to swallow live rodents whole again.

"I've been thinking about the idea of wearing disguises," Branwen said, averting her eyes from the slavering owl-girl. "I think I know how it can be done." She threw a gnawed bone into the fire. "At first light we can hunt for another of these pigs, or for a deer or something similar. Then we will take it to the nearest village or farmstead and barter the fresh meat for clothing."

"And if we are recognized?"

"I do not think we will be," Branwen replied. "The prince's soldiers will not have had time to visit every hamlet and farm." She glanced at Blodwedd. "We can leave *her* in the forest with the horses and my war-gear. We enter on foot, with a fresh-killed deer or two over our shoulders, and leave the rest to luck and destiny!"

Rhodri grinned. "That is a good plan," he said.

"But if we're to go hunting at first light, we should sleep now."

They piled more wood on the fire so it would keep burning through the night. Then Branwen made herself as comfortable as possible by curling up on her side, her face to the warmth of the flickering flames, with Geraint's cloak pulled up to her ears.

She woke once in the night. Blodwedd was sitting hunched by the fire, her arms folded around her up-drawn shins, her chin on her knees, her eyes closed.

She sleeps sitting up, Branwen thought drowsily. *Like a bird on a branch!*

She looked for Fain, but the falcon was invisible in the night-shrouded tree. She dropped her head and fell quickly asleep again, but the silent, soaring shapes of owls haunted her dreams.

9

"KEEP OUT OF sight, do you understand?" Branwen said to the owl-girl. "And don't let the horses stray. We'll be as quick as we can."

Blodwedd gazed at Rhodri with worried eyes, as though the thought of parting from him disturbed her.

"Don't be alarmed," Rhodri said. "No harm will come to us."

Blodwedd made a curious snapping motion of her lips and teeth, as though in her mind she was fretfully closing a beak. "Very well," she murmured. "But do not leave me overlong with these great beasts—I know not how to control them."

"They're tied fast," Branwen reassured her. "Just make sure the knots on the reins do not slip."

They were in the eaves of a patch of forest that

skirted the ridged foothills below the mountains. Ahead of them the land rose and fell in buckles and ripples, much of it still wild but some parts showing the hand of man. Coppiced woodlands could be seen, the tall, straight, slender branches thrusting up like spears in the silvery early light. Muddy pathways criss-crossed the land, and there were fields where wheat and flax and rye grew.

At the edge of the forest, the hill fell away at their feet. Below them in a cupped valley, they could see the huts and pens and houses of a small hamlet.

Branwen looked at Rhodri. "Ready?" she asked, hefting the young roe deer that lay across her shoulders.

Rhodri nodded. He had the female's fawn over his shoulder: a buck, no more than two moons old. It would make sweet eating.

The hunting had gone well—they had come upon mother and child at first light, feeding upon leaves and shoots. Branwen had paused for a moment, regretting the necessity of harming the gentle creatures, but she had a hunter's instincts and knew she had no choice but to go for the kill. The best she could do for the two animals was to make sure they died quickly and painlessly.

So now they had two fine deer to offer in exchange for clothing. The people of the hamlet would be eating venison that night, and Branwen and Rhodri would have new clothes to fend off prying eyes.

It was a good plan.

Still, Branwen's eyes narrowed as she took a last look back at Blodwedd. Could they trust her? Did they have a choice? She was uneasy about leaving behind her brother's sword and shield and chain-mail coat, but those were items they would not have been able to explain to the people of the hamlet—no more than they would have been able to account for such fine horses in the possession of two young travelers.

But Branwen still had her slingshot, and Geraint's hunting knife was at her hip. No one would find that odd—anyone seeking game in the forest would carry such things.

Branwen and Rhodri trudged side by side down the hill toward the hamlet. Branwen suddenly heard a soft swishing sound behind her. She turned and saw Fain following.

"No!" she called to the bird, gesturing it away. "You can't come. People would be suspicious if they saw you with us."

Fain circled them, his eyes staring down, his wings barely moving.

"We will not be long," Branwen called up. "Go! Wait with Blodwedd."

Fain gave a single harsh croak and then flew back into the trees.

"Remember," she said to Rhodri. "Speak as little as possible. It was your accent that gave you away as a half Saxon before. These people are unlikely to be as well traveled as Gavan is, so they may not know a Northumbrian accent when they hear it—but the less said, the better."

When they reached the hamlet, the ground was bare and a little muddy underfoot. Chickens scratched for grain on and around the path. Goats bleated in pens made from wattle hurdles. There were only three buildings in all, low huts with shaggy, thatched roofs hanging close to the ground and walls of daub and wattle. Two men were making repairs to the wall of one of the huts, scooping the wet paste of mud and straw from wooden buckets and slapping it over cracks and holes where the weather had got in and the wattle framework was visible. Once dry and firm, the daub would insulate the house against the worst that winter could throw at it.

A boy and a young woman were busy threshing, their arms rising and falling as they wielded their long wooden flails to beat the grain loose from the ears of corn that were spread thickly upon the ground. Chaff and straw stalks danced in the air as they worked. Branwen knew that this must be the remnants of the previous season's harvest, hoarded and stacked and kept dry to provide bread throughout the year.

A woman in a brown apron and a white linen wimple stood by the doorway to the nearest hut. There was a wooden crib at her feet. She was spinning wool, letting the cone-shaped bobbin dangle down for a small infant to grab at ineffectively.

"That's my good, strong boy," she crooned as the pudgy fingers snatched at the thread. "That's my clever one." The infant gurgled and blew bubbles in delight.

She looked up as Branwen and Rhodri walked toward her.

"Good morrow," she said, a tinge of suspicion in her voice, although Branwen guessed it was no more than the normal caution reserved for strangers. She eyed the carcasses stretched across their shoulders. "Those are fine looking beasts, fresh from the forest, if I'm any judge."

"That they are," said Branwen with a smile. "We killed them ourselves before the sun came up this very morning. Mother and child caught napping in the twilight. I felled them with my slingshot."

"*You* felled them?" the woman said with an arch of her eyebrows. She looked at Rhodri. "And what were you doing, my fine young fellow, while this girl-child was at the hunt?"

Rhodri hesitated for a moment.

"He helped," Branwen said quickly. She stepped forward, stooping and letting her burden down. She crouched, patting the golden-red hide. "They would make many a good meal," she said, smiling up at the woman. "Would you be interested in a trade?"

"I might," said the woman. "If you can prove that you have come by these beasts honestly, and are not thieves and vagabonds."

"And how would I prove that?" Branwen asked lightly. Usually she would have bridled at such a suggestion, but she was wise enough to keep her temper with the doubtful woman. Anger and hard words would get them nowhere.

The woman gestured to the slingshot that hung from Branwen's belt. "Show me your skills," she said.

Branwen stood, slipped the slingshot from her belt, and felt in her pouch for a stone. "Tell me what to hit," she said.

The woman looked around. "That wooden pail yonder," she said, pointing to a pail that stood by the goat pen some fifty paces away.

"Hmmm," Branwen said, eyeing the easy target. "You mean to test me well." She smiled. "I can but try." Then, quick as a flash, she spun the slingshot twice around her head and let fly. The stone cracked on the side of the bucket.

A smile broke on the woman's face. "A skillful maid, indeed," she said. "And who taught you such skills?"

"My brother," Branwen replied. She straightened her shoulders and looked the woman keenly in the eye. "These carcasses are mine, and I would take it badly if anyone disputed it. Shall we trade?"

"Aye, lass, we shall," said the woman. "Come inside, and we shall speak at our ease." She glanced at Rhodri. "And will your silent companion enter, too? I have stew prepared, if the two of you are hungry. I can heat it while we come to some fair agreement."

Rhodri laid the young buck down beside its mother and followed Branwen and the woman in under the low lintel of the door. The windows of the house were unshuttered, and the interior was full of light. As was usual among such dwellings, the rectangular house had a beaten earth floor with an oblong firepit in the center, girdled with stones. A ladder stretched up to a hayloft under the thatch. There were straw mattresses against the walls, and to one side of the firepit, a pair of quern stones were set in a wooden frame. A young girl of seven or eight years old was slowly turning the stones, and fine white flour was trickling into a stone trough. She glanced up curiously at them as they entered.

"Stop that now, Ariana," said the woman. "Go and feed the goats—and milk them, too. Don't you hear them bleating, girl?"

"Yes, Mama," said the girl, getting up and trotting from the hut.

"Now then, sit you down," said the woman. "Bartering is made easier in comfort, I find." She took a pair of black iron tongs and lifted a stone out of the fire. "You look healthy and hale," she said, carrying the smoking stone over to a large wooden bucket of stew. "So I don't take you for beggars." She looked at Rhodri. "Despite your rags and tatters. Whence come you? Whose daughter are you, maid?" She lowered the stone into the bucket. There was a hiss and a gout of steam.

Branwen leaned forward, watching the thick brown stew already bubbling from the heat. They hadn't eaten yet that morning, and a bowl of stew would be very welcome.

The woman put down the tongs and folded herself up to sit on the floor. Branwen and Rhodri sat in front of her.

"My father is a farmer of Cyffin Tir," Branwen told the woman, reciting a tale she and Rhodri had worked out earlier that morning. She was aware of Rhodri staring intently at her, his lips moving a little as though he was mouthing silently to himself the words they had rehearsed together. "We met with bad fortune. The Saxons came raiding, and our home was burned and all our possessions along with it. I was sent over the mountains to seek clothing and goods to help us build our life again."

The woman's face clouded. "Ach! Saxons," she spat. "The devils that they are! Would that King Cynon were a stronger man—a great, bold leader like our Prince Llew—then maybe those ravaging dogs would be sent to the rightabouts!" She looked at Rhodri. "And what is your tale, boy?"

"I worked on the farm with Branwen," he said, his foreign accent all too obvious in Branwen's ears.

She winced inside and wished he had not used her real name. Why hadn't they thought to come up with aliases? But the woman showed no sign that the name had any significance to her.

"Did you? Did you, indeed?" said the woman. "Well now." She leaned over, stirring the stew with a wooden spoon. "So, you wish to trade meat for clothing and . . . what? Pots? Farm tools? What else?"

"Clothing would suit us best," said Branwen. "Perhaps a dress and a wimple, and a jerkin and leggings, and maybe a woolen cloak or two—if you are willing to part with them."

"We have spare garments," said the woman, hooking her head to a simple wooden box under one of the windows. "But it is a lot you ask for only two deer, my child. If your need is so great, maybe you would be willing to work to make up the difference? The boy could set to the winnowing, and perhaps you could spend a morning at the loom?"

Branwen glanced at the tall wooden loom that stood against the wall. There was already cloth in the frame. Branwen had seen women at the loom daily in Garth Milain, but she had never been asked or expected to join in the time-consuming and laborious task.

All the same, if a morning of weaving would get them what they needed, she was willing to accept the woman's offer and try her hand at the loom. But could they afford that kind of time? Neither her vision of the coming carnage nor Blodwedd's message from Govannon of the Wood had given any indication of when Ironfist's attack was due to fall on Gwylan Canu. Today? Tomorrow? By the new moon? When?

"I see you have your doubts about my offer," said the woman, now spooning the steaming-hot stew into two bowls. "Eat now and think it over. For the two deer, I can offer little more than a cloak or two and a gown. If you need more, you know what I'd have you do." She handed the bowls to Rhodri and Branwen then heaved herself to her feet. "I must check on the babe," she said. "Talk it over—you'll find it's a fair offer, and the longer you are prepared to work, the better you will serve your folk back in Cyffin Tir."

So saying, she went stooping out through the low doorway.

Branwen waited until she was sure the woman was out of earshot. "You shouldn't have called me Branwen," she hissed to Rhodri.

"I know," he said, his face troubled. "The moment I said it, I knew it was a foolish thing to have done." He shook his head ruefully. "You were right—I should have kept quiet. We should have told her I was mute!"

"All the same, no harm was done," said Branwen. "Just be more careful from now on." She lifted a spoonful of the stew. The meat was chicken, and she could smell cabbage and onions, too, as well as parsley and a hint of rosemary and savory. It smelled wholesome and appetizing, and she ate it with pleasure, speaking between mouthfuls. "But what are we to do? Can we afford to spend time here? There's little purpose in us telling our tale to Iwan ap Madoc if we arrive in Doeth Palas too late for it to do any good."

"I think we have a few days," said Rhodri. "It will take Ironfist a little time to organize his men and take them to the coast—it's not something that can be done all of a rush."

"So, you think we should stay here and work?"

"I would rather not, if we had the choice." Rhodri glanced over to the wooden box of clothes. "I'm thinking that if I were a little less honest, I'd be sorely tempted to grab what we need and make a run for it."

"Steal from her?" said Branwen in dismay. "How can you think such a thing while you're filling your belly with her food?"

"Not steal," said Rhodri. "Borrow. As we did the horses—remember, you said when you took them that you would be glad to bring them back to their rightful owners when your need of them was done. So it would be with this woman's clothes. That's all I was suggesting."

Branwen shook her head. "It's work or nothing," she said. "We could offer to bring them more game—but it's hard to catch deer or wild pig in full daylight—and we'd be as well off working through the day as wandering the forest till dusk. But I'm concerned about Blodwedd. What might she do if we do not return soon?"

"She's not our enemy, Branwen," said Rhodri. "You should learn to trust her. If we . . ."

He was silenced by a shadow across the doorway. The woman had returned. But she was not alone. The two men who had been repairing the walls came in after her—and Branwen saw to her dismay and alarm that their faces were set and grim, and that one was armed with a heavy wooden club while the other held a hunting spear in his two hands.

"Do you think the eyes of Bras Mynydd are blind?" spat the woman. "Last night a rider came from Doeth Palas—speaking of two runaway Saxon spies—a black-haired girl dressed in hunting clothes, and a boy in rags."

Branwen and Rhodri scrambled to their feet, their bowls spilling their contents across the floor. The woman knew who they were! She had tricked them—putting them at their ease while she fetched the men.

"Our prince has offered a rich reward for you treacherous swines!" snarled the man with the spear. "And the offer holds good whether you be alive or dead." He grimaced with anger. "So? What is it to be? Delivered alive and in bondage to Doeth Palas—or dragged there lifeless by the heels?"

10

BRANWEN BACKED AWAY from the two men, almost stumbling over the stew bucket, as she fumbled for her slingshot. Her knife would aid her only in close combat—but with the slingshot maybe she could keep the two men at bay until escape was possible.

She could not believe she had been taken so completely by surprise. She—the stealthy, keen-witted hunter—caught by the farm woman's pretense like a fly in a spider's web.

Rhodri held his hands out. "Whatever you have been told, it is not true," he said. "We are not spies. We mean you no harm."

"Listen to his voice!" snarled the man with the club. "He tells us his lies in a foreign accent!" He spat. "Saxon cur! You should not be given the offer of

84

life—you should be killed where you stand."

Branwen's eyes moved quickly from man to man. Their expressions were cold and hard—this was not a situation she would be able to talk her way out of. She ground her heels into the earth floor, balancing herself, quickly fitting a stone into her slingshot and lifting her arm above her head. "The first man to approach me will regret it," she said, her gaze flickering from the spearman to the man with the ugly, knobbed club. "My aim is true—ask the woman. Make a move on me and you will lose an eye!"

"Ware!" called the woman, stepping in behind the two men. "She's a devil with that thing."

Rhodri took a quick step forward and picked up the iron tongs from beside the firepit, jumping back again as the spearman made a stab at him.

"There's no need for this," Rhodri said, his voice trembling a little. "Let us go on our way and all will be well."

"You'd have us let you go and tell your tales to Herewulf Ironfist?" scoffed the man with the club. "Betray us to the Saxon pestilence? Do you think us fools?" The man pounced, lunging at Rhodri with the club. Rhodri fended it off with the tongs, but they were struck from his hands. As he tried to avoid being hit by a second swing of the club, he lost his footing and fell backward with a gasp.

Branwen swung her slingshot and loosed the stone. It cracked off the man's wrist and he shouted in pain, dropping his club and reeling sideways, his hand clutched to his chest.

"That could have been your eye if I wished it!" she shouted.

The spearman surged toward her with a roar of rage. She felt for another stone, but he was on her before she could reload the slingshot. She shifted her weight, sidestepping as the spearhead skimmed past her. Bringing her arm up, she caught the man across the throat as he staggered forward from the impetus of his missed blow. She ducked down, her shoulder hitting him in his stomach.

Flexing her legs, she heaved upward, using all the power of her limbs and her back to lift him off his feet. His own momentum betrayed him, and he was tossed onto his face behind her. She turned quickly, coming down heavily on him and straddling his back. Snatching the spear from his hand, she threw it out of reach. Now she slipped the knife from her belt and held it to his neck.

"Be still!" she shouted. "Or I shall cut your throat where you lie!"

He lay gasping, his face in the dirt. She knew he was no match for her—he was a simple farmer who probably had never wielded a weapon in anger before. Not that he wouldn't have run her through if she had given him the opportunity—she was all too well aware of that. But he could do her no harm now, and she wished to avoid hurting him further.

Keeping the knife blade steady against his skin, she turned to see how Rhodri was faring.

It was not good. He was lying on his back and the woman stood over him with the iron point of the spear against his throat.

Fool! Branwen cursed herself for not having thrown the spear out of reach.

"Let Baddon up, or I'll skewer your friend like a pig," the woman said grimly.

Rhodri shot Branwen an apologetic glance, as if blaming himself for the turn of events. Blood trickled down his neck where the spear point had nicked his flesh. From the look in the woman's eyes, Branwen had no doubt as to whether she would make good on her threat. One wrong move on Branwen's part, and Rhodri's life would end.

"Leave him be!" gasped Branwen. "See! Your man is safe and sound!" She took the knife from Baddon's neck and stood up, stepping back to let the man scramble to his feet. His face was red with anger and his eyes were ablaze.

"Drop the knife," the woman said. Branwen hesitated. Geraint's knife was her last hope of survival. With it she might be able to slash her way to freedom. Without it she would be bound and delivered over to the justice of Prince Llew.

But she faltered for only a moment before letting the knife slip from her fingers. She could not make an escape for herself and leave Rhodri's corpse as proof of her faithlessness. Better to suffer at his side than to live with that burden on her soul.

"And the slingshot, if you please," said the woman.

Branwen let the strip of leather fall.

The man with the wounded hand moved toward her, his face livid with pain and ire, his lips tight. "You will wish we had killed you!" he spat, coming close. She stood her ground, gazing levelly at him and expecting the worst. He drew back and struck her hard across the face with his fist.

She staggered, her whole head exploding into pain, white lightning stabbing across her field of vision.

"A taste of what is to come!" he raged, spittle flecking on his lips. "I hope your death will be a slow and lingering one, and I hope I am there to see it."

Branwen straightened, holding up her aching head, looking into his face. Refusing to show him any trace of fear.

"It's cowardice to hit an unarmed prisoner!" shouted Rhodri. The woman spun the spear in her hands and struck him in the stomach with the butt end. Rhodri doubled up on the ground with a stifled moan.

"Have your revenge on the girl later, Newlyn," chided the woman. "Fetch rope now and tie them up." She turned to Baddon. "And when they are secured, go you and harness up the oxcart. I'd have us drive to Doeth Palas and turn them over to Prince Llew as soon as we can."

"And take our reward," Baddon said.

"Aye, lad, and take our reward!" replied the woman. "It will be some recompense for the hardship and loss of this past winter."

Newlyn turned to leave the house, but he had not taken two steps before he was halted by the sound of scuffling from close outside. A moment later there was a shrill cry of pain. The young boy who had been threshing the grain came stumbling through the doorway, grimacing and holding a hand to the side of his face.

He stared at the woman. "Mama!" he cried, "she hurt me!" Then he fell onto his knees, blood showing between his fingers. Sharp nails had raked four cuts across his cheek.

"Fodor!" cried the woman, rushing forward, her arms outstretched. Before she had even reached him, the sound of a baby's cries outside the hut could be heard, along with a young woman's weeping, fearful voice: "No! No! Please don't!"

Another shape stood in the doorway, casting a long, ominous shadow into the house.

"Blodwedd!" breathed Branwen. "By all the saints, *no!*"

The crying baby hung from the crook of the owl-girl's arm, held as carelessly as a bag of grain. In her other hand she held Branwen's sword, its edge steady above the baby's bent neck.

"Release them or I will cut its head off," Blodwedd said, her deep voice cutting through the wailing from outside and the sobs of the woman, who had flung her arms around the kneeling boy.

"Put the child down," said Baddon, moving away from Branwen. "See? Your friends are unharmed." His voice was filled with dread.

"He's only an infant!" gasped Newlyn. "An innocent babe!"

"What is that to me?" demanded Blodwedd.

"Let us go free," said Rhodri desperately. "She will do as she threatens."

The woman pulled Fodor to his feet and drew him away from Blodwedd, her face gray with fear. "Do not harm the babe," she said, her voice quavering. "If you must spill blood, kill me instead."

Branwen crouched to pick up her knife and slingshot. "Stand back against the wall," she said. "Let us leave, and there will be no more bloodshed."

The two men backed away.

"You will pay for this deed," said Baddon. "Escape now, but you will be hunted down and slaughtered."

Branwen walked over to Blodwedd. "Give me the baby," she said.

Blodwedd hesitated for a moment then nodded. Branwen drew the crying infant out of her arm and turned to the woman. "Take him," she said. "And thank the saints that you are all still alive!" She looked into the woman's anguished face, feeling pity for her. She regretted that her own lack of foresight had put them into this situation, and wished that the boy had not been hurt, that none of this had happened. But the wishes were fleeting—she dared show no remorse or compassion to these people. They would see it as weakness, and she could not afford to have it spoken abroad in Bras Mynydd that she was weak—she had no doubt that she would need to show a ruthless face in times to come.

The woman stood and grasped the squalling baby to her chest, her eyes hollow and her cheeks wet with tears.

Branwen held out her hand for the sword. Blodwedd's eyes narrowed momentarily then she handed it over.

The owl-girl turned in the doorway. "Get you inside!" she said. The little girl Ariana and the young woman who had been at the threshing with Fodor came into the house, cringing. They ran quickly to be near the two men.

"Look in the chest," Branwen said to Rhodri. "Take what we need."

Rhodri knelt by the open wooden chest and began to go through the piled clothing.

Blodwedd's eyes shone eerily as she stared at the men. "Do any more live here?" she asked.

"No," said Baddon, glaring at her. "This is all of us. Go—take what you wish and leave us."

Blodwedd looked at Branwen. "It is not safe to leave them alive," she said. "They will raise the alarm. We must kill them all."

Branwen stared at her, revolted by the indifference in her voice as she condemned these people to death. But she realized the truth of what the owl-girl was saying. If these folk were left alive and free, they would spread the alarm.

"No!" gasped Rhodri, looking up at Branwen in horror, as though sensing her indecision. "No matter how great our cause, nothing good can come of such a cruel deed. Tie them up—gag them—but we can't kill them." His voice rose with emotion. "These are not Saxons, Branwen. These are your own people— the people you are destined to protect!"

"I will not kill them," Branwen said. "But they must be tied hand and foot." She looked at the huddled family. The woman was now near the others, with the baby swaddled in her clothing. His wailing ebbed to sobs as she rocked him in her arms. Fodor clung tightly to her skirts. Branwen hated the look of fear and loathing in the woman's face.

"Where is there rope?" Branwen demanded.

"In the barn yonder," said Newlyn. "But if you leave us tied, you may as well kill us now—seldom and few are the folk who come nigh our farm. Belike we should be dead of starvation before we were found."

Branwen pointed her knife at him. "Be silent!" She turned to Rhodri. "Go to the barn—fetch the rope."

Glancing uneasily at her, Rhodri left the house, dropping a pile of clothing by the door as he went.

Branwen was angry. It was a fiercer, more wrenching anger than she had felt even on the battlefield when the Saxons had swarmed around her. A deeper anger than she had ever felt toward Rhiannon. It was an anger that gnawed in her belly and boiled in her mind, ignited by the fact that for a few terrifying moments she had actually considered heeding Blodwedd's words—because for that fleeting time she had weighed in the balance these people's lives against her own safety.

"It would be safer if we cut their throats," Blodwedd said, her voice totally emotionless.

Branwen turned on her. "You've hurt the boy and terrified the others—aren't you satisfied with that?"

The great golden eyes blinked. "Satisfied?" she echoed, as if she didn't understand what Branwen meant. "I will be satisfied when our quest is done and the place of singing gulls is swept clean of the Saxon hawks," she said. "I will be satisfied, Warrior-Child, when I am set free to soar the open skyways once more." Her eyes glowed. "And until that glorious time, all who block my path will be struck down."

"Surely she is not human," Branwen heard the woman murmur. "See! Her eyes! She is a demon." She turned to look at Branwen, and there was dread and disgust in her face. "You have called up demons to aid you," she said, her voice shaking. "I have heard of such things from my mother's mother—of creatures that have slept long in forest and stream and mountain. Things that slumber deep and should never be awoken." Her eyes flashed. "Beware, girl—they will serve you only while it pleases them. Such creatures have their own dark purposes and desires."

Branwen gave a harsh bark of laughter. "You think I do not know that?" she said. "You think I would choose the life of a hunted fugitive if I were free to do otherwise? You have *no idea* of the burden I bear! Count yourself lucky that the demons did not choose you or yours for their 'dark purposes and desires'!"

Rhodri came back into the house, lengths of hempen rope in his arms. He looked sharply from Branwen to Blodwedd.

"Branwen, I think the man spoke true," he said. "If we tie them up, they may well die of thirst and starvation before they are found."

"Blodwedd would have me slaughter them, you'd have me set them free to condemn us," said Branwen. "And I am left with the weight of decision."

"And what is that decision?" asked Rhodri.

Branwen frowned, considering his question. She turned to the gathered family. "Ariana," she said. "Come here."

The girl clutched at the woman, whimpering.

"I will not hurt you," Branwen said. "Be brave and true and you will be the protector of all your family. Come!"

"Go to her," murmured the woman. "Do not be afraid."

Trembling and unsteady on her feet, Ariana walked to where Branwen was standing. "You will come with us for part of our journey," Branwen said, resting her hand gently on the child's head. "And when we release you, you will come back here and set your kindred loose. Can you do that?"

The girl's eyes were huge as she looked up into Branwen's face. "Do not let the demon kill me," she said, her voice quavering.

"She will do you no injury, I swear," said Branwen. "Rhodri—tie the others up good and tight."

Slowly and methodically, Rhodri moved among them, getting them to sit and then tying them securely, passing the ropes around their ankles and wrists with many tight knots. He found a piece of clean cloth to bind the wounds on Fodor's cheek before tying him as gently as possible and seating him with the men. He left the woman's hands free so that she could keep hold of the baby, silent now in her arms. But he took her away from the others, and had her sit with her back to the quern stones while he wound the rope around and around the heavy milling block and tied it beyond her reach.

He stood up, his task complete. "There," he said. "And now let us get away from this place."

"Take some food," Branwen told him. "Only what we need."

Rhodri explored the house and found bread and cheese. He walked to the door and picked up the bundle of clothing, wrapping the food in a fold of cloth.

"Do not fear," Branwen murmured to Ariana as she led the girl from the hut. She rested her hand on the girl's shaking shoulder. "All will be well."

11

THE HORSES WERE waiting, still tethered to a low branch.

Fain watched from a stump as they sorted through the bundle of clothes. Rhodri flung off his old rags and drew on a woolen jerkin and leggings—new-made, it seemed, and unworn. He knelt, slipping on a pair of soft leather shoes, cross-gartering the thongs up his calves.

Branwen saw the doubt and concern in his eyes as he glanced occasionally at Blodwedd. A bond had been growing between him and the owl-girl, but Branwen wondered if that bond had now been broken.

Branwen picked out a simple brown gown for herself, and a white linen wimple that she could use to cover her hair and keep her face in shadow if necessary. She pulled the gown on over her hunting clothes, thinking it prudent to wear the dress during their journey, just in case they were seen from afar. It would be hot once the sun was up, she knew, but she was not prepared to leave her leathers behind. She tied the gown at the waist with a strong leather belt that had an iron clasp. Into the belt she thrust her sword and knife, along with her slingshot and the pouch for her stones.

Her more precious belongings—everything she kept hidden away—were tucked under that gown. Firestones and tinder, kept in a leather pouch, were necessary to their survival. But there were other items, too—less practical but indeed vital to her nonetheless. A small bag containing a handful of white crystals that Geraint had found on the mountains. A comb gifted by her mother. A small golden key her father had given her on her tenth birthday—found in an old Roman temple, he had told her, although no one knew what lock it might open. These last things were virtually all she had left of her old life; they pained her and comforted her at the same time, and she would never be parted from them.

Folding the wimple and tucking it into her belt, she looked around and saw that Rhodri was helping Blodwedd into a dark-green gown. The owl-girl stood like an awkward child while he settled the gown into place on her small body, tugging at the hem to straighten it, and then took a rope belt and knotted it around her waist. He had picked a wimple for her, too, to shade her face and hide her peculiar eyes from view.

A dull wave of confusion sickened Branwen. How could Rhodri bear to have anything to do with her? She wasn't human. She was just an animal in human form—a cruel, murdering *thing*, with no compassion, no mercy or kindliness in her heart.

Branwen saw Ariana watching the owl-girl with frightened eyes.

She knelt, resting her hands on the small girl's shoulders and looking into her face. "Have no fear," she said softly. "You will not be hurt, I promise."

"She hurt Fodor," Ariana replied, her eyes still on Blodwedd. "She wanted to kill all of us."

"Your brother's injuries are not severe," Branwen said. "He was more scared than hurt, I believe."

Ariana shook her head. "He is not my brother," she said.

Branwen frowned.

"Fodor is my cousin," the girl said in a whisper. "His mother was my aunt—she died in the winter. My papa died, too. And Teithi died, and Aunt Yestin and Hafgan. They got ill and they all died."

"I am sorry," said Branwen. "My papa is dead, too. And my brother. The Saxons killed them."

The girl's forehead crinkled. "Saxons are bad people," she said. "Papa used to tell tales of the Saxons. He said they want to kill us. Why are you helping them?"

"Believe me in this, Ariana," Branwen said solemnly. "We are not Saxon spies. We hate the Saxons as much as you do. More, probably, because you hate only what you have been told, but my friend Rhodri and I have *seen* their brutality. We know the deeds of which they are capable!"

"Why do they wish us harm?" asked Ariana.

"They envy us the good fortune of living in such a beautiful land, Ariana," Branwen said, her heart going out to the little girl. "But I will not let harm come to you or to this land, not if I can help it. Now— have you ever ridden a horse? Do you know how?"

Ariana shook her head.

"Then I shall show you. You will sit in front of me and I will keep you from falling."

The girl's worried eyes turned to Blodwedd. "Was Aunt Aberfar right? Is she a demon?"

Branwen stood up, avoiding the question. "She will not hurt you," she said. "Come, now—let me help you mount up."

"Are you going to kill me?"

"No! I promise you, no." On a sudden impulse, Branwen took her knife from her belt. "Here—take this. Hold it tight, it is heavy." Ariana grasped the long hunting knife in both hands. "Keep it with you as we ride," Branwen said. "Hold it against my throat if it makes you feel safer." She grasped the little girl under the arms and lifted her up into the saddle. "We will ride until the sun is high," she said. "Then you will be let down and allowed to return home."

The girl looked down at her from her perch on the horse's back.

"I wouldn't want to kill you," she said. "I don't think you are bad."

Branwen put her hand on Ariana's knee, deeply moved by the girl's faith in her. If only she had the same faith in herself—the faith that she could fulfill the burdensome destiny that the Shining Ones had thrust upon her. Somehow she needed to *find* that faith—despite her misgivings, despite her feelings of inadequacy—if only to justify the look of trust in Ariana's eyes.

"Listen to me, Ariana," she said. "My name is Branwen ap Griffith. One day, perhaps, you will hear my name again. People may speak of me as the Savior of Brython—because that is, apparently, my destiny. To save this land from the Saxons." She lifted her hand and touched her fingers against the girl's heart. "But if that day ever comes, and people sing songs of the deeds of Branwen ap Griffith, remember how very brave and strong you have been today—remember that Ariana the farmer's daughter is as courageous as any hero in the ballads!"

So saying, Branwen mounted up, with Fain flying over her head and Rhodri and Blodwedd following behind. She curled one arm around Ariana's waist and sent her horse off at a brisk walk along the forest eaves and into the north.

* * *

The beat of the horses' hooves was soft in the dense grass, and the air was still and quiet, with hardly a leaf stirring as they passed. Branwen could hear Rhodri speaking with Blodwedd as they rode. As before, the owl-girl was seated behind Rhodri, her thin arms around his waist.

"How did you know to come to our aid when you did?" he asked.

Branwen turned her head a little to better hear the owl-girl's response, realizing she had been too caught up in her anger at Blodwedd's callous behavior to give any thought to that question—though it was a good one. What had caused her to come to their rescue when she did?

"Lord Govannon spoke in my mind," said Blodwedd. "'Blodwedd of the Far-Seeing Eye,' he said, 'you fail in your duty to the Warrior-Child. You have let her go into great peril. Go now to the habitation of the humans and do what you must to bring her back to the safe path.' So, I took the sword and came down to the human place. And I looked in through a window and saw you upon the floor with a spear at your throat, and I saw everything." A bitterness entered her voice. "The Warrior-Child believes I struck the boy out of malice, but it is not so. I did not wish him pain, but the others needed to know that I was resolute—that if they sought to harm the Warrior-Child, then my retribution would be swift and deadly."

"Because unless you look after her properly, you will never be an owl again," Rhodri murmured. "I understand."

There was a keen edge to Blodwedd's response. "You think that is all?" she asked. "You think I care only for myself? Do you not know the peril that this land is in? Lord Govannon has shown me horrors, Rhodri. He has shown me what will come to pass if the Saxons rule here. How the land will suffer and groan. Forests cut down or burned. Rivers dammed and fouled. The green hills scarred and gouged and riddled with maggot holes where the humans gnaw at the rock to feed their fires and to forge their weapons and to fill their pockets with pretty gems. The entrails of the world spewed up in a black slurry that will kill all things—bird and beast, tree and flower. And the air choked with filth, and the fish dead in the rivers and lakes, and nothing—*nothing* of beauty and grace left in the land.

"That is why the Warrior-Child must not fail," continued the owl-girl. "That is why her destiny must be fulfilled. That is why no one can be allowed to stand in her way."

They rode silently on through the morning, keeping to the forest's edge while the sun rose bright in a clear blue sky. A little before midday, Branwen brought her horse to a halt. She swung down from the saddle, reaching up to help Ariana dismount.

Wordlessly, Ariana held out the knife. Branwen took it and slipped it in her belt. She walked over to where Rhodri had halted his horse.

"Give me one of the loaves," she said, avoiding eye contact with Blodwedd. He passed down a wheaten loaf and she tore it in two, handing half back to him.

"Take this for your journey home," she told Ariana, going back to her and giving her the bread. "You know the way, don't you?" She pointed south along the forest.

Ariana looked at her. "I have never been so far from home," she said uneasily. "Must I go back alone?"

Branwen frowned. What other choice was there?

"*Caw!*"

She turned at Fain's sharp cry. The falcon was perched on the saddle of her horse, his eyes glittering. He rose into the air, spreading his gray wings.

"*Caw! Caw!*"

The bird flew higher and circled southward, back the way they had come. He flew for the length of a single bowshot, then swooped down and landed on the bare limb of a gorse bush. He turned to stare at them.

"*Caw!*"

"Fain will lead the child," said Blodwedd. "He will see her safe home."

Ariana stared after the falcon, her face uncertain.

"Trust him," Branwen said. "He is a wise creature. He will lead you true." She called, "Fain! She is under your protection. Take her to her folk, then return to me as swift as you can."

"*Caw!*"

"Go, little one," said Branwen. "Have no fear."

Giving her a final look, Ariana turned and ran.

Branwen stood on the hillside, watching the little girl as she raced through the tall grass. As she came close to where Fain was perched, the falcon flew up and winged its way farther southward.

The little girl turned and gave Branwen a last look before following the bird.

Branwen mounted up again. Now they could travel at speed. With good fortune, they would arrive at Doeth Palas before nightfall.

12

THEIR LUCK HELD. Or perhaps luck had nothing to do with it. Perhaps it was fated that they should reach Doeth Palas without being caught by Prince Llew's soldiers. Branwen hoped that it was so. She hoped the Shining Ones were watching over her.

She had given a lot of thought to what she had overheard the owl-girl saying to Rhodri: *That is why the Warrior-Child must not fail. That is why her destiny must be fulfilled.* She still questioned her ability to live up to the expectations of the Shining Ones—but she now found herself clinging to the hope that she *could* be the person they thought she was.

They traveled quickly through the afternoon, avoiding any sign of human habitation—passing hamlets and farmsteads at a distance, moving into the cover of trees or valleys, concealing themselves behind hills at the first sight of smoke or thatched roofs or men and women working tilled fields. They avoided the roads, keeping always to deep countryside as they headed northwest across Bras Mynydd.

Sunset found them in the forest that spread at the very foot of the huge mound upon which the great and formidable citadel of Doeth Palas was founded. As they slid between the trees, Branwen saw torches ignite atop the high stone ramparts. More lights flickered to the south, where an ancient Roman wall ran along a sharp ridge, lined with iron braziers.

The sight of the mighty fortress of Prince Llew brought memories swarming into her mind. Although it felt like a lifetime ago, it had been only a short time since that night when she had first arrived here, raw with the pain of Geraint's death, overawed by the size and the grandeur of the citadel. Her whole life had been overthrown in a day. Doeth Palas was to be a staging-post on her journey south to Gwent, where she would be married to a boy she had met only once, ten years ago—when she had been five and he had been a mean-spirited and spiteful child of six. Her marriage to Hywel ap Murig was intended to cement an alliance between Powys and Gwent. She was meant to be the great hope of the House of Rhys—the *mother* of heroes!

But she had hated life in Doeth Palas and kicked against the rules and the pointless daily rituals of the life she was forced to lead while she waited there for the roads south to become safe for travel. She could still see the prince's wife, the lady Elain—her mouth puckered with disapproval. And she could still hear the carping voices of their two daughters, Meredith and Romney, high-born princesses who had done their best to make Branwen feel like an uncultured barbarian.

And then there was Iwan, handsome son of the House of Puw—a thorn in her side from the very night of her arrival. He seemed to delight in tormenting and criticizing her. But here she was, risking her neck to warn him of a Saxon attack on his home.

Branwen was vividly aware that they were close to Rhiannon's pool—the ring of bright water set in a forest clearing where she had wrestled with the enchanted salmon—where she had first encountered the Shining Ones and learned of the fate toward which they wished to guide her. She did not try to find the clearing again—she remembered Rhiannon's parting words.

My part is done, Warrior-Child. Let others now light your path.

As night gathered under the trees, the three travelers huddled together, eating cheese and bread and drinking from the water bottle filled recently from a bubbling spring.

"Why do we not build a fire?" asked Blodwedd, sniffing skeptically at a piece of cheese that Rhodri had given her. "Why do we not hunt and cook?"

"There are too many men about," Rhodri explained. "They come and go upon the road from the citadel to the outer wall—they may see the flames. It's not safe."

"A pity," said Blodwedd. "Roasted meat is good in the mouth."

"You like cooked food, then?" said Rhodri. "I thought you might prefer the taste of raw meat."

Blodwedd frowned. "The food I ate had no taste," she said. She reached out a hand, two fingers pointing. "I see it move." She linked her thumbs and spread her fingers in mimicry of a bird's wings. "I float on the wind." She almost smiled. "A snap of the beak. I swallow, and it's gone. There's no taste, Rhodri. No taste at all. Human food is . . ."

"Better?" Rhodri offered.

"Different," said Blodwedd. "Perhaps I shall miss it when I get my true form back."

"So, being human isn't all bad?"

Blodwedd tilted her head, her eyes thoughtful. "It is hateful to be without flight," she said at last. "You folk—you crawl along the ground, bound to the earth. You never feel the keen north wind in your faces as you rise high into the sky." Her voice took on an almost elegiac quality, and Branwen found herself gazing at the owl-girl in surprise. "Never know the joy of the silent swoop. Ahhh!" Blodwedd sighed. "To glide above the forest roof on a moonless night!

There is joy indeed—there lies contentment."

"You wouldn't be able to do much soaring with your injured arm," Rhodri said. "Not for a while yet."

"You think not?" Blodwedd pulled the bandage loose from her arm.

"Branwen, look at this!" Rhodri exclaimed in amazement. "There's no inflammation, and the wound is already scabbed over and healing."

"Good," Branwen said curtly. "I am glad."

"Did I not tell you, Rhodri?" said Blodwedd. "We heal quickly or not at all. Were I in my true form, already I would be winging over the treetops."

"Do you not hate Govannon for taking that away from you?" Branwen asked quietly.

Blodwedd gave her a startled look. "Hate Lord Govannon?" she said. "How could that be? I *am* Lord Govannon!"

Branwen almost choked on a piece of cheese. "What do you mean?" She coughed, half rising.

"All creatures of the woodlands are a part of the great Lord of the Forests," said Blodwedd. "He is in all of us, warm as blood, rich as rising sap, sharp as claws and thorns, bursting with life like a new-hatched chick or a seedling striving for the sun. We are his children and his limbs and his heart and eyes, his fingers and his arms and legs, his muscles and sinews and bones. We are all of him, the great Lord, Lord of the Forest—Govannon of the Wood." Her strange eyes turned to Branwen. "How could I hate him?"

Branwen sat down again, swallowing hard. "Does he have no physical form, then?" she asked. "I have heard that he was like a man—or half man, half stag. A man with antlers."

Govannon of the Wood. He of the twelve points. Stag-man of the deep forest, wise and deadly . . .

"I know nothing of that," said Blodwedd. She touched a finger to her forehead. "He comes into my mind as a great eagle—greater than all others, greater than any that have ever been. His wings span the land from sea to sea, and when he rises into the sky, the sun is dimmed and his shadow covers the world." Her eyes shone. "With one claw he could pluck a mountain out by its roots, and when he lifts up his voice, the stars shiver and the moon cracks. That is the Lord Govannon."

"I don't understand," said Branwen. "Rhiannon was a woman—a woman in white who rode a white horse. But . . . but you say that Govannon is a *bird*?"

Blodwedd gave a throaty laugh. "The Lady Rhiannon is not a woman," she said. "The Shining Ones are not *human*, Warrior-Child." She laughed again, as if the absurdity of the idea delighted her.

"You mean the Shining Ones can be anything they wish?" said Rhodri. He looked at Branwen. "Do you see?" he said. "Rhiannon showed herself to you as a woman—because you're human. For Blodwedd, Govannon is a bird. A huge eagle. They change their appearance to fit their surroundings—and their needs."

Blodwedd nodded enthusiastically. "That is the truth, Rhodri," she said. "To the fish of the wide rivers, Rhiannon is an ancient pike. To the trees of the forest, Govannon is a mighty oak." She raised her hand. "Lord Govannon is *all* trees, he is *all* birds, he is *all* creatures: deer, shrew, wren, and raven, oak, ash, and thorn. The lark in the morning and the owl at night. The white snowdrop in spring and the acorn of the late summer. Open your eyes, Warrior-Child— see truly who the spirits are that guide you!"

"We will sleep tonight in the forest," said Branwen. "We must take it in turns to keep watch. If there is any sign of people in the woods, we must know it—and avoid them." She glanced at Blodwedd. "We cannot risk being discovered."

"I will watch through the night," said Blodwedd.

"No, we should take turns," Rhodri suggested. "We all need to get some sleep."

Blodwedd smiled. "I can both sleep and watch together," she said. "Not a mouse shall stir but I will know of it, no matter how deep my slumber." Her eyes turned to Branwen. "I will serve as lookout through the night—if the Warrior-Child trusts me."

Branwen looked at her. The owl-girl was a dangerous and disturbing creature, and Branwen was certain that she would never grow to like her, but she had no doubt that Blodwedd could be relied on as a vigilant lookout.

She nodded. "Do it, then—and wake us at the least sight or sound of people. And in any event, wake us before first light. If we are to mingle unseen with the folk who come to Doeth Palas daily to trade, then our disguises will require some items for barter. A few fresh hares should suffice." She lay down, wrapping Geraint's cloak around herself and bringing the warm, woolen cloth up over her head. "And then we shall learn whether Iwan ap Madoc is to be trusted!"

13

ONCE AGAIN, FLYING shadows and the sinister beating of wings haunted Branwen's dreams. There were golden eyes, too—round as wheels, rimmed with flame, watching her unblinkingly from the black pit of the night.

She awoke in darkness to the flutter of wings. Fain had returned. He came to rest close to her head.

"Is the girl-child safe?" she whispered.

Fain dipped his head as though to say *yes*.

"Good." She reached out and gently stroked the bird's chest feathers. "You did well. I'm glad you're back." She turned her head. She could see the dark hump of Rhodri nearby. Blodwedd was in her usual pose at his side, sitting up gawkily with her limbs gathered up, her chin on her knees. Her golden eyes were wide open—staring straight at Branwen.

The owl-girl's head tilted and an accusatory glint came into her eyes, as if she assumed Branwen was checking on her and resented it.

Branwen nodded to acknowledge Blodwedd's gaze, her lips spreading in a tight smile intended to convey that it was no lack of trust that had awoken her. Then she turned away and drew the cloak over her head again.

A pale mist came to the forested valley in the still, cool time before dawn. Branwen crouched, shivering a little, and stared through the trees. She had taken off her brown gown and was in her hunting leathers. The long skirts of a gown were useless for forest work, and woolen garments were forever snagging on twigs and branches. Fain had disappeared into the mist to scout ahead for quarry. Rhodri had stayed behind with the horses—he had no skill at the hunt and was not especially adept at moving with stealth and silence.

But someone else was. Branwen watched the slim shadow of the owl-girl as she glided through the mist like a wraith, passing in absolute silence from tree to tree. Adept as Branwen was in forestry, she felt heavy and clumsy in comparison.

Blodwedd turned and beckoned. Branwen followed, moving forward on tiptoe, making sure that every step was soundless.

Blodwedd's hazy form slid forward, heading

deeper into the forest. A dark, winged shape exploded from the mist at eye level. It circled the owl-girl twice, then vanished again. Fain. On the hunt.

Blodwedd turned and beckoned again, this time waiting until Branwen caught up to her. The owl-girl pressed her lips to Branwen's ear and whispered in a barely audible voice.

"Fain has found two hares. I will go around. You wait here. Be ready."

Branwen nodded. Blodwedd sped away as silently as a shadow and was swallowed in the mist.

Just like an owl on the hunt! Branwen thought, stepping cautiously forward. The dawn was close now. She could feel it in the air and see it in the way the deep dark of night began to soften to shades of slate gray. The mist coiled its tendrils around her legs as she moved, the air still cold in her lungs.

She came to a place where the trees thinned a little and the mist was fading. A shape stirred on a branch above her head. Fain. He stared down at her.

She crouched, her head low, her eyes scanning the ground.

There!

A gray-brown hump in the grass. A crouching hare. She took in a shallow breath and held it, taking her slingshot and fitting it with a stone from the pouch at her elbow, leaving the mouth open to allow her to quickly take out another stone.

Then she waited, judging from experience how long it would take Blodwedd to circle the hare. She saw a long ear twitch.

Geraint's tutoring came back to her.

Be calm, be silent, be swift, be still. . . .

Branwen rose, twining the leather ends of her slingshot between her fingers. She lifted her right arm above her head slowly and stretched the left out in front of her—elbow locked, hand flat, fingers pointing toward the hare—creating a line along which she could aim.

Twice she spun the slingshot, her eye never leaving the dark hump—her focus aimed on the long narrow head from which the ears folded back along the spine. Then she flicked her fingers open, loosing the stone. Even as it flew through the air, she was reaching for a second stone and fitting it to the slingshot.

The first pebble struck the hare, and it slumped into the grass with barely a sound. A second hare—an animal Branwen had not even noticed—bolted from the shallow depression in which the two had been resting. It raced to Branwen's left, dashing for the cover of denser trees. Branwen spun and threw—but the hare jinked at the last moment, and the stone missed.

Annoyed at herself, she snatched up a third stone. Blodwedd appeared in the hare's path as if out of nowhere, lifting her arms and shouting. The hare turned sharply, scudding back and zigzagging through the long grass, so it was almost impossible for Branwen to aim at it.

Fain lifted suddenly in the air, arrow-fast on his

scythe-shaped wings. He rose then stooped, stalling midair before plummeting toward the hare. The terrified animal turned again, its wide eyes desperate. Blodwedd came running at it with her arms spread wide.

The hare sped toward where Branwen was waiting. Her stone struck it between the eyes. It flipped, tumbling through the grass, dead before it came to a slithering halt almost at her feet.

Blodwedd picked up the other hare by the ears and walked toward Branwen, holding it aloft. "That was well done!" she said, smiling her pointed smile. "As an owl, I might have taken one, but never the pair. You hunt well, Warrior-Child."

Branwen almost smiled—the rigors and the necessary focus of a good, clean hunt had cleared her mind. "Another half dozen, maybe, and then we go to the citadel. Pray that good fortune attends us."

"I don't like this plan," said Rhodri. "I should go into Doeth Palas with you." He gave Branwen an uncomfortable look. "I don't want to lurk uselessly in the forest with the horses while you walk into who knows what dangers."

"What would you do, Rhodri?" asked Branwen. "Even if you pass without any of the gate-guards recognizing your face, you cannot speak to answer their challenges—your accent would give you away before you spoke a handful of words."

"Then I shall be dumb," said Rhodri. "And this

hooded cloak will hide my face as well as those wimples hide you and Blodwedd from prying eyes."

"Prince Llew's soldiers are hunting for a male and a female traveling together," said Branwen. "Two females traveling together will not arouse their suspicions, but add a man and our chances of succeeding are diminished."

Rhodri stared at her for a long moment, then his eyes dipped. "Very well," he said. "Rhodri the beggarly runaway will skulk in the forest with Fain and our two horses while the brave young women go alone into the wolves' lair!"

"Do not fear for the Warrior-Child," said Blodwedd, lifting her hand to show the crooked fingers and white, claw-sharp nails. "Any that look askance at her will lose their eyes."

"No!" said Branwen. "We only fight if all is lost."

Blodwedd gave her a curious look. "I will defend you *before* all is lost, Warrior-Child," she said. "Thus *all* shall never *be* lost. But have no fear—I will not kill needlessly. And I will touch no child, if you wish it so."

"Good. That's good, then," said Branwen. She turned to Rhodri. "We should return before midday—but if we have not come back by nightfall, flee this land. If we are captured, I want to know you will not share our fate."

Rhodri's eyebrows rose. "You think I would run and hide and leave you to the mercies of Doeth Palas?" he asked.

"No, I don't," said Branwen, her mouth curling in

a faint smile. "But it would be wise."

"I've never been known for my wisdom," said Rhodri. "But for now, good luck go with both of you. Be wary and cunning, and take no risks—and if Iwan proves false, do not hesitate to cut his throat."

"It will not come to that," Branwen added quickly.

"It may," Rhodri warned.

Branwen saw the apprehension in his eyes. She rested her hand on his chest. "We will not be long," she said. "Keep yourself safe!"

"For you, always," he murmured.

Nodding, Branwen stooped and picked up the long, slender branch to which they had tied three of the hares they had caught. Blodwedd already had a second branch over her shoulder; four hares dangled from it, blood clotted on each of their muzzles.

Branwen glanced down at her shield and sword and chain-mail shirt, lying on the ground with her leathers and hunting knife. She and Blodwedd were dressed now in gown and wimple, but Branwen had her slingshot and stones with her, tucked well out of sight. Two young peasant women from a farm or hamlet of Bras Mynydd would not draw undue attention from Prince Llew's guards. They would pass unnoticed among the crowds that made their way every day into the markets of the great citadel.

Or so Branwen hoped.

14

"SO MANY HUMANS!" murmured Blodwedd, her eyes wide in the shadow of her wimple. "Such danger!"

"Stay close to me and all will be well," Branwen said. "Do not speak unless you have to, and keep your eyes on the ground at all times."

"Why?" asked Blodwedd.

"Because you have an owl's eyes!" Branwen hissed. "Do you think they will go unnoticed if anyone looks directly into your face?"

They were in the midst of a slow-moving crowd of peasants, jostling and shuffling and knocking and barging up the steep, narrow road that led to the rearing, white stone ramparts of Doeth Palas, citadel of Prince Llew, lord of Bras Mynydd.

The citadel towered above them, its blanched

ramparts shining in the light of the sun as it climbed over the eastern mountains. The massive fortifications of Doeth Palas were cloven by a deep passage; the road to the gates passed through this gap, rising sharply, the earth beaten iron-hard through the years by the passing of thousands.

Branwen and Blodwedd were pushed together as the traders, hawkers, and farmers pressed toward the gates. Some rode in ox-carts, while others had their wares packed in wicker baskets suspended from the backs of donkeys. Some drove geese and goats and pigs. The rising heat of the day filled the air with the heavy, pungent smells of grain and animals and closely packed people. There was shouting and grumbling and the honking of geese and the squeal of pigs and the calling of traders as they greeted one another.

The procession slowed almost to a stop as the crowd of peasants came to the bottleneck at the open gates. Branwen waited impatiently to be let through. This would be the first test of their disguises. Armed guards stood atop stone slabs on either side of the road, scrutinizing the people as they made their way past the gates. Other guards shoved their way roughly in among the crowd, spears in their hands, keeping some semblance of order and checking that all was well.

Branwen linked her arm with Blodwedd's, determined that the bumping and barging of the people would not separate them. They were almost through now—she could see the wide, paved road that led deep into the heart of the citadel. At the path's end, she saw the high, thatched roof and the stone walls and gold-sheathed doorways of Prince Llew's Great Hall.

Stalls and carts already lined the road where those peasants at the head of the procession began to set out their wares and prepare for trade.

A burly man elbowed Branwen aside, and she stumbled into one of the guards.

"Now then, maid," growled the guard, fending her off with the shaft of his spear. Branwen swallowed her irritation as he pushed her back. She kept her head down, the white linen wimple drawn over her forehead.

Still clinging to Blodwedd, she passed the guard, and the mass of people began to loosen. They were within Prince Llew's fortress and all was well.

"Hoi! You there—maiden!"

Branwen's heart pounded. It was the voice of the guard she had bumped into. Was he calling to her? She didn't dare look around. *Keep walking! Just keep on walking!* she thought, nearly in a panic.

"Hoi! Stop when I speak to you!" A hand came down on her shoulder, bringing her to an abrupt halt.

"I will kill him," muttered Blodwedd in an undertone. Branwen was grateful that the general hubbub prevented the guard from hearing the threat.

"No! Wait!" Branwen whispered under her breath. She turned, her head still lowered. "What do you want of me?" she asked aloud.

"Use a less haughty tone with me, girl," warned the guard. "Those are fine hares you have for sale. I'd have a brace for the cookpot. What price are you asking?"

Branwen had to think quickly. Money was seldom used in the less sophisticated cantrefs east of the mountains; in Garth Milain virtually all trade was for barter—a fine, plump goose for two bags of rye grain, or a wheel of fresh-churned cheese for a basket of tench or trout or grayling. She had no real idea of the value of coins here.

"What would you consider a fair price, sir?" she asked.

"An eighth of a silver piece for the pair," said the guard, his fingers delving into the leather pouch at his waist.

"A half would be closer to the mark, sir," she said, keeping her voice low and humble. She assumed the guard had named a price lower than the true value of the animals; to agree to his first offer would rouse his suspicions.

"Ha! Would you make your fortune out of me, girl? A quarter and no more."

"Done!" Branwen shifted the branch from her shoulder and slipped off two of the hares. She hoped the guard did not see how her hands were shaking as he dropped the cut silver coin into her palm.

She bowed her head, hefted the branch back onto her shoulder, and walked on, away from the gates. Her racing heart slowed, and she blew out a relieved breath.

"What did he give you?" asked Blodwedd. "Show me."

Branwen displayed the quarter-circle coin on her palm.

"*That*—for two hares? What purpose does it serve?"

"I'll explain another time," said Branwen. "We must find Iwan."

"There are many people here," Blodwedd said, staring out across the thronging market. "Where is he to be found?"

"I have an idea," said Branwen. "Follow me."

She led Blodwedd into the heart of the market. It was a noisy, boisterous affair. People crowded and elbowed and jogged and jarred one another, some laden with panniers from which they traded, others arguing and bickering over the stalls. Stilt-walkers, jugglers, and acrobats entertained the passersby. Metalsmiths came with heavy carts, selling pots and pans and knives. Grain traders cried their wares, competing with the loud shouts of their neighbors. A hundred different smells filled the air—sweet, sour, savory, and foul—rising from the uneasy animals and from wicker baskets and hempen sacks. There was the clank of metal on metal as goods were weighed on handheld balances, and the slap of palm against palm as deals were done. Oxcarts rumbled; gaggles of geese waddled underfoot; wattle pens were set up to house sheep and goats and pigs. There were earthenware jars of honey, fresh from the hive, as well as wheat and rye and barley by the poke, and beans and peas and lentils. And in the odd corner, rings of men and women watched cock fights and wrestling bouts.

But Branwen wished only to pass through the melee as quickly as possible. The noise of the market formed a constant backdrop as she led Blodwedd between the huts and dwelling places. She had in mind a courtyard, hidden close to the walls—a dusty square where she knew the young men of the court often gathered to practice archery and hone their battle skills.

As they turned a few corners, moving away from the marketplace, Branwen recognized the long building whose wall formed one side of the courtyard.

"Stay back," she murmured to Blodwedd. The owl-girl nodded. Branwen slid along the wall and peered around the corner.

Three lads were in the courtyard. There was gangly Andras, red-haired Bryn, and Iwan ap Madoc, tallest and most handsome of the three. Branwen felt a strange fluttering in her stomach as she caught sight of him, smiling his usual cocksure smile as he leaned on his bow and watched Bryn aiming for the wicker target.

"Elbow up more," Iwan remarked.

"I do not need your advice," said Bryn, his lips to the bowstring, his arms shaking a little as he strained against the tension of the bow.

He loosed the arrow. It struck the head of the wickerwork figure with a sharp *thuk*. "Now you do better!" demanded Bryn.

"With pleasure," said Iwan, setting an arrow to the string and pulling back on his bow.

Branwen didn't bother waiting to see his shot. She knew he would hit the target with ease. "He is there," she whispered to Blodwedd. "But he is with others. I need to speak to him alone—the others cannot be trusted. One of them in particular has no love of me—a big redheaded lad who thought he could best me with a staff in his hand." Her fists clenched as she remembered their fight. "I proved him wrong, but he would delight in giving me up to the prince if he knew I was here."

"Then what shall we do?" asked Blodwedd.

"We'll leave the hares here—they have served their purpose, I hope." They laid the two long poles down against the wall. "Now, I want you to watch and wait," Branwen continued. "Be my lookout—I need to know if any others approach. Look out especially for an older man with gray hair and a white scar down the left side of his face." This would be Gavan ap Huw, warrior and hero of Powys—briefly her mentor, the man whose teachings had saved her life during the battle outside the gates of Garth Milain. How he must hate her now! He must think her a traitor—to have released a condemned spy and fled with him.

Gavan ap Huw often schooled the lads of the prince's court in weaponry and battle skills. Above all others in Doeth Palas, Branwen did not want to come face to face with him. She didn't want to see the disgust and abhorrence in his flint-dark eyes; she didn't want to suffer his disappointment and displeasure; and she did not want his to be the hand that dragged her to Prince Llew's feet.

She crept back to the corner. Skinny Andras was aiming at the target now, but Branwen saw that his stance was all wrong—it was obvious to her that he would miss.

He did, and his two companions roared with laughter.

She watched from behind the wall as the three boys took turn and turn about. Her intention was to follow Iwan once the training session was done and to somehow get him alone.

A fourth boy came running into the courtyard. "Hoi! Come quickly—Padrig has challenged Accalon of Rhufoniog to a wresting bout in the market. Gold coins are being gambled."

"On Padrig's swift slaughter, surely!" laughed Iwan. "Accalon is unbeaten in fifty matches. He will pound our little Padrig to a sticky paste."

"Padrig is as slippery as an eel," said Bryn. "I'll risk a silver half piece on him!" He hooked his bow over his shoulder and strode off. Andras followed.

"Oh, it will be amusing, I suppose—albeit brief!" said Iwan, following the others.

Branwen had to act quickly. She fumbled under her gown for her slingshot. Bryn and the fourth boy had already left the courtyard by the time Branwen loosed a stone.

It skipped on the hard earth a fraction away from Iwan's foot. He paused, staring down at where the small white pebble had come to rest. Then, quick as an adder, he turned and stared along the obvious trajectory of the stone.

Branwen leaned around the corner, pulling back her wimple so that he could see her face. His expression changed from puzzled curiosity to amazement as he caught sight of her. She beckoned to him, then slid out of view before any of the others saw her. She leaned against the wall, her heart hammering and her legs trembling. Blodwedd looked questioningly at her, but Branwen gestured for her to keep silent.

Everything depended on Iwan's reaction to seeing her. Would his instinct be to call the guard? Would he give her away?

"Go on ahead," Branwen heard him call. "I will follow shortly. Put a gold quarter piece on Accalon for me."

Branwen bit her lip. Soft against the distant

hubbub of the market, she could hear footsteps padding toward her across the courtyard.

Iwan turned the corner. "Well now," he said, an arrow point aimed at her heart. "The barbarian princess has returned to the scene of her great treachery. How very interesting. Prince Llew will think better of me now, when I bring him such a prize!"

15

BRANWEN GAZED INTO Iwan's eyes. "Kill me now rather than hand me over to the prince," she said.

"As you wish," said Iwan. He glanced for an instant at Blodwedd, his arrowhead still aimed at Branwen's heart. "But I'd like to know first why you threw your whole life away for that Saxon vagabond—and what madness brought you back here." An uncharacteristic urgency entered his voice. "Prince Llew *will* have you hanged, Branwen, have no doubt about that—princess or no. And your feet will be dangling long before your father could bring a force over the mountains to seek your rescue."

"My father is dead," said Branwen flatly.

Iwan let out a long, regretful breath and grimaced in dismay, lowering his bow. "Then it is true."

There was sympathy in his eyes now. "One of the men sent to seek you in the mountains returned here on a foaming, exhausted horse late yesterday eve. He came staggering into the Great Hall, speaking of battle and disaster in Cyffin Tir. He said Garth Milain was burning and all were slain. The prince and Captain Angor bade him be silent, and we were sworn to speak nothing of his grim tidings. Then they took the rider to the private chambers, and we were told nothing more." He frowned. "But how do *you* know of this?"

"I was at the battle, Iwan," said Branwen, her voice trembling at the memory. She was aware of Blodwedd chafing at her side. "I have traveled far since last we met. I fought at my mother's side. The Saxons were beaten back."

"So Garth Milain is not lost?"

"Not lost to the Saxons," said Branwen. "But it was burning when I left, and my father lay dead upon the battlefield."

At last, the owl-girl could keep her silence no longer. "Tell the boy why we are here," she said. "Tell him of Lord Govannon's prophecy."

"Lord Govannon?" breathed Iwan, staring at her. "Govannon of the Shining Ones? There is no such creature! What madness is this, Branwen?"

"A great madness indeed," said Branwen.

Blodwedd's eyes suddenly narrowed. "It is not safe here," she said. "People approach. I hear their voices—I smell them—they are close."

There was a wooden entrance in the wall of the long building. "What's beyond this door?" Branwen asked.

"A storage hut for animal feed," Iwan replied. He walked rapidly toward the door. "Come. We will speak within, away from prying eyes." He gave her a wry look. "And if our discussions turn bad, we shall see whether I can loose an arrow more speedily than you can a stone."

He opened the door and they entered a long room piled with sheaves of wheat. The air was stuffy under the thatch, smelling strongly of the dry wheat. Behind them, Iwan swung the door to, leaving it open a fraction so that a strip of bright light was thrown across the piled sheaves. Branwen blinked, her eyes slowly adjusting to the dimness.

"Tell me your tale," Iwan said. "Although if you truly believe you have come here as the emissaries of a dead god, then I fear there is little I can do for you." He looked closely at Blodwedd. "Who *is* this, Branwen?" he asked, lowering his head to look into Blodwedd's wimple. He gave a low gasp at the sight of her wide, golden eyes, bright even in the half-light. He looked at Branwen. "By all the saints—what is she?"

"Her name is Blodwedd," Branwen said. "If I told you more, you would think me out of my wits." She looked into his confused face. "I have come back here to give you a warning, Iwan."

"A warning?" An eyebrow arched. "Of what would you warn me?" he asked. "To be more vigilant when I am assigned as sentry over a Saxon spy? That is a lesson I have already learned, Branwen, to my great discomfort. I got Captain Angor's rod across my back for allowing you to make a fool of me like that. I'll not be duped by you a second time."

"I'm sorry you were beaten," said Branwen. "I would not have wished that upon you. But I had to save Rhodri. He would have been tortured and hanged otherwise, and he is *not* a spy. It was his warning that took me to Garth Milain in time to beat the enemy back. I told Prince Llew that Garth Milain would be attacked, and he called me a fool and a dupe!" Her eyes blazed. "He knows otherwise now." A thought struck her. "You say the horseman came last night with the news of the battle? What has the prince done? Is he gathering a force to pass over the mountains and come to the aid of Cyffin Tir?"

"Not that I know of," said Iwan. "I am not privy to the prince's high councils, but I have seen and heard nothing to suggest that he intends to send a troop of men into the east. And word has certainly not gone abroad in Doeth Palas of the battle. The people here go about their daily lives, and their only fear is that their throats may be cut by a Saxon spy and the lunatic princess who set him loose!"

"So the prince does nothing," Branwen said bitterly. "A noble ally in times of woe! The garth burns,

134

and he sits on his hands!"

"You want me to go to the prince and ask him to ride to the aid of Cyffin Tir, is that it?" asked Iwan. "He would not heed me, even if I were allowed to speak with him. But no—you said you were here to 'warn' me of something."

"The Saxon hawks circle above the house of the singing gulls," said Blodwedd. "That is the warning we have come here to give you. How will you act, boy? What will you do?"

Iwan stared incredulously at her, clearly non-plussed by her enigmatic speech. "She talks in moonstruck riddles!" he snapped, turning to Branwen. "What does she mean?"

"She means that Gwylan Canu is in danger of Saxon attack," said Branwen.

"As are we all," replied Iwan. "This is no news."

"Herewulf Ironfist already leads an army north-ward," said Branwen. "They will come upon the fortress of your father by land and by sea. All will be slaughtered. A Saxon pennant will fly over the broken gates of Gwylan Canu." She chose not to mention that in her vision, Iwan himself was also slain and mutilated.

"How do you know of Ironfist's movements?" Iwan demanded. "And how are you so sure that my father will not throw back the Saxons from his walls? You cannot know for certain that defeat will be the outcome of a battle that has not yet been fought."

"I was shown it!" cried Branwen. "Please, Iwan. Trust me!"

Iwan hesitated, his face twisted by confusion and doubt. "What do you mean when you say you were *shown* it?" he asked. "Branwen! If you want me to believe you, I must know more."

"Would you know more, boy?" growled Blodwedd, drawing back her wimple so that her inhuman eyes caught the strip of sunlight and reflected it like molten gold. "Would you have me show you more?"

She moved forward, silent and swift, deadly as a feathered barb. Iwan gasped and stepped back, his eyes staring from his pale face.

"Blodwedd! No!" breathed Branwen, pressing quickly between Iwan and the owl-girl. "Do not do this!" She knew what was coming—what the owl-girl intended for Iwan.

Blodwedd pushed Branwen aside with ease, her clawlike fingers coming up on either side of Iwan's startled face. She pulled his head down and stared intently into his eyes.

"See now, and *understand*!"

Branwen saw a look of horror burn across Iwan's face as his gaze was caught and held by Blodwedd's. He stopped struggling and dropped heavily to his knees, his arms hanging limp—a marionette with its strings cut, held up by the owl-girl's two thin hands and by the power in her blazing eyes.

As he knelt there, transfixed by Blodwedd's

gaze, his expression grew ever more alarmed and appalled.

His lips moved. "No . . . no . . . no . . . Father! They come from all sides! Ware! Ware!" Then he cried out, tears running from his eyes. "No . . . ! Father—*no!*"

"Blodwedd, stop!" gasped Branwen, pulling at the owl-girl's arm. The vision of Iwan's severed head rose ominously before her mind's eye.

Blodwedd let out a low, threatening hiss.

"No!" shouted Branwen. "Enough!" She clasped her arms around the owl-girl's waist and heaved her backward, breaking her grip on Iwan—severing the dreadful link between them.

Iwan groaned and fell forward onto his hands, panting, his head hanging.

Blodwedd looked at Branwen. "It was necessary," she said. "It is done."

Iwan lifted his head and stared at her. "What are you?" he gasped.

"I am Blodwedd of the Far-Seeing Eye," replied the owl-girl. "I was sent by Lord Govannon to guide the Warrior-Child on her true path. The Shining Ones have chosen her to be the Savior of Brython. The Old Gods do not sleep—they are watching over her."

"But is . . . is my father already . . . dead?" gasped Iwan. "Is Gwylan Canu fallen?"

"No!" exclaimed Branwen. "I do not believe so. You must go to Prince Llew, Iwan. Speak with him.

137

Tell him of your father's peril and beg him to send a force of warriors along the coast to Gwylan Canu."

Iwan gaped at her. He staggered, still disoriented and dazed by the intensity of Blodwedd's vision. Branwen caught his arm. He leaned heavily on her, panting for breath.

"This is madness," he gasped. "Visions and dead gods? Am I a gullible child to be told such things and believe?" He glared at Blodwedd. "This she-devil is a sorceress!"

"Believe me," said Branwen, her fingers digging into his arm. "I know how the mind revolts. I, too, denied these things—until denial became impossible." She tugged at his arm. "Look at me, Iwan. Have I lost my wits? Am I a stranger to truth and reality? Is that how I seem to you?"

He rubbed his arm across his face and peered at her. His eyes were on hers for a long time, as though he was trying to pierce her mind and stare deep into her soul.

"Even were I fool enough to trust you, Branwen," he said at last, his voice slow and heavy, "the prince would not send warriors to Gwylan Canu on my word alone. And you can be quite certain that I would not go to him with the tale you tell—not unless I wanted the madness whipped out of me."

"Then tell him a different tale," said Branwen. "Tell him you met with a messenger riding hard from your father's fortress—a messenger with grim and urgent news! Tell him you learned that Gwylan Canu is in deadly danger, that the Saxons are coming in force. Tell him you told the messenger that you would pass this news onto the prince, and you sent the rider back to Gwylan Canu with all the speed he could muster, back to your father to let him know that he should hold firm, for aid would swiftly follow. Tell the prince all that!"

"A messenger from Gwylan Canu?" murmured Iwan. "Dagonet ap Wadu, perhaps—he would know me well and take orders from me. But, no! He could not have entered Doeth Palas without drawing the attention of the guards on the gate."

"Then tell the prince you met him on the road, outside the citadel," urged Branwen.

"Yes, yes," muttered Iwan. "It is possible that I could have met with Dagonet on the east road while wandering abroad, exercising my horse." He ran his hand over his forehead. "Ach, but to take such a tale to the prince? Would I be able to convince him that I am telling the truth?"

"You have shown no difficulty in being plausible in the past, Iwan," Branwen said. "The first time we met, you played me for a fool with ease."

Iwan nodded. "I can playact most blithely, for certain," he said. "But this is a deadlier game by far, Branwen. And if I am believed, and you prove false, it will be the end of me at Prince Llew's court. I will be disgraced—or worse."

"I will not prove false," said Branwen. "You have looked into Blodwedd's eyes and seen the same things she showed me. The danger is real. Ironfist is coming for Gwylan Canu—you cannot think otherwise."

There was a long silence. Branwen could see Iwan was thinking hard—deciding whether or not to give credence to what he had seen. At last, he took a long, slow breath. "No, I do not think otherwise," he said. "I will go to Prince Llew. I will make him listen—I will make him believe. But what of you, Branwen? You cannot show yourself in Doeth Palas."

"I shall not," said Branwen. "We came here only to speak with you—to convince you that your home is in peril. We will go now."

"Will this prince of men believe—and act?" asked Blodwedd. "Is it certain that warriors will be sent to the place of the singing gulls?" She looked sharply at Branwen. "Unless our actions work to the salvation of the citadel on the seashore, we will have failed in our task. Should we not go with this boy to the prince and add the weight of our words to his argument?"

"You cannot do that," said Iwan. "Branwen is a condemned fugitive—the prince would never listen to her." He looked at Blodwedd. "As for you," he shook his head, "one glance into your eyes and Prince Llew would know you for a demon of the old times. You would be slaughtered on the spot."

"That would not be such an easy task," Blodwedd growled.

"Nevertheless, I doubt even you could hold out against fifty warriors," Branwen said. "You would die and I would soon hang, and all would be lost. No. Iwan must go alone."

"I shall," said Iwan. He stood in the doorway, the door half open so that he was bathed in sunlight and his long shadow stretched across the floor. He looked at Branwen. "Thank you," he said. "Thank you for trusting me." He gave her the ghost of a smile. "Did I not say you would have an interesting life, Branwen? I never knew till today that I was gifted with prophecy! But if it is so, then here's one last foretelling: We *will* meet again, barbarian princess, and you will see you were right to put your faith in me. But for now—farewell." He turned and ran from the building.

Branwen stepped outside cautiously and watched until he turned a corner and vanished. All the time that her eyes were on him, she could feel rage rising within her. She had kept it suppressed so long as Iwan was with them, but now she turned to Blodwedd, free to give voice to her fury. "Did you show him his own death?" she demanded, her voice trembling. "Did you make him see his own head hanging from a Saxon fist?"

"No, I did not," Blodwedd said. "All but that, Warrior-Child."

"I'm grateful for that, at least," Branwen said, her anger abating a little. "We should go now. I would be out of this place before Prince Llew's warriors begin to gather."

"We cannot depart," said Blodwedd. "Not until we are certain that the boy's warnings will be heeded."

"It will take time for a host to be mustered," said Branwen. "Yet we will know soon enough. We will keep watch from the forest." She thought for a moment. "If soldiers have not taken the road to Gwylan Canu by the time the sun is low in the west, we will know Iwan has failed. And then . . ." Her voice faded.

And then?

Return to Doeth Palas. Give herself up to the guards. Hope to be taken to the prince—hope to convince him where Iwan failed.

Hope to live long enough to do what she had come here to do.

16

BRANWEN HAD BEEN apprehensive ever since she nervously stepped foot on the road that led up to the citadel; and once within Doeth Palas, she had been on edge, wary of every shadow, of every eye turned toward her. But true fear of capture did not strike her until she saw the gates ahead, through the crowds, and knew that escape was near. The terror—the thought that safety lay so near but that danger could still strike her down at any moment—it was overwhelming.

The market bustled, riotous and unruly, and she had to force her way forward, forging a path in the opposite direction of the mass of people. Blodwedd was close behind her, struggling to keep up. Branwen could see from her stumbling, uncertain walk and her hunched shoulders that the owl-girl was having trouble coping with the crowds that pressed in all around her. A woman crossed Branwen's path, leading a donkey loaded with sheaves of flax. Branwen was pushed to one side as the woman barged through the crowd. The donkey came between her and Blodwedd. More people shoved past, knocking her aside, forcing her to use her arms to fend them off. The crush took away her breath, and she was unable to see where she was going.

She fell over an earthenware pot and struggled to raise her hands over her head to avoid the trampling feet. There was something nightmarish about the surging crowds. She had to get up again! She had to find Blodwedd!

A hand plucked her from the ground. Her arm was twisted roughly behind her, fingers locking on her wrist and wrenching the joints of her arm to force her out of the crowds and into a narrow passage between two buildings.

"Release me!" she demanded, wincing from the pain in her arm and shoulder.

The fingers loosened from her wrist. She turned and looked up into the face of Gavan ap Huw. His gray eyes glowered down at her, and his mouth was set in a grim line.

"What are you doing here?" he asked, and Branwen was surprised to hear a quaver in his gravelly voice. "Are you moonstruck to come back here, girl?"

She didn't know what to tell him. The truth? Gavan

did not believe in the Old Gods, and he would not listen to talk of Rhiannon of the Spring and Govannon of the Wood.

"Do you know what happened at Garth Milain?" she asked him, her own voice shaking.

"The battle? Aye, I know. All dead, child—all burned. Your home . . . gone. Is that why you have returned? It was lunacy to do so. Do you not know what kind of welcome Prince Llew will have prepared for you, Branwen?"

"No! You're wrong about the battle," said Branwen. "Not all are dead. My mother still lives, and although the garth was burned, the Saxons were thrown back. I was there, Gavan. Rhodri spoke the truth; everything he told me was true. He is no spy."

"That is not for you to decide," said Gavan. "Come, I must take you to the prince."

"No!"

"Be calm, girl. I will speak on your behalf in front of the full council. The fell deeds in Cyffin Tir will weigh in your favor. Prince Llew is not a tyrant, Branwen—he will treat you justly when all is known." His eyes glittered. "Where is the boy?"

"Far from here," said Branwen. "Where you will never find him."

"Is that so?" Gavan's voice was thoughtful. "He means us naught but good, and yet he flees us?"

"You would have hanged him," said Branwen. "He has no reason to trust to kinder treatment were you to capture him again. Let me go! Let me leave Doeth Palas. I give you my word that neither I nor Rhodri will do anything to cause harm to a single soul of Bras Mynydd." She looked fiercely into his eyes. "I have a task to perform, Gavan ap Huw—you would do well not to hinder me in it. You do not know what peril you put yourself in!"

His great hand gripped her shoulder. "Tell me of this peril."

"You would not believe me."

"You are the daughter of Alis ap Owain. Open your heart and speak honestly with me, and I will believe you."

Branwen paused, uncertain of how Gavan would react to the things she was about to tell him. "The Shining Ones have awoken," she said at last. "They would use me to beat back the Saxons. They call me the Emerald Flame of my people. They call me the Bright Blade. They call me the Sword of Destiny. Release me, Gavan ap Huw, or you stand in the way of the Old Gods!"

A look of alarm crossed Gavan's face. "No!" he gasped. "It cannot be. You are deluded, Branwen. Tell me that you know this to be untrue."

She laughed without humor, and his face became even more grave and troubled.

"She is telling you the truth," came a man's voice from behind the old warrior. "Now, do nothing foolish. Do you feel the blade in your back? Twitch but the tips of your fingers, and it shall be the end of you."

"Rhodri?" breathed Branwen, as stunned as Gavan. Her companion had come up behind the old warrior without a sound.

"Yes, and not a moment too soon, it seems," said Rhodri. "Hoi! Hold still, old man—I may not be a great swordsman like you, but it will take little skill to skewer you like a wild pig!"

Gavan's eyes narrowed. "It seems he is not so very far from here after all, my lady," he muttered. "Boy! Do you know the danger you are in? Were I but to cry out, a hundred men would fall upon you like thunder before you could run ten steps."

"I am sure you're right in that," said Rhodri. "But you'd not be alive to enjoy the sight!"

Gavan winced as Rhodri pressed the tip of the knife into his back.

"I have offered my life to my liege lord many a time," said Gavan, speaking without a trace of fear or anger. "Think you I fear death if my duty requires it of me?" He twisted in an instant, taking Rhodri completely by surprise, and before Branwen was able to react, the knife was wrested from Rhodri's grip and he was pressed up against the wall with its keen edge against his throat.

"Now, boy, let's see how *you* face certain death," Gavan growled.

There was dread in Rhodri's face as Gavan pulled his head back by the hair to stretch his neck under the blade. "Kill me, if you must," Rhodri croaked. "But let Branwen go. She has told you the truth." He swallowed hard. "My life for hers, old man. Willingly."

For a few long moments Gavan held Rhodri against the wall, his slate-colored eyes staring into Rhodri's brave, frightened face.

Branwen didn't dare move—nothing she could attempt would be quick enough to prevent the cold iron from slicing across Rhodri's flesh.

At last, Gavan took the blade from Rhodri's neck, turning the knife in his hand and offering the handle to him. "Three fine fools together are we, I think—but I will not be the cause of the downfall of the House of Griffith," he said somberly. "I will not have it weigh on my heart that the daughter of Alis ap Owain died because of my actions." He turned to look at Branwen. "I fear for you, child—truly I do. But for all your ravings, I cannot believe you mean us harm. Go now, return to your mother—and seek her wisdom, for pity's sake. For you are mad, Branwen, if you believe you are guided by gods."

"If I had my way, I would be by my mother's side at this very moment," Branwen said. "My heart aches to be with her."

"Then go to her!"

"I *cannot!*"

A slender figure appeared at the end of the alley. She walked forward, drawing her wimple back and looking keenly up into Gavan's face.

"Beware, warrior of Powys," Blodwedd murmured. "Beware lest your eyes be opened by the gods themselves—for they will pour their truth into your heart like molten iron, and you will be seared and destroyed by it!"

Gavan stared at her, his face blanching.

"What . . . are you?" he breathed.

"What am I?" Blodwedd's voice was a low rumble. "I am the silent wing in the still of night. I am the swift slaughter in twilight. I am the claw that clutches the heart, the beak that pecks the soul. Would you know me better, warrior of Powys?"

Gavan shook his head. "No," he murmured, and for the first time, Branwen heard fear in the powerful old man's voice. "No, for the life of me, I would not. I know now what you are. But the world has changed since your kind walked abroad. You are wrong for these times. You come here from beyond sanity's shores."

"You thought we would slumber for all eternity?" Blodwedd asked him. "You thought that if you never spoke our names, you would be free of us? Free of the ache for air in your lungs? Free of the need for earth beneath your feet? Free of the howling hunger? Free of the unslakable thirst? Free of all things that bind you to this land?" She smiled. "Not while you breathe and walk and eat and drink, warrior of Powys." She turned to Branwen, her head bowed. "I failed you again, Warrior-Child," she said. "I should not have let us become parted."

"No harm was done," Branwen said. She looked into the disturbed face of the old warrior. "Do you see now, Gavan? Do you see that I am not mad?"

"That may be," said Gavan. "But heed my words, Branwen: These ancient powers that call you are like a mighty river, and you are but a leaf on their flood. They will bear you to your doom, child."

"Perhaps," Branwen said. "But you must leave me to walk the path laid out for me by the Shining Ones. If you truly honor me for my mother's sake, tell no one that you saw me here."

Gavan bowed his head. "I will pray for your soul," he said.

"For that, much thanks," Branwen replied. She looked from Rhodri to Blodwedd. "Come. He won't give us away." And so saying, she pulled her wimple close over her face again and led her two companions along the narrow alley between the two huts and out into the marketplace.

17

"WHAT GORAIG GOBLIN put it into your mind to risk your life like that?" Branwen demanded as she and Rhodri moved through the trees toward where the two horses were quietly grazing. "Don't you know that Gavan could have slaughtered you in an instant if he had so chosen? I told you to stay with the horses where you would be safe."

"I left Fain to watch over the horses," said Rhodri. "And here they are—safe and sound. And your armor remains untouched. As for the rest," he shrugged, "I asked myself, 'What would Branwen do in these circumstances?'" He smiled. "The answer came very easily."

"Then perhaps such questions are better left unasked," retorted Branwen.

"*Caw! Caw!*"

Branwen smiled at the falcon, perched on a branch, watching them with its clever, knowing eyes.

"Thank you, Fain," she said. "You are more true to your duty than some I could mention."

Blodwedd looked from Branwen to Rhodri. "Why do you chide him so?" she asked. "He acted out of loyalty and concern."

"He could have been killed," Branwen snapped.

"Well, I was not," said Rhodri. "Now that we are safely returned and out of earshot, tell me all that happened in Doeth Palas. Did you find Iwan?"

"We did," said Branwen. "He will speak with the prince."

"And will Prince Llew act, do you think?"

"That we shall see," said Branwen, staring up through the leaves at the midday sun.

The afternoon wore slowly away. The forest was full of drowsy air, the light thick and golden through the canopy of leaves. An insect buzzed in Branwen's ear. She flicked her hand at it, fretting at the delay.

She and Rhodri and Blodwedd were seated under the trees, waiting. Blodwedd was sitting as she always did—bolt upright in the grass, her legs folded, her arms wrapped around her shins, her chin on her knees. Her eyes were open, but she did not seem to be looking at anything. She had not moved for some time. Branwen wondered whether the owl-girl was watchfully asleep, perhaps, as she had been the previous night.

Rhodri was whittling a stick with the hunting knife, his head bowed in concentration. Branwen envied his calmness. She felt anything but calm. She had no idea how long ago it was that she had sent Fain to gather news, but it seemed like a whole lifetime. And still they hid in the forest, and still they knew nothing of what was happening in Doeth Palas.

What if Prince Llew did not act? What were her options then? She had gone over this many times in her mind, turning her thoughts like heavy rocks, not liking what was revealed beneath.

A gray sickle-shaped form came winging through the branches.

Branwen jumped up. "Fain!"

The falcon gave a succession of sharp calls as it circled her.

She looked over to Blodwedd, who was alert now and also on her feet. "What is he saying?"

"Horsemen," said Blodwedd. "Many horsemen have left the citadel, armed and caparisoned for warfare. They have taken the coastal road to the east, traveling swiftly."

Branwen let out a breath. "Then it is done!" she gasped, relief thrilling through her body like a rush of cool water. "The prince has sent soldiers to Gwylan Canu. Ironfist will be thwarted!" She looked over to where Rhodri was standing. "It is done!" she called to him.

He smiled, looking at Blodwedd. "The place of singing gulls will be safe from the Saxon hawks, Blodwedd," he said. "You will be a bird again!"

"When all is fulfilled, with my lord's blessing, I shall," said Blodwedd. "The bird is on the wing and the prey is under the claw, but the kill is not yet certain." She looked at Branwen. "We must go to the place of singing gulls," she said. "We must know for sure that all is well. Only then will our duty be complete. Only then will Lord Govannon release me."

The stone-clad citadel of Doeth Palas stood on a lofty peak rising from a forested valley at the northern limits of the kingdom of Powys and indeed the entire land of Brython. The solitary hill sheared down in precipitous cliffs to the restless sea, and from its shoulders long, undulating bluffs of timeworn limestone stretched into the east.

A road ran along these cliffs, hugging the coastline, rising and falling like a pale ribbon as it threaded its way into the cantref of Teg Eingel—longtime seat of the House of Puw—a narrow stretch of land between the Clwydian Mountains and the sea.

It was a road much used, traversed by merchants, hawkers, and travelers in peaceful times—a conduit for trade and commerce. And in unsettled and violent days, the hooves of war-horses and the feet of soldiers echoed among the cliffs and glens as armies swept back and forth with the tides and fortunes of battle.

Although Branwen had no patience for dry lists of names and dates, she had always loved the thrilling tales of the old wars that were told and retold around the hearth in the Great Hall of Garth Milain. So she knew it was almost twenty years now since a Saxon warrior had walked this road—twenty years since Powys had been in such peril as now haunted these regions.

Branwen, Rhodri, and Blodwedd tracked the horsemen of Doeth Palas as they made their way along the road. They were careful to keep out of sight, wary of showing themselves against the horizon or to coming close enough for a vigilant eye to catch a glimpse of them.

Fortunately, the northern reaches of Bras Mynydd were less hospitable than the fertile lowlands, and there were no farms or hamlets to be avoided. There were hills and forests enough to provide cover, and when the difficulties of the landscape forced Branwen to lead them away from the warrior band, there was always Fain to keep watch from on high and guide them back to the road.

They shadowed the horsemen through the long afternoon and into the evening.

They were drawing close to the mountains now; the dark-green bulk filled the eastern sky as the sun set, the highest peaks turning to gold in the fading light.

* * *

Night fell. The horsemen made camp in a sheltered dell south of the road, building fires and setting the horses to graze while they prepared their evening meal.

Branwen and Rhodri watched from a high ridge, lying flat on their stomachs as they peered down the wooded slope to where the cooking fires flickered. Branwen was in her hunting leathers again. She felt much more herself now that their disguises had been shed, and she was glad to feel the knife and slingshot at her belt. Her sword and shield were with Blodwedd and the horses, further up the hill and well out of sight. It had been difficult to convince Blodwedd to let the two of them patrol alone, but in the end the owl-girl had agreed to remain behind while they scouted the land.

"How many men, would you say?" asked Branwen. "Fifty, perhaps?"

Rhodri nodded.

"Why so few?" Branwen wondered aloud. "He has twice ten times that number of armed men in Doeth Palas. What can fifty men do against Ironfist's army?"

"They can hold the tide till the foot-soldiers arrive," said Rhodri. "My guess would be that these are just an advance party, sent as a show of force—to let Ironfist know that the prince of Bras Mynydd is coming for him." Rhodri grinned, his eyes bright in the darkness. "Ironfist will be livid to find that his tactics have been discovered. His whole purpose was to strike without warning—first, Garth Milain, then another citadel, and another and another—his enemies never knowing when or where he will come at them next. This will sour his milk for him! Closed gates and men armed and ready. Ha!"

"The prince is not with them, I think," said Branwen, staring down through the gloom. "But who is leading them, then? We have never come close enough to find out. And is Iwan with them? That's something I'd like to know."

"Go down and ask," Rhodri suggested. "And while you're at it, beg some food from them. We have hardly anything left to eat. I have to say, being linked to your high destiny would be more comfortable if the Old Gods gave thought to our bellies once in a while."

"Don't joke about such things," Branwen warned.

"Was I joking?" Rhodri sighed, lifting his head to gaze off into the east. "How far is it to Gwylan Canu, do you think?"

"Why ask me? I don't know these lands," Branwen replied distractedly. She was staring down the long slope and calculating how close she could get to the encampment without being spotted by the sentries. "Another day? Half a day? It cannot be too close, or they would not have made camp for the night." She lifted herself onto one elbow, looking at Rhodri. "I'm going down there," she said.

"Are you out of your wits?" Rhodri hissed. "Why

would you want to do that?"

"I may learn how soon they expect to come to Gwylan Canu," Branwen replied. "And find out whether you are right about more warriors coming, or whether fifty is all Prince Llew is willing to spare for a neighbor in peril."

"What are you saying? I don't understand."

"Neither do I," said Branwen. "But doesn't it seem odd to you that the prince did not send his warriors over the mountains to Garth Milain when he learned of the Saxon attack? Why did he not come to our aid?"

"The battle was over, so far as he knew," said Rhodri. "Your army scattered or slain, your mother and father dead, and the triumphant Saxons warming their hands as Garth Milain blazed. It was too late to help. That seems reason enough—and there's little purpose in risking your neck to be certain of it."

"I'll be careful," assured Branwen.

"All the same," Rhodri said, "you'll probably find that they're talking of nothing more elevated than saddle sores, or grumbling about having to sleep under the stars instead of snug in their own beds with the furs piled high."

"We shall see," said Branwen. "Wait for me—I shan't be long. And don't let Blodwedd know I've gone. The last thing I need is for her to go crashing down there causing chaos."

Rhodri gripped her arm. "Branwen—be careful."

"I will, I promise." She pulled away and slipped silently over the ridge and down the forested slope.

"Be calm, be silent, be swift, be still." Branwen mouthed the familiar instructions to herself as she made her way down the steep fall of the hillside. Occasionally the bulk of trees blocked the sight of the fires down in the vale, but most of the time she could see the flames flickering through branch and bole as she slipped lithely from trunk to trunk, her fingers running over the rough and ridged bark. The acrid smell of smoke drifted toward her, tingling in her nostrils, blotting out the other nighttime forest scents.

She began to hear the voices of the warriors . . . the clank of metal against metal . . . the restless thud of horses' hooves . . . the crackle of the flames. And with those sounds on the night air mingled the rich aroma of cooking meat, filling her head and making her belly growl. She had not tasted hot food since the half-finished bowl of stew in the farmhouse, where they had almost been captured.

She rested her back against a wide fir, listening intently. The nearest campfire was no more than twenty paces away, and now she could clearly hear the voices of the soldiers.

"I'm telling you, there's a storm coming," one was saying. "I can smell it on the air. We'll sleep cold and wet this night. We should have found a more sheltered spot to make camp."

"We should have ridden on through the night," said another voice—one that Branwen knew. Iwan. So, he *was* traveling with them. She felt uneasy, remembering the vision of his severed head dangling from a Saxon fist. Was he riding to his death? A third voice interrupted her troubled thoughts.

"And arrive to fight red-eyed and yawning?" it said. "That were wisdom, indeed, young pup!"

"Captain Angor knows his business, lad," said the first voice. "Don't you fret. We'll be up and on the move with the dawn. It makes no sense to travel by night. Look you at those hills—wooded from end to end—trees enough to hide an army! You'd have us ride such terrain at night? Why, if old Ironfist was lying in ambush, we'd not stand a chance."

"Aye, I don't like the look of these forests," said a different voice. "Pass that pig's foot, Digon—fetch it out of the flames before it's charred. Mark me, boys, there's something uncanny about these old woodlands. Don't you feel it? Eyes watching. Minds turning."

Branwen felt a shiver run down her spine. There was something almost sinister in the way that flecks of firelight trembled and danced on trunk and branch and leaf all around her. But what did the man mean? *Eyes watching. Minds turning.*

"They say there was a Druid temple hereabouts in the way-before times," said the first voice in a husky growl. "They performed strange rites and rituals in these hills, sacrificing to the Old Gods—"

Ahhh! The Old Gods . . .

"Be silent, you fool," the third voice said angrily. "Do not name them! Not here. Not in this place. Are you moonstruck?"

"Why do you fear them?" asked Iwan. "Do the Old Gods hate us?"

"How would you feel, boy?" commented the first voice, ominously. "To be a god no longer worshipped or feared?"

"Speak no more of these things!" snapped the third voice.

There was a lull in the conversation for a few moments. Branwen could hear the sounds of meat being gnawed from the bone and of drink being swallowed.

"I still say we should have pressed on through the dark," Iwan said at length. "Scouts could have ridden on ahead to scour the road for danger. And isn't it as dark for Saxons as it is for us? My father could be lying slain this very moment, while we sit cramming our bellies and gossiping!"

"If your father is already slain, there's little need for haste, boy," said the first voice lightly. "He won't begrudge us our respite—not where he'll be watching from!"

There was some laughter at this, but Iwan broke angrily into it. "If Gwylan Canu is taken while we slumber and snore, every death will be on our heads."

"Calm yourself, boy!" ordered the third voice. "Dagonet ap Wadu will have reached the citadel by now. They will know of our coming. The gates will be closed. Why do you fret? Gwylan Canu is a strong fortress and your father a fearsome warrior. We will arrive in time, Iwan, have no fear."

Branwen heard Iwan give a snort of anger. She knew why he was angry and frustrated by the delay; he alone knew that Dagonet would not be arriving at Gwylan Canu with hopeful tidings. There had been no messenger to begin with.

"Don't stray, lad," called the first man.

Branwen realized that Iwan must have got up from the fireside and walked away from the men.

"I'm going to check on the horses," called Iwan, his voice farther away now. "Perhaps they'll make more sense than you bunch of old women!"

The soldiers roared with laughter.

Branwen moved stealthily across the hillside, careful not to rustle a branch or snap a twig. She peered around a trunk. The horses were gathered a little way off from the fires, haltered by reins looped around fallen branches and large stones. A slim shadow moved among them.

She slipped from cover and was among the horses in an instant, smelling their distinctive scent, listening to their breathing and their nighttime movements.

She ran her hand over flank and neck, enjoying the rough texture of their hair, wishing she had some morsel—an apple or something—to offer them as they turned their huge, noble heads toward her.

And then one horse in particular nuzzled against her—and even in the dark of night, she knew him. A tall bay stallion, the bold and true friend she had been forced to leave behind when she had fled to save Rhodri from the gallows. Her own horse.

"Stalwyn!" she breathed, lifting her hands to stroke his neck and run glad fingers through his glossy black mane. "I thought I'd never see you again, boy." She pressed her face into his neck and breathed in deeply, her head filling with his warm, horsey scent. "So, they knew your worth, did they, the men of Doeth Palas? Who rides you now to war, boy? Someone equally worthy, I hope." Stalwyn lifted his head, his liquid black eye shining. He pushed his soft nose into her shoulder, as if glad to be reunited with her. "I'd ride off with you now, if I could," she murmured. "But we'd be seen and that would not be good. Be brave and steadfast, and with luck we will be together again in time."

Oh, but the smell of him brought back such memories! There was a thickness in her throat and a prickling in her eyes as she remembered carefree days riding on the heaths with Geraint, the wind slapping her skin red as berries, Stalwyn's body moving powerfully under her as she gripped him tight with her knees and thighs and they raced away the long summer days.

She thought of him in wintertime, fetlock-deep in snow, his breath white like the smoke from a smithy's fire when the bellows are blown. The trill of a hunting horn. The chase for a stag. And Stalwyn sweating in the paddock afterward, leaning into her as she wiped him down with sacking, his hot horse smell filling her head.

Lost times. Never to be recovered, except with the bittersweet stab of memory.

"Branwen?" The voice was a low murmur, breaking the reverie into which Stalwyn's scent had thrown her. She looked around sharply, her fingers gripping her knife. Iwan was staring at her, his face just a pale blur in the night. He came closer, lowering his voice to a whisper. "You followed us?"

"I had to know your home would be saved," Branwen whispered back. "But why are there only fifty of you? Prince Llew could have spared more, surely?"

"More are coming," murmured Iwan, his head close to hers, his eyes dark and deep. "Two hundred or more—on foot, as soon as they can be mustered. But fifty horse was all that the prince could bring together on such short notice."

So Rhodri's guess had been right—these were only the vanguard of the force that would be sent. Good. Very good—so long as they came quickly!

"At least Prince Llew believed you," Branwen said.

"Aye, I played the part well. But you should not be here. It isn't safe. What if you are discovered?"

"Don't worry on my behalf," Branwen replied.

He looked closely into her face, his breath warm on her cheek. "Oh, but I do," he whispered, his eyes glinting in the dim light. "I knew from the first time I saw you that you'd stamp a heavy foot on my heart, Branwen."

She stared at him, confused, not understanding what he meant. Was he playacting again?

"You should not have come, Iwan," Branwen murmured.

He looked puzzled. "Why so?"

Because I fear you will be killed!

A deep voice called. "Hoi! Iwan!"

He spun, his face perturbed. "Here, Captain— I'm coming." He glanced briefly at Branwen, moving away, holding his arm out toward her, warning her to stay hidden. Without thinking she reached out, and their fingers touched for a moment.

Then he was gone among the horses.

"Who were you speaking to, Iwan?" came Captain Angor's voice.

Branwen shrank away between the horses, a cold sweat starting on her face and the blood throbbing in her ears.

"Gwennol Dhu was fretful," Iwan replied smoothly. "I calmed her with a few gentle words."

"The horses are agitated, for sure," said the Captain. "They care not for this forest. It has an ill name in legend: the Ghostwood. Perhaps ancient memories linger."

"Memories of the Old Gods, do you mean?" asked Iwan.

"There are no Old Gods, boy," Angor said abruptly. "There are Saint Cadog and Saint Dewi and Saint Cynwal. Look you how they watch over us. We need no others."

"But the saints have gentle hands and they watch from afar," Iwan responded. "It is said the Saxons have terrible gods. Gods of thunder and lightning, blood and iron. Gods of death and mayhem. Can the saints protect us against such gods?"

"Aye, lad—that they can, have no fear on that score. Come now—get you to sleep, Iwan ap Madoc. It is stern work that awaits us with the coming of the new day."

Branwen heard them move away, back toward the campfires. She let out a long, slow breath.

She waited among the horses until she felt it was safe to slip into the sheltering darkness under the trees and up the long hill to where her companions were waiting.

The Ghostwood, haunted by memories of ancient things. But *what* ancient things? Branwen wondered as she climbed whether Blodwedd would be able to tell her more. Yes, if anyone knew the secrets of this place, it would be Govannon's messenger.

18

"ARE YOU THISTLEDOWN that you think you can move among men without being seen?" In the darkness under the trees, Blodwedd's eyes were like angry fires.

"No one saw me except for Iwan," Branwen retorted, stung by the owl-girl's rebuke and refusing to be browbeaten. "And I won't answer to you for my movements. You're here to be my guide, not my master." She held Blodwedd's eyes.

"Did you find out anything of use?" Rhodri asked, obviously wanting to break the tension between his two companions.

"More soldiers are coming," Branwen said, turning to Rhodri. "Iwan told me so. And one of the soldiers thinks there's a storm coming." She peered up through the branches. "But I'm not so sure." In the clear sky, stars were twinkling, cold and remote.

"He is right," said Blodwedd, looking at Rhodri. "I can smell it on the air. It rides in on a brazen west wind. There will be rain before dawn."

"Then we should get what sleep we can," said Rhodri. "For a while, before the heavens open." He pulled his cloak around his shoulders and curled up on his side.

Branwen settled back against a tree trunk, pillowed on dead leaves, with her knees up, her feet splayed, and her arms folded over her chest. She closed her eyes but was vividly aware of Blodwedd's presence on Rhodri's far side, bundled up like a grasshopper on a stoop of hay. Did the girl never lie down?

Girl? Is that what you called her? Careful, Branwen—don't forget what she truly is.

Branwen opened an eye. She was surprised to see Blodwedd gazing at Rhodri with a curious, conflicted expression on her pale, wide face. It seemed part fascination, part joy, and part . . . what? *Longing*, almost. Yes, that was it exactly—a look of quiet, almost regretful yearning.

Has she fallen in love with him? Branwen wondered. She found the idea faintly repellent. And what feelings did Rhodri have for the owl-girl? He was kind to her, as was his nature, and he was obviously intrigued by her. But surely it was no more than that? Surely he could not have deep feelings for a creature so inhuman that she had come close to slaughtering a helpless baby?

Blodwedd's eyes turned toward her and her face became blank and unreadable again. "You may speak freely," Blodwedd said. "He will not wake."

"Why?" Branwen asked sourly. "Have you put a spell on him?"

"Not I," Blodwedd replied. "There are things you wish to ask me, but you fear the answers. Ask anyway, Warrior-Child—it is the fears that are never faced that gnaw the deepest."

"The men were talking about this place," Branwen began hesitantly. "About this forest. Something about it scares them, like children frightened of the dark, except not quite that. One of them started to talk about the Old Gods, but he was told to hold his tongue." She sat up now, suddenly sleepless. "Do the Shining Ones live in this forest?"

"I have told you already," Blodwedd said, as though speaking to a child. "The Shining Ones live in all things—trickle and torrent, shoot and tree, pebble and crag, breeze and blizzard. *All* things."

"So why do the men call this place the Ghost-wood?"

The huge eyes shone. "Perhaps because this was a place of worship in the young days, in the days before the counting of days. It was here they venerated the guardians of the land and gave thanks for their stewardship."

Branwen tried hard to understand what the owl-girl was telling her. "You mean there was a temple here—a Druid temple—before the Romans came?"

"A sacred place," said Blodwedd. "A blessed place. A glorious place. If men fear it now, it is only because they know in their hearts that they have turned away from the father who seeded them and the mother who bore them and watched over them. They fear to come here because this place speaks to them of who they once were, and shows them the folly of the path upon which their feet are now set." Blodwedd rose to her feet. "It whispers of their peril, Warrior-Child. It murmurs of their doom."

"A Saxon doom?" Branwen asked, gazing up into the owl-girl's face. She trembled as Blodwedd stared at her; she felt in danger of losing herself once more in those golden eyes. But she could not tear herself free from the gaze.

Her head throbbed, and white lightning flashed at the edges of sight. Her skin prickled hot and cold, and she felt dizzy and disoriented as though in a nightmare or a high fever. Blodwedd seemed somehow to have grown taller; she towered over Branwen, her head among the stars, her feet sunken deep into the earth, her arms as wide as the night sky.

"The riddling Saxons will come, Warrior-Child," cried Blodwedd, her voice booming in Branwen's mind, "and the high-hearted Angles and the flaxen Jutes and the runewise Danes." Lightning flashed around the owl-girl like knives, and white sparks rose from her hair, forming forked, antlerlike shapes against the dark sky.

"What are you talking about?" shouted Branwen. "I don't understand!"

But Blodwedd didn't seem to hear her.

"And also will come the butchering Vikings," she raged on, "steeped to the shoulder in crimson gore, cutting the blood eagle and sprinkling salt in the wounds. And in their wake will come the courtly Normans and Owain Gwynedd, first prince of the Walha. And in time upon bad time, Edward Longshanks will awaken to slaughter the four brothers of Gwynedd and to hack off the head of Llewellyn Ein Llyw Olaf—the last leader of your people—and carry it as a trophy through the streets of London."

"Stop! Stop!"

"And then, in the reign of Henry Plantagenet, third of that name, the great hero Owain Glyndwr will arise—a warrior descendant of warrior stock, the far-flung son of the daughters of the sons of the women of the House of Griffith!"

"For pity's sake—enough!" cried Branwen, screwing her eyes shut tight, pressing her hands to her ears to try and hold back the thundering and crashing of Blodwedd's voice in her head.

And suddenly the voice was gone—and all Branwen could hear was the hiss and spatter of rain. She held her breath for a few moments to be sure. Yes, Blodwedd's rantings were over.

Branwen could still hear the thunder, but there were no longer words in it. She could still see the cold fire of the lightning through her closed eyes. She could feel rain on her skin.

She opened her eyes. Blodwedd was standing over her, small and slender again, gazing unfathomably down at her through a curtain of slanting rain. Branwen gasped, her head aching and her limbs tingling as though the lightning had got into her body and was burning her from within.

Blodwedd stretched down a thin hand. Branwen took it and got up. She glanced at Rhodri, sleeping still in all the tumult, curled under his rain-speckled cloak. The horses stood close by, lost in imperturbable horse dreams.

Wordlessly, Blodwedd led Branwen through the trees. The rain tapped on the leaves like impatient fingers, but beneath their feet the ground was still dry. Thunder rumbled and growled, and blades of lightning bleached the world black and white, so that sable trees stood stark against a backdrop of blanched nothingness, like a veil thrown across eternity.

They came to a grove where there was no rain and no thunder. The sky above was vibrant with uncountable stars. The air was sweet and warm. Branwen saw that the skulls of animals had been nailed high on the trunks of the trees that ringed the glade, their staring eye sockets black in the light of flickering torches.

A rhythmic drumming filled the trees, throbbing

in the air and making the ground shudder under Branwen's feet.

A circle of gray, shoulder-high standing stones dominated the grove, rough-hewn into shapes like pointed leaves or spearheads. Designs and patterns had been engraved on the stones, but the hollows and ridges were blurred by lichen and fungi.

Branwen had the certain feeling that the stones had been there for a long time—girdled with snowdrops in festive spring, scorched by the sun in high summer, marooned in an ocean of brown leaves in autumn, snow-crowned in deepest winter—enduring and outlasting all that the shifting seasons offered for years beyond count.

A woman stood in the middle of the stone circle, dressed in deep-blue robes, her arms spread wide and her face lifted toward the starry night sky. She was chanting, her deep, resonant voice keeping time to the drum.

> *In the summer comes love and devotion*
> *Like a stallion galloping, courageous for*
>   *his lady and his lord.*
> *The sea is booming, the apple tree in bloom*
> *The thirsty earth drinks deep*
> *The sun shield-shining*
> *Lightning comes as arrows from the blue*
>   *sky*
> *Cloudless rain like a falling of spears.*

I long for and I crave thee, guardians of
  our land
Eternally renewed from ever was to ever
  will be
Earthshakers, with the sky on your
  shoulders
With your feet in the sea
Movers of the rolling world, the Shining
  Ones.
I stand among the slender hemlock stems
In bright noon and in blessed night
Awaiting the fair, frail, fragile form
Awaiting thy light.
See, silent she comes as the deer's footfall
Comely and bountiful,
See, mighty he comes, root deep, leaf bright
Loving and giving,
See, solemn she comes from out the hollow
  hills
Constant and true,
See, merry he comes, the liquid acrobat who
  carves the quartered sky
Laughing and leaping

As the woman threw her words up into the immense darkness, four figures moved around her in a slow ritual dance. One was a woman, turning and turning, dressed in white; her long, fine white hair spun with her, and in her hands she held the white skull of a horse. The second was a man dressed all in green, stamping with heavy feet, antlers bound to his forehead. The third figure, bent-backed, stumbled forward, its gnarled fingers clutching a twisted stick; it was masked with an ancient and ugly face, wrinkled and wise. The last of the four was a man in gray who tumbled and cavorted and pranced and leaped like cloud-wraiths in a gale.

"What is this?" Branwen asked, her mouth dry, her head hammering.

"The midsummer rites from the years of man's innocence," said Blodwedd. "Do you recognize the players, Warrior-Child?"

"The woman in white is like Rhiannon," said Branwen. "I imagine the green man is Govannon of the Wood."

"Yes. And the crone is Merion of the Stones and the cloud-man is Caradoc of the North Wind. This is from the days of belief, Warrior-Child—from the days of bone-deep faith and loyal blood. This is from the days of *understanding*."

"Geraint told me that the Druid priests sacrificed children to the Shining Ones," Branwen said. "That they used human blood to placate the Old Gods. That they were terrible and full of vengeance."

"Do you see spilled blood, Warrior-Child?" asked Blodwedd. "Do you feel fear in the air?"

"No." There was certainly no sensation of fear in the glade. Instead Branwen sensed joy and awe, as though this worship she was witnessing was a pleasure and a privilege. She turned to look into Blodwedd's golden eyes. "Why did we turn our backs on them?"

"You are human—you tell me."

"I don't *know*!"

"Humans are weak and changeable," said Blodwedd. "All the same, the parent loves still the wayward child, foolish and errant though it be. But when danger threatens, then the children must return and guard the home, lest the house fall and all are consumed in the flames." A sinister, dreadful light glowed again in Blodwedd's eyes. "The Shining Ones dread the coming of the Saxons, Warrior-Child. They dread the things these folk bring with them."

"What things?" Branwen whispered.

"The dark and brutal gods that dwell in their hearts," Blodwedd murmured. "Gods of warfare and avarice who have no love for Brython nor its people. Gods with iron teeth and hearts of stone. Gods whose footsteps burn, whose touch withers, whose breath is plague and damnation. Gods who will enter the hearts and minds of the people of Brython and destroy them."

Branwen felt her eyes widen in horror. "So the Shining Ones would have me fight not only the Saxons, but their gods as well?"

Blodwedd smiled. "Now you have wisdom, Warrior-Child," she said. "Now you see all! But the task is not as heavy as fear makes it appear. The Saxon gods follow behind the armies, feeding on death and despair as carrion birds feed on the fallen in battle. Hold back the Saxons and their gods will never darken this land. Do this thing and you will turn the long hard winter into glorious summer, Warrior-Child. That is what you must do. That is why the Shining Ones have called you. That is your destiny!"

19

THE STARS WERE snuffed out by a mass of seething black cloud. Thunder roared. Branwen blinked the teeming rain out of her eyes, trying to see in the sudden darkness.

"Blodwedd?" she screamed as storm-winds buffeted her and tore her hair.

Forked lightning cracked the sky open and showed Branwen the world around her.

She was at the edge of the glade still, but it was overgrown now, bereft of magic. The stones were half buried in fern and flower, their heads mantled in climbing plants. Tall trees grew where the woman had chanted and the four god-players had danced. But from high on the trunk of a nearby tree, the dead black eye sockets of a goat skull stared down mournfully, the last remnant of lost love and failed devotion.

"I am here," came Blodwedd's crackling voice. "We must return—there is mischief afoot! I smell wolves in the night! Rhodri cannot fight them alone."

Wolves!

Branwen drew her knife as she ran, and she felt the dark ecstasy of impending combat thrilling through her body. Here at last was an enemy she could strike at! Here was a prey to vent her frustration on! She gripped the knife tightly, chasing hard after the owl-girl as she flitted through the trees, praying Rhodri had not been caught unawares.

As she neared their camp, she could make out the frightened neighing of horses and the keening screech of Fain the falcon—but she could also hear harsh snarling and the growling of wolves.

Rhodri was on his feet, freed now from whatever spell had caused him to sleep so deeply earlier in the night. He was held at bay against a tree, his face twisted in fear, his clothes and hair saturated from the rain. He was holding off four or five wolves, Geraint's sword gripped in both fists as he swung it to and fro in a wide arc before him. As the blade scythed the rain, the wolves backed off and came snapping forward again.

Fain was doing his best to help, wings fluttering as he rose and swooped, flying into the wolves' eyes with outstretched claws, screaming, distracting them from their prey.

Even had Branwen been in a position to shoot a stone into a wolf's eye, the rain would have made it impossible for her to aim accurately with the slippery wet leather slingshot. No! Knife work was needed now—and quickly, too, before one of the wolves got close enough to Rhodri to draw blood.

Blodwedd let out a fearsome shriek, throwing herself forward with her arms raised and her fingers crooked into claws. Far more owl-like than human at that moment, she threw herself on the back of one of the wolves, sending it tumbling. As the two rolled over and over, Blodwedd's arms and legs wrapped around the shaggy body of the fearsome creature, its vicious head twisting and the wide jaws snapping red.

Branwen sprang forward, stabbing fiercely, and caught a wolf in the hindquarters. Blood spurted as the wolf turned, howling in anger and pain; its eyes were poison-yellow, and its black lips drew back from slavering fangs. She slashed again with the long hunting knife, rending the wolf's shoulder to the bone. As lightning flashed, she saw a second wolf turn and leap toward her.

She dropped to her knees in the wet earth, and mud sprayed up around her. Claws raked across her back as the flying wolf overshot. Without a moment's hesitation Branwen lunged forward and sank her knife deep into its throat. It gave a hideous yowl as dark blood gushed from the wound, and then the wolf crashed in front of her in a tangle of twisted legs.

She took one quick look into the dead eyes and saw the jaws still open, the tongue hanging, red with blood. Then she stumbled to her feet, dashing the rain out of her eyes, and whirled about as she heard a scrabble of claws behind her—the wolf with the injured shoulder.

She had no time to use her knife as the huge creature pounced. Instead she thrust her forearm between its jaws, forcing the mouth wide so that it could not bite together, fighting to stay on her feet as the weight of the animal came hammering down on her. There was the stench of its breath and the horrible smell of its rank, wet fur, followed by the scrape of its hooked and broken claws along her skin. Branwen wrenched her arm to one side, forcing the creature's head to twist on its powerful neck, and drove her knife upward, cutting through flesh and sinew and throbbing veins. Hot blood splashed over Branwen's face as the bulk of the wolf suddenly became lifeless, bearing her down into the mud.

Using all her strength, she pushed and kicked the hairy corpse off her. She scrambled to her feet, her shoes slipping, her face whipped raw by the rain. She saw Blodwedd rise from a dead wolf, her arms blooded to the elbow, her mouth red and dripping, her eyes ferocious. The wolf's throat had been bitten out.

Branwen turned away from the dreadful sight, desperate to get to Rhodri's side. He was still fighting for his life but managing to hold off the last two wolves, slashing and swiping at them as if the sword was a stick. He had no battle skills—no training as a warrior. All he had was courage and the strength of his two arms. Fain was still with him, plunging with outstretched claws, rising in a flurry of wings as the deadly teeth snapped at him.

Behind the tree against which Rhodri was trapped, Branwen saw the two horses rearing on their hind legs, kicking the air, their eyes terrified as they dragged at their tethers.

"Hold on!" she yelled to Rhodri. "I'm coming!"

Screaming in rage, she flung herself on the nearer of the two remaining wolves, using her momentum and weight to drive her knife up to the hilt in its back. The wolf twisted and writhed in its death agonies, ripping the knife from her fist and knocking her feet out from under her, sending her slamming hard to the ground.

She blinked as she lay gasping on her back. Pain wracked her body, and the rain filled her eyes, mixing with blood and veiling her sight with a red haze. She heard snarling. She felt blindly for her knife. A great dark, shaggy head appeared above her. Claws dug into her chest. Crimson jaws opened, yellow eyes gleamed. Fetid breath blasted her face.

Her fingers scrabbled in mud and grass, finding no weapon. She dashed the red water from her eyes as the gaping maw plunging toward her throat. There was a shout from above her. The wolf's head jerked up and its neck arched back. It fell sideways, kicked for a few moments, then lay still.

Branwen sat up, coughing and choking. Blood bubbled from a wound in the wolf's back. Rhodri was standing over her, panting for breath. He held the sword in both his hands, its blade swimming with gore.

She got up, grimacing, aching from her fall. Blodwedd walked toward them through the rain.

Rhodri gave Branwen a wry smile. "A fine time to go for a walkabout, Branwen!" he said. "If not for Fain waking me up, you'd have returned to find me being enjoyed as a late supper by those fine fellows!" He looked around at the five dark corpses. Fain had come down to perch on one wolf's unnaturally bent head. Branwen looked away as the curved beak pecked for juicy morsels among the bloody fur.

"Do you think the soldiers in the valley below will have heard us?" Rhodri asked. "I'd rather we did not have to face them as well!"

"The storm is loud enough to drown out all else," said Branwen. "And I doubt they would come to investigate the howling of wolves."

Blodwedd came up to Rhodri and looked into his eyes. "Are you hurt?" she asked.

He flinched for a moment at the gruesome sight of the owl-girl; her teeth and lips were still red with wolf's blood, and her long fingernails were dripping.

When Blodwedd saw his dismay, her forehead wrinkled in concern. She crouched quickly and washed her hands in the long, wet grass, passing the back of her hand across her mouth to wipe the gore away before standing again.

"No. I'm not hurt," Rhodri said, his face softening as though he was touched that Blodwedd should have cared enough to clean herself for him. "You arrived before my strength gave out. I was more worried for the horses, truth be told. I thought they might . . ." His voice trailed away. He turned and Branwen became aware of something that she had not noticed until that moment.

The horses were gone. In their dread of the wolves, they had torn loose from the stump to which they had been tied.

"Curse the luck!" groaned Branwen. "We cannot follow their trail in the dark—and there's little chance of hearing them in this storm." She pulled her cloak around her shoulders. "Let's hope they do not stray far. We must find what shelter we can from this downpour. With good fortune, we may find them in the morning."

"We may," Blodwedd said. "If we live out the night."

"Why shouldn't we?" Branwen asked her. "The wolves are dead."

"Five is a small pack, is it not?" Blodwedd asked. "I have lived in these mountains all my life, and I have observed many things and counted many beasts, both great and small. This was not the whole pack, Warrior-Child. These five were but out-runners— scouts sent abroad to lead the pack to food."

A cold fear swept over Branwen. The owl-girl was right—and she should have known it! She had often accompanied her father and brother and the court warriors in winter, hunting the starving wolf packs that came ravaging down from the mountains through the deep snows. Even in the frozen heart of the worst winters, when their numbers were thinned by starvation and unendurable cold, the packs were always large—twelve or fifteen wolves at least, and sometimes as many as twenty.

"Perhaps this was a single family," Rhodri suggested.

As though to mock his wishful words, a drawn-out howl sounded through the rain. Not the distant baying of a wolf on a lone crag—but the blood-chilling howl of a rapacious predator, sounding out his rallying call from far, far too close.

"They come!" hissed Blodwedd.

Branwen stared into the heavy curtain of the rain. Yellow eyes shone like jewels in the darkness. She turned slowly, her heart beating fast under her ribs. Two pairs of eyes . . . five . . . ten . . . twenty! *Even more!* Those eerie, luminous eyes were all around them— surrounding them in a deadly, unblinking ring.

There was a second, ghoulish howl, rising and falling in the night. It scraped at the inside of Branwen's skull like fingernails drawn down slate.

As the howl faded, the eyes began to move forward.

20

THROUGH THE RAIN, the wolves began to take form, moving in from all directions. Branwen took two swift steps and grasped the hilt of her knife, still jutting from between the ribs of her last victim. It would not come loose easily, so she pressed her foot down on the carcass and pulled to rip it free.

She moved back to be near the others, her eyes flickering from wolf to wolf, from eye to gleaming eye. These were nothing like the half-starved, bony animals of winter; these wolves were large and well fed, powerfully muscled and filled with the courage of the pack. Their narrow shoulders came up to her waist, and from their bulk, she guessed that each one probably outweighed her. Formidable foes, indeed, especially in such numbers.

They had killed five, taken them by surprise and

from behind. But twenty-five?

"Can you communicate with them?" Branwen asked Blodwedd. "Animal to animal? Tell them we are under Govannon's protection!"

"Owls do not speak with wolves, Warrior-Child," hissed Blodwedd, and Branwen could hear terror in her voice. "You must escape. See you the scar-faced old gray? He is their leader, I think. I will attack him while you break out of the circle. Run fast and swift, Warrior-Child. If you hear pursuit, find a tall tree and climb for your life. I will come to you when I may, and if not, Lord Govannon will send a more worthy creature to watch over you."

"I'm not leaving you to be killed!" exclaimed Branwen.

"You must!"

"No!"

"Branwen, she's right," Rhodri's voice was dull, as though he already knew that Blodwedd was lost. "I'll stay with her—hold them off. You must get away if you can."

Branwen eyed the massive gray wolf that Blodwedd had indicated. He was old, she could tell, but there was strength and murderous intent in his yellow eyes, and when he came to a halt, about five paces from them, the rest of the pack halted also, their heads down, watching and waiting.

Branwen spread her feet, grinding her heels into the mud and squaring her shoulders. She lifted her knife hand above her head; the blade ran with rainwater.

"Come, old gray-muzzle!" she shouted, staring into the wolf's deadly eyes. "Do you know who I am? I am Branwen ap Griffith! Come, if you dare—I don't fear you!"

The wolf's eyes burned into hers, lurid as candle-light—ravenous, impassive, unknowable.

Rhodri raised his sword, holding the hilt firm in both hands. Blodwedd's fingers curved and her lips drew back. Death hovered above them, impatient, expectant.

Branwen took a step forward, ready to fight for her life.

A peal of thunder shook the world, and the whole mountain seemed to rock, taking Branwen's feet from under her and throwing her in the mud. Gasping, she got to one knee, her ears ringing.

Lightning split the sky into fragments. A fizzing whiplash of blinding white fire struck a tree, bursting the trunk open and sending the tall branches tumbling in flames. Branwen was dazed by the lightning flash, but in the blur of partial vision she thought she saw a pathway opening through the trees—a shimmering pathway of coruscating green light. She knelt, her shoulders down, her mouth open, staring in wonder as the pathway unwound itself into the distance.

The trees seemed to bend away from the green pathway; their branches were bathed in the flickering emerald light, and every leaf and bud sparkled. The path ran up a hill, and on its crest, caught in a mesh of trapped lightning, she saw a standing shape.

A man, but much larger than a man.

It was a great silhouetted man, dark as caverns, tall as mountains. He was standing spread-legged, and from his head rose twelve-point antlers flickering with lightning. Although she could not see his face or his eyes, Branwen knew he was looking at her—looking into her. One massive arm rose and the hand beckoned.

Then the thunder rolled again, and Branwen closed her eyes against the noise. When she opened them again, the green path was no more and the stag-man was gone.

"Branwen!" It was Rhodri's voice, calling through the numbness that clouded her ears. "Quickly! Get up!" There was joy and relief and disbelief in his voice. "The thunder frightened them away! The wolves have gone!"

A hand helped her up. The rain was falling like spears, splashing knee high, beating into her face. She turned to Rhodri, her mind full of green clouds.

"Branwen?" There was a sudden alarm in his voice. "What's wrong? What's happened to you?" She stared at him, groggy and befuddled. Blodwedd was also looking into her face with apprehension.

"She has seen marvels," said the owl-girl.

"What . . . is it . . . ?" Branwen asked.

"Your eyes!" said Rhodri. "They're . . . they're filled with green light."

"This is not good," said Blodwedd, her voice fearful. "There are few whom the wendfire light does not change."

"Why?" gasped Rhodri. "What is it?"

"It is the light that fills those who have looked into the eyes of the Lord Govannon," said Blodwedd. "Alas! Death lies often in that light."

"What did you see, Branwen?" urged Rhodri. "Tell us. What did you see?"

"I . . . don't . . . know . . . ," Branwen mumbled, trying to think. "A man . . . with antlers. He beckoned. . . ." She turned, pointing through the trees. "That way!" she said. "We have to go that way!" A few ragged thoughts managed to come together in her head. "The wolves!" she gasped. "What of the wolves?" She stared around, lifting her knife.

"Did you not hear my words? They're gone," Rhodri said. "Branwen, can you *see*?"

"Yes." She caught hold of his arm. "Come on—we must go this way."

Without waiting to see whether they were following, she began to run unsteadily over the slippery ground, her body battered by the rain.

She went stumbling into densely packed trees where the ground rose sharply under her feet. Beneath the sheltering arms of the forest, she no longer felt the full fury of the storm, though the rain splashed down all around her in huge heavy drops, beating on the leaves above her like the sound of ten thousand spears pounding against ten thousand shields.

There was a cave ahead. She had not known what she was running toward until she saw the black mouth open in front of her—and then suddenly she knew, as if she had known all along. A deep cave. Shelter from the storm.

She stood in the wide cave-mouth, her head suddenly clear again.

Rhodri and Blodwedd were running toward her through sheets of rain. His arm was around her shoulders, and their heads were down, their backs bent against the torment of the weather.

"Where is Fain?" she shouted above the din of the pounding rain.

"He will have found a safe place to weather the storm," called Blodwedd. "Have no fear for him."

They came into the shelter, panting and dripping. Rhodri pushed his hair out of his eyes. "It has gone," he said, looking into her face.

Branwen frowned. "What has?"

"The green light—it's gone from your eyes." He shook his head. "You saw Govannon?"

"I don't know." She turned to Blodwedd. "Did I?"

"I believe you did," said the owl-girl. "Indeed, so." She looked even thinner and stranger with her saturated clothes clinging to her body, and her long hair plastered against her skull. Her round eyes seemed to fill half her face.

"He led me here, I think," said Branwen. "Look!" she pointed. Brushwood and small branches and twigs were strewn across the cave floor. "We can build a fire."

"If we can see what we're doing . . . ," said Rhodri, staring into the black depths of the cave. "Are you sure we haven't been led to a wolves' lair or a bear's den?"

"I'm sure," said Branwen. She gathered the brittle branches and twigs and set them in the center of the floor, just deep enough into the cave that she could still see by the dim light. She took tinder and fire-stones from the leather pouch at her belt and knelt to arrange the wood. Picking the thinnest twigs, she made a nest into which she placed a small amount of the dried moss tinder. She held the firestones close to the tinder and struck one against the other. Sparks flew, flashing and fading in an instant. The rain hammered down. Rhodri and Blodwedd stood close by.

Strike and chip.

Flying sparks.

Patience and concentration.

Strike and chip.

Branwen watched for the spark that would live long enough to cause a smolder in the tinder—smolder to scorch to smoke to flame.

Branwen could see from the corner of her eye that

192

Blodwedd was shivering. She saw Rhodri put a tentative arm around her shoulders. The owl-girl pressed close against him, and Branwen saw him wrap his arms protectively around her; Blodwedd's skinny body relaxed against him, her head resting against his chest.

She tried not to care that her friend's hand had come up gently to rest on the owl-girl's head. Rhodri was only showing kindness to the bedraggled creature—even a stray dog would deserve comfort on such a night. And besides, she did not envy Blodwedd the warmth of his embrace—it was only the thought that his affections were leading him astray that caused her concern. The last thing Rhodri needed was to lose his heart to something that was not human. At the end of that thorny path waited only despair.

Clear your mind.

Concentrate on the stones.

Strike and chip.

Watch for the one heroic spark.

Strike and chip.

A wisp of smoke curled. Branwen leaned low, doubling over to blow gently on the smoldering spark. A tiny white flame quivered. She blew again, nursing the budding flame, then carefully fed it more moss.

More flame rose now from the pile, leaves of fire with red and yellow edges. She offered twigs to the flame. Soon they would have a fine, leaping fire. Soon they would be warm and dry.

* * *

They huddled around the fire while the rain fell like molten iron and the thunder bellowed all around them, beating the hills like drums. The incessant noise made Branwen's teeth ache. Garish lightning came and went, turning the rain from black to silver.

The fire gave light enough to illuminate the whole of the small, round cave. The walls were of stooping gray stone, striated with bands of minerals that sparkled blue and yellow in the light. The earthen floor, strewn with pebbles, sloped slightly toward the mouth so that the rain did not seep in.

Rhodri spotted something that disturbed them: Scattered among larger stones at the back of the cave were human bones—a skull, a complete rib cage, other long bones. Evidence, perhaps, of some poor soul devoured by wild animals. Maybe dragged in here from the forest . . . or attacked within while sheltering from bad weather.

It was not a comforting discovery.

The fire spat and crackled fiercely, making Branwen's eyes smart.

"I'm hungry," Rhodri said, gazing into the flames.

"So am I," said Branwen.

"What little food we had is with the horses."

"I know."

"At least we don't need to go thirsty," he said, turning his head to the cave mouth, where torrents

of water splashed and foamed. "That's a good thing."
He looked at her. "Where were you—when the wolves
first attacked me?" he asked. "Where did you go?"

"I don't know," Branwen said. "A place . . ." She
shook her head. "An *old* place."

"A young place," said Blodwedd. Branwen gazed
into her eyes for a moment, then looked away.

"Yes. A young place."

"I don't know what you mean. What kind of
place?"

Branwen gnawed a torn fingernail. "It was a
clearing in the forest—but we were seeing a scene
from long ago. Lifetimes upon lifetimes ago. There
was a woman. . . . She was singing—chanting—a
song about the Shining Ones. It was wonderful . . .
glorious. . . ."

"One of the druades, she was," Blodwedd murmured. "Woman priests of the old ways. Wise heads.
Full throats. Great hearts." There was sadness in her
voice. "Long gone now. Hunted down. Betrayed." She
clutched at her arms. "The smooth-faced conquerors
came. But theirs is not the blame. They had their own
shrines and wells—their own gods. The Druid blood
they shed had no divinity for them. It was her own
followers who led them to her. Wickedness."

Blodwedd dropped her head and became silent,
her eyes darkly reflecting the fire.

Branwen spoke hesitantly, drawing her thoughts
out like tangled, knotted threads. "People fear the

Shining Ones," she said. "They say that these Old Gods—they are not real. They never *were* real. Stories for children! Make-believe! And yet they fear them—fear to talk of them—fear to have their names spoken aloud." She looked at Rhodri. "I think I begin to understand why that is."

"They turned their backs on the old ways," said Rhodri.

Branwen nodded slowly. "My father told me once to be honest and true always in your dealings with others, because you can never trust a man you have betrayed—you will always fear his revenge."

"And if a man's revenge is fearsome, how much worse would be the revenge of a betrayed god?" said Rhodri. "Yes. I see the problem."

"The Shining Ones are not vengeful," said Blodwedd. "They are wild and perilous, like an avalanche—like deep water—like a thunderstorm. But they are not cruel—not vengeful."

"No, maybe they aren't, but they're pitiless, all the same," said Branwen. "Pitiless in shaping people to their needs." She stared across the fire. "Why did they choose *me*, Blodwedd?"

"You think the Shining Ones chose you, Warrior-Child?" said Blodwedd. "No. They did not choose you. The mountains chose you. The forests and the rivers chose you. The land of your birth chose you, Warrior-Child. Be honored!"

"I want you to stop calling me that," said Branwen.

"Use my real name."

Blodwedd gave a mysterious smile. "Ahhh, but what *is* the real name of the Warrior-Child?" she asked in a low, thoughtful voice. "*Now* she is Branwen ap Griffith—but it was not always so. Once she was Addiena the Beautiful, daughter of Seren. And before that she was Ganieda, forest girl and sister to Myrddin Wyllt. Celemon was her name in the long-ago—Celemon, daughter of Cai the Tall." Blodwedd smiled again. "Many are the names of the Warrior-Child down the rolling years," she said. "Many the names and many the lives. You are but a thread in the tapestry, Branwen ap Griffith, a single footprint upon the eternal road." She laughed, low and soft, a sound that made Branwen shiver. "But I shall call you Branwen, if it eases your mind."

21

B RANWEN LAY CURLED on her side, her head pillowed on her arm, her eyes half open as she gazed into the dancing flames.

Blodwedd's words had given her a lot to think about. *What did she mean, I am "but a thread in the tapestry"? And who were those other women she named?*

An odd image came into her drowsy mind, as though formed in the flames. She saw herself standing on a hilltop under a bright sky, on the crest of a long white road. All along this road, women were walking. Women armed and armored. Women with faces strong and proud. A line of women stretching back along the road forever—a line of women stretching onward down the road forever. A thousand generations of warrior women.

The image faded, but it left Branwen with a feeling

of deep well-being—of *belonging*.

The fire cracked and fizzed. Beyond the flames she could see Rhodri, bare-chested, leaning against the cave wall. His face was peaceful in sleep, and one hand rested on the shoulder of the small figure that lay with her head in his lap, her limbs relaxed and her huge amber eyes closed for once.

So, Blodwedd had finally learned the art of sleeping like a human. *Good for her.*

True, Branwen was still haunted by the image of Blodwedd's impassive face as she held the sword over the neck of that baby. But inhuman and monstrous as the owl-girl could be, she had offered without hesitation to give her life in exchange for Branwen's safety when the wolves had surrounded them in the forest.

That was something to remember.

At last, Branwen's eyes closed, and her mind drifted off into velvet darkness.

Branwen dreamed that it was daytime—a bright morning. She stood at the cave mouth, gazing out over the forest. The breeze was fresh and cool, but there was an ominous feel in the air, as though the hills and the woods were holding their breath in anticipation of some horror.

She heard voices calling through the trees, urgent and excited.

One rang out above the others. "This way, masters! She goes this way! Follow closely—she may shift her shape in order to evade us!"

Other voices called in response—male voices—breathing hard and speaking a language she did not know, a strange, silken language of words that seemed to flow together without pause or break.

Now she could see movement among the trees—dark, blundering shapes under the arching branches. The smell of fear wafted to her, knotting her stomach. Something dreadful was about to happen.

A woman burst from the forest, dressed in ragged and stained blue robes. Her face was livid with fear; her mouth opened and closed, gulping the air; and her eyes were wild and staring. There were cuts and bruises on her face, and her hands were bloody, with torn and dirty fingernails.

Branwen stared at the fleeing woman, her heart beating fast.

I know you! I saw you in the glade—speaking those beautiful words to the Shining Ones. You're the chanting woman—the druade from the ancient forest. But who is chasing you?

The woman scrambled desperately up the long slope. A spark of faint hope came into her eyes as she looked up toward the cave. At first, Branwen thought the hunted woman had seen her—but then she realized the woman was looking straight through her, staring into the mouth of the cave. Perhaps she hoped that the cave wound on deep into the hills—perhaps she hoped to escape her pursuers that way.

It was a forlorn hope. The cave was no more than a rounded hollow in the hill—once in, there was no other way out.

Don't come this way. It's a dead end. You'll be trapped.

The woman ran on with renewed strength, passing Branwen as if she didn't see her and entering the darkness of the cave.

Perhaps they would not look there for her. Perhaps they would search elsewhere.

A man plunged out of the trees. He was dressed all in furs and untanned animal skins, and his hair was ragged and unkempt, but he had on his top lip the thick, drooping mustache worn by the men of Brython.

"I see her! She has gone into the cave! Now we have her!"

He came pounding up the slope.

No! She didn't come this way! Go back! Go back!

Five more men emerged from the trees.

Branwen could see that they were soldiers, although their clothes and weapons were unfamiliar to her.

They wore gray iron helmets with thick ridges and curved cheek-guards, and there were curved plates of iron over their shoulders and around their chests. Underneath the armor they wore short-sleeved tunics of a vivid red, and instead of trews or leggings they had short red kilts that left their legs bare, save for leather sandals with thongs tied to the shin. Their shields were oblong, curved, and painted deep red with iron bosses stamped into them. Short, broad-bladed swords bounced at their hips, and each carried in his free hand a long wooden javelin with an iron point.

The skin-clad man paused, waving back to them and pointing toward the cave mouth. "Come, my masters—she is trapped now!"

He was speaking Branwen's own language—a man of Brython, guiding alien soldiers to the woman's hideaway. *Traitor!*

They came plodding up the hill, breathing heavily, the sweat running down their faces. Olive-skinned faces, Branwen could see now—far swarthier than the hunted woman or the man in the animal skins.

One man pulled off his helmet and wiped his face—and Branwen saw that he was clean-shaven and had dark hair clipped short around his head. He spoke to the others in a voice of authority, handing his javelin to one of them and drawing his sword.

No! You cannot do this! What harm has she done to you?

The soldier pushed the skin-clad man aside, his face grim as he strode into the cave, his sword jutting forward.

No!

Branwen could not bear to look. She heard the woman pleading. The man spoke harshly. There was a scream, cut short.

Then silence.

The soldier came out of the cave, wiping his sword on a piece of blue cloth.

"That is the last of them, Principalis Optima Flavius," said the skin-clad man. "All the old priest-hood is dead now, my master—dead and gone forever."

The soldier said something to his companions, then sheathed his sword and took back his javelin. He strode down the hill, and the other four men fell into line behind him.

The skin-clad man of Brython peered into the cave, a look of woeful regret disfiguring his face for a moment before he turned and trotted along in the soldiers' wake like an obedient dog.

22

"*CAW! CAW! CAW! Caw! Caw!*"

Branwen awoke at the strident, insistent falcon cry. Daylight filled the cave, sparkling on the embedded minerals so that skeins of moving light wavered across floor walls and roof. Cool morning air flowed in. She had slept close to the fire and saw now that it was finally dead, the rowan branches transformed to a lacework of white ash on the blackened ground.

"Fain!" Branwen gasped, dream-drunk still and fighting to gather her wits. She sat up and saw Rhodri and Blodwedd lying together close to the cave wall— Blodwedd curled on her side with her arms across her chest and her knees drawn up, and Rhodri at her back, an arm thrown protectively across her.

"I'm glad he survived the storm unharmed," came Rhodri's sleepy voice, "but I'd wish for a more melodic introduction to the day!"

He lifted his head and gazed at Blodwedd, his face amazed—as if he had awoken from an outlandish dream to find it real. He withdrew his arm from her and pulled himself up against the cave wall, rubbing the heels of his hands into his eyes and yawning.

"Caw! Caw! Caw!"

The falcon was in the cave mouth, moving impatiently from foot to foot, ruffling his feathers and bobbing his head.

"The horses have returned," said Blodwedd, her eyes opening sharp and bright as she switched from sleep to waking in an instant.

Puzzled but relieved, Branwen got to her feet and stepped out into the day. Fain rose into the air and circled high above the cave, calling loudly.

It was early, and the sun was low in a sky banded with innocent white clouds running before a strong west wind. Of the black storm clouds from the night there was no sign, although the ground was still wet underfoot and the rocks and the leaves shone jewel-bright.

The two horses were standing side by side, just under the trees, their heads down to tear at the grass. When they had made camp the previous night, Rhodri and Branwen had taken the saddles off, but now they were strapped onto the horses' backs once more. All the things that had been left in the clearing were slung over them—cloaks and clothing, Branwen's chain mail and shield, even their bag of food.

"How could this be?" Branwen wondered aloud, walking quickly down the hill toward the animals. *Who brought them here? Who put their saddles on? Who gathered our things?* The horses lifted their heads as she approached. Branwen gasped and stopped.

An eerie green light flickered in their eyes.

As she moved closer, though, the light paled and went out, and the large eyes were brown once more. She stood between the horses, touching them, stroking their hides, as though to reassure herself that they were real.

"Did Fain bring them back?" called Rhodri as he came out of the cave, pulling on his jerkin.

"I don't think so," Branwen called back. "Govannon, perhaps?"

"Govannon, indeed," said Blodwedd, emerging behind Rhodri. "Fain warns that the soldiers have already broken camp," said Blodwedd. "They are riding hard to the place of singing gulls. We must be swift if we are to keep track of them."

"Then we will follow now," Branwen said as she ran back up to the cave to retrieve her sword, knife, and leather belt.

"What of the things we left in the forest when the wolves attacked?" asked Rhodri as she moved past him. "Your shield and chain mail and our cloaks."

"Look more carefully, Rhodri," Branwen called back as she entered the cave. "Someone has already seen to that."

He peered down at the horses. "Even our bag of food was remembered," he said with wonder in his voice. "At least we shan't go hungry."

"We'll eat in the saddle." Branwen buckled the belt around her waist and slipped the sword and knife into place. She paused for a moment. The early light reached all the way to the back of the cave, splashing her shadow over the rocks and up the far wall.

She walked deeper into the cave and gazed down at the scattered bones, consumed by an aching sense of sorrow and loss.

Suddenly she was aware of Blodwedd at her side. "Did you dream her death, Branwen?" the owl-girl asked. "The chanting woman from the holy glade?"

Branwen's throat was thick. "Yes."

"The cave remembers—old stones do not forget." Blodwedd sighed. "Ah, but man is fickle and full of fear. It was ever so."

"Does that excuse him for leading them to her?"

"No," murmured Blodwedd. "And yes."

Branwen turned her back on the pitiful sight and walked out into the daylight once more. She strode down the hill, staring up into the sky. "Fain! Fain! Guide us!" she called, and leaped into the saddle. A sudden urgency had filled her, a burning need to be on the move.

Fain glided down, flying so close that his wingtip almost brushed her shoulder. He gave a single commanding cry.

"Come on!" Branwen shouted as Rhodri and

Blodwedd came racing down the hill. Hardly waiting for them to mount, she urged her horse to follow the falcon. She had the feeling that before this day had run its course, they would be caught up in events both great and deadly.

"Gwylan Canu," Branwen murmured, gazing down with narrowed eyes. "The place of singing gulls."

It was a little after midday. Fain had led them through the long, warm morning, winging away under trees that dripped still from the previous night's storm. At times he would leave the troop as they traveled along the coast road, rising up and up till he was only a dot against the blue sky. Occasionally he had vanished altogether—but always he'd come back with news of the progress of the prince's horsemen.

Down through valleys he had guided them, where ferns curled like reaching fingers through a waxen ground-mist, where the trees were garlanded with spiders' webs. Upward they'd followed him then, to summits where the wind sang and played and flicked their hair into their eyes. Down again, through bleak ravines running with white water, and then back up around brown peaks that tore the clouds. Northward, always northward—until, rounding a blunt, fern-clad knob of rock, Branwen had heard for the first time through the trees the sound of surf breaking on rocks, and smelled the evocative tang of the sea.

They'd come to this high ledge where the pines stood like sentinels at the world's end, where the ocean stretched out before them, a sheet of blue silk strewn with diamonds. At their horses' hooves, the land crumbled away in rugged, boulder-strewn precipices down to a rubbled shoreline of pocked and fissured rock, where the waves broke in plumes and flurries of white foam.

Now, standing proud and strong on a narrow outcrop of seaworn limestone was the citadel of Branwen's vision—the fortified village of Gwylan Canu. Its back was to the ocean, and its landward side was protected by a long, sloping rampart of drystone, pierced by a massive timber-framed stone gatehouse. Many houses and huts huddled beyond the wall, and on a high point near the sea Branwen saw the Great Hall of the House of Puw, its stone walls and thatched roof rising proud above the other dwellings.

As Branwen gazed down, the endless tide pounded in on the black rocks, sending up spouts of foam that gushed from sea-gnawed blowholes and cracks; it almost seemed that the entire shoreline was boiling like a cauldron in a firepit. To either side of the rocky headland, the land fell back to form deep, sandy bays. Some ways westward along the shore, sheltered from the full fury of the sea, a small knot of huts was gathered—a sparse fishing village with its boats drawn up onto the beach like black leaves. There was no sign of activity or movement in the village. It seemed deserted.

Beyond the fishing village, Branwen saw the pale tongue of the road from distant Doeth Palas, skirting the cliffs, winding in and out to follow the contours of the land. She traced this road with her eyes, all the way to the gatehouse of Gwylan Canu.

Now Branwen turned her eyes eastward, where the road continued chasing away along the coastline. Somewhere out of sight in that direction, she knew the road branched and sent a tributary striking southward into the wild lands of Cyffin Tir, where it would lead a weary traveler at long last to Garth Milain.

Branwen felt an ache as she thought of her homeland—and of her dear, brave mother, bereft of son, husband, and daughter—at the farthermost end of that long pale road.

By all the saints, when will this be over? When will I be allowed to go home?

"That's strange." Rhodri's voice brought her back to the present. "Why are they waiting outside the walls?"

To the west of the gatehouse and a little way from the sloping walls of the citadel, the rocks formed a flat plateau blanketed with scrub and wild grasses. It was here that the fifty horsemen of Doeth Palas had come to a halt at the roadside. The horses had been gathered together as though Captain Angor had ordered them to make camp.

"I do not know," said Branwen, shading her eyes against the glare of the sunstruck sea. The men were marshaled in rows, but she could not make out enough details to understand what was going on.

"This is all wrong," Rhodri said, his voice uneasy.

"It makes no sense. Why are the gates closed? And look—there are armed men on the gatehouse. Why would the gates be closed against Prince Llew's men?"

"Unless we have come too late and the Saxons have already taken the citadel," said Branwen in alarm. "By Saint Cadog! I wish I could see more!"

In response to her words Fain took to the air, wheeling in long, graceful loops down toward the citadel.

"Move back under the trees, just in case they look this way," Branwen said. She dismounted, and Rhodri and Blodwedd did the same, leading the horses a little farther into the woodlands.

Blodwedd stared back over her shoulder, her owl eyes wide and full of apprehension. Her expression was one that Branwen had never seen on a human— pure, primal unease.

"What is it?" Rhodri asked her.

"The sea . . . ," murmured the owl-girl, as if struggling to find the words. "It . . . puts a chill . . . in my heart!"

"Why is that?" Rhodri asked gently, his hand resting on her shoulder.

"My lord Govannon holds sway only over the land," Blodwedd replied. "Beyond the shores of Brython, he can no longer protect me."

"I'll protect you," Rhodri said. "Trust in me."

Branwen smiled to herself. The thought of gentle Rhodri protecting the wild owl-girl was as odd in its way as learning that there was something in nature that made Blodwedd afraid.

Blodwedd turned to him. "I fear you cannot protect me, my friend," she whispered.

Branwen left Rhodri and the uneasy owl-girl under the trees. She pushed forward again to cliff's edge, pressing herself against a tree, watching in growing apprehension as Fain zigzagged above the citadel.

What would he find? Echoes of her dreadful vision? Corpses and bloody Saxon banners?

It seemed an age till Fain came flying back up to them. She lifted an arm, and he came to her with wings curving and claws outstretched.

He landed gracefully on her wrist, and she carried him to the others. Folding his wings, he stared at Blodwedd and gave a succession of carping cries.

"What is he saying?" Branwen said anxiously, staring at the owl-girl. "Are we too late?"

"There are no Saxons in the citadel," Blodwedd said. "But there is fear and dismay—women weep, and the menfolk are armed and grim."

"Why do they not allow the prince's horsemen in?" asked Branwen.

"Caw! Caw! Caw!"

"Fain does not know," said Blodwedd.

"Then we must go and learn for ourselves why Iwan's father slammed the gates on his own son," said Branwen. She looked into the falcon's bright black eye. "Stay with the horses, my friend," she said. "You are a worthy guide and see much, but I don't want you to draw attention to us. Do you understand?"

At her words, Fain took wing, coming to land on the saddle of her horse.

"Blodwedd—I want you to stay here as well."

The owl-girl looked levelly at her. "Twice now have I left your side and let you walk into peril," she said. "It will not happen again . . . *Branwen.*"

Branwen held her eyes for a moment, then nodded.

"Don't bother asking me to stay behind either," Rhodri said. He peered down the long slope scattered with boulders. "But it will be a perilous descent, I think."

"Then we must take great care," said Branwen.

Indeed, the way down was not easy, and it was all the more difficult because it was vital that they shield themselves from Captain Angor's men. They climbed down in an unspeaking single file, Branwen first, then Blodwedd, and Rhodri in the rear. They used every scrap of natural cover, crouching, often pausing, seeking a safe path, then moving forward again, sometimes on hands and knees. Branwen worked her way slowly and cautiously down the hillside, summoning all her powers of stealth and silence despite her eagerness to unravel the conundrum of the locked gates. On such a precarious hillside, one carelessly placed foot could easily send stones bounding down the slope to alert the soldiers below.

But at last they made it unseen to a deep, narrow cleft that ran just above the landward side of the plateau where the soldiers were gathered. From here, they could hear the men's voices on the fresh salt breeze that blew in from the sea.

Cautiously, Branwen climbed the side of the cleft and lifted her head above the sharp rim of dark rock. Ensuring that her footing was secure, she edged up till she could see to where Angor's men were standing.

Branwen stared down in shock. Iwan was being held between two of the men, and ropes bound his arms at the elbow and wrist. His usually impassive face was pale and angry, and there was a trickle of blood at the corner of his mouth, as if he had been struck.

Captain Angor was speaking. "If they will not heed the voice of reason," he growled, "let us see whether threats will force their hand."

"They will never surrender Gwylan Canu to you!" It was Iwan's voice, filled with rage. "My father will die first, traitor!"

Angor turned on Iwan with a snarl. "You had better pray your father sees sense, boy," he said, grasping Iwan's hair in his fist and forcing his head back. "If he does not, the next sight he will witness will be his son's severed head on the end of my spear, dripping blood as I raise it up in front of his gates!"

23

BRANWEN'S MIND REELED. She had risked the dangers of Doeth Palas in order to warn Iwan of the coming Saxon attack. He had trusted her word—he had gone to Prince Llew, and the prince had sent fifty horsemen to Teg Eingel. But this war band intended to invade Gwylan Canu rather than protect it! And Captain Angor was threatening Iwan with death if Madoc ap Rhain refused to unbolt the gates and surrender the citadel to the prince's men.

And all but Iwan were party to the betrayal. That explained the small number of men sent riding east— all had to have been handpicked for the willingness to betray the House of Puw. But it was madness that in such times men of Powys would fight one another!

An insistent tugging at her tunic made Branwen look back. Rhodri had climbed partway up the slope

215

toward her. His anxious face stared up at her, his eyes questioning. She shook her head and gestured for him to leave her be.

Iwan was speaking again, his voice defiant. "I thank the saints that you have among your men such fools as cannot hold their tongues!" he spat. "If I had not heard them speaking of your intentions to take my mother and father captive, I would not have been able to call out and warn them to bar the gates against you! As it is, you can sit here till you rot, you treacherous dog! Gwylan Canu will never fall to you!"

Branwen winced as Captain Angor swung his arm round and slammed his fist into Iwan's mouth. "Be silent!" he shouted. "Unless you wish to share the fate of those men whose loose lips came close to ruining all!"

At those words, Branwen realized that what she had taken for a bundle of bags and provisions thrown down in the grass was actually two dead bodies. Her stomach churned, and she had to press her lips together against a rising sickness as she saw that their throats had been savagely cut.

Iwan spat blood and glared defiantly at the captain. "Kill me quickly, then, and have an end to it!" he shouted.

Angor grinned crookedly. "Oh, no, my fine young cockerel," he said, and now his voice was deadly calm. "That would never do. Kill you quickly? That will not serve my purposes at all. When I said that the next thing your father would see would be your dripping head, I neglected to mention the long and painful road you would travel before it came to that." Iwan blinked and looked away. Angor thrust his hand under Iwan's chin, wrenching his struggling prisoner's head so their eyes met once again.

"You know me, Iwan ap Madoc, do you not?" he hissed. "You have seen me at my work. Trust me when I tell you that I am an absolute master at the craft of teasing a man's soul from his body. You will beg for death long before I am done with you—unless you beg first for your father to open his gates to us."

Iwan's face went ashen, but there was still audacity in his eyes as he stared with contempt at the vicious old soldier. Branwen's heart went out to him—so brave and defiant against such terrible odds.

"That will never happen," Iwan said thickly, his lips bubbling with blood.

"A bold claim," said Angor. "But make no rash promises, boy—not until you have learned the full extent of your courage." He patted Iwan's cheek. "It's a rare privilege, Iwan, that I offer you. Few are the men given the opportunity to be taken to the uttermost end of their endurance. It will be an interesting journey."

He stepped back and spoke to the two men holding Iwan upright. "Come, we have wasted enough time on this. Let us see if Madoc ap Rhain has yet come to greater wisdom."

He strode toward the gatehouse, the two men following close behind, half dragging Iwan between them. Branwen's soul ached as she saw the way Iwan struggled to keep to his feet. Anger blazed through her, and she closed her fingers around the hilt of her sword. She couldn't leave Iwan to the vile practices of Captain Angor. She would reveal herself and come to his aid—even thought she knew her chances were limited of surviving a reckless assault on so many armed men.

She started along the cleft, knowing she must keep hidden for as long as possible. But her rage betrayed her as she made her first move hastily along the gully, and her foot came down on a loose stone. It spun away, cracking against others and sending a small flurry of rocks tumbling noisily down to the bottom of the cleft.

Branwen ducked, her heart hammering. Angor spun around, his eyes searching along the ridge. "What was that?" he shouted.

Fool! Clumsy fool!

"Loose rocks, Captain," a voice called. "Nothing more."

"Be certain!" shouted Angor. "Go up there and check. Madoc may have men on the ridges, waiting to fall on us unawares!"

Branwen grimaced at her blundering stupidity. Now men would come up here and scour the hillside. If they were discovered, all would be lost.

Something touched her leg. She looked down. Blodwedd was just below her on the slope. "Do not fear," whispered the owl-girl. "I know I said I would never leave your side—but now I must. I will give them something to chase!"

Branwen nodded, and the owl-girl slid away down the slope. She paused for a moment, her gaze lingering on Rhodri's face. Then she went running along the cleft, her long, thick hair flying.

Branwen watched as Blodwedd scrambled lithely up the far slope. She came into clear view, leaping and bounding among the rocks, moving more swiftly than any human as she skimmed the loose scree, turning this way and that along the face of the precipice, kicking up clouds of gray dust that billowed in her wake.

Even as she watched, Branwen could not quite believe her eyes. Clad in her simple gown of dappled brown, and only dimly visible through the dust, Blodwedd's shape suddenly seemed quite different. Was she still a slender young woman—or had she now taken on some animal form?

Stone and rock rained down. Branwen heard the men shouting out.

"There! There it is! On the hill!"

"What is it?"

"A hare, I think!"

"No, it's too large. A fox, maybe?"

"A young deer? No—see how it throws up the dust

as it runs! A wolf of the mountains? What is it?"

"Whatever it is, it moves with rare speed! See? It's in among the trees already."

"Captain Angor—did you see? It was only an animal."

"Yes, I saw it," came Angor's voice. "A wild dog, I thought."

The voices dropped to murmurs. No men came up the hill toward them. Blodwedd's diversion had worked—for the moment, Branwen and Rhodri were safe.

Paying close attention to her footing, Branwen moved across the face of the cleft. Rhodri kept pace with her at the bottom.

A strident voice called out.

"Madoc ap Rhain! The time for deliberation is done! What is your answer? Will you open your gates and surrender to me, or will you look on as I torture your son to death?"

A woman's voice responded. "For pity's sake, Captain Angor—do not harm my son!"

"Get you from the walls, woman," shouted Angor. "It were best you did not see what is to come if your husband does not relent!"

Branwen lifted her head over the ridge again. She was almost opposite the gatehouse of Gwylan Canu. Angor stood under the great wooden gates, staring up at the high ramparts. Many armed men lined the walls, but no weapons were drawn and there was a deathly silence from the battlements.

Above the gates stood a portly, elderly man with long gray hair and a gray mustache—a warrior past his prime. Branwen vaguely recognized the man from her childhood; he had visited Garth Milain once, this merry-faced old lord. She remembered that he had roared with laughter that day, till his round belly shook. But there was no laughter in him now—his face was pale and drawn, as though he were looking into the very pits of Annwn.

A woman was at his side, clad in green and with plaited flaxen hair. She seemed young, many years the old man's junior—and by the look of her, a woman of old Viking stock. Even from a distance, Branwen could see that she was weeping.

"Angor, I implore you," Madoc called down, his emotions made plain by the quavering of his voice, "look not through your master's greedy eyes. He can take as many lands as he wishes, but he creates enemies of his countrymen. You must see this. What of the old alliances? What of our long fight against the Saxon hordes?"

"What of them?" Angor shouted. "This is not about territory. Too many years lie on your gray head, Madoc ap Rhain! You are aged and fainthearted and weak. You cannot defend this cantref. Step aside now! Prince Llew commands this for the good of Powys— and any who stand in opposition to that greater good will suffer the consequences! Open your gates and all will be well. You have my word on that!"

"Old I may be, Angor of Doeth Palas, but faint-hearted I never was!" shouted Madoc. "You shall not usurp me nor enter my citadel, though you come at my walls with ten times your present number. Do your worst! If my son dies, I will unleash such vengeance upon you that the very stones of Gwylan Canu will sicken at it!"

"We shall see," called Angor, drawing his sword. "I have many skills, Madoc. Your son shall not die—not for a very long time." He turned. "Bare his chest!" he ordered the two men holding Iwan fast. Iwan struggled as the men tore his tunic open.

Branwen's fist tightened on her sword hilt.

A long, keening wail sounded from the gatehouse. Iwan's mother was leaning out over the old stones, her hand reaching uselessly toward her son.

"Let me tell you what wonders await the boy," Angor called out callously, turning and pressing the point of his sword to Iwan's abdomen just above his belt. Iwan winced as the point cut his skin and a thin thread of blood trickled down. "A small cut made here will give access to his innards. I have a tool—a clever little hooked implement—forged for this very purpose." He drew a thin loop of iron from his belt and held it up for the watchers from the battlements to see. "It goes into the belly, do you see? Great care and skill are required to turn it just so—allowing it to hook around the boy's guts. And then, very slowly, very carefully, I will draw it out again—and the guts will come unraveling with it."

Angor stared up at Iwan's mother. "I will draw out your son's guts, woman. You will be surprised how much of a man's innards can be pulled out without causing him to die on the spot." His voice rose to a fearsome roar. "No, my lady, even then your son will live for half a day—and in that time, he will learn how to scream. Trust me on this—he will learn how to scream his lungs out!"

Branwen felt sickened by Angor's threats, and she could see the horror that swept over the faces of Iwan's parents. Iwan himself was white-faced, staring blankly ahead of him as though in utter disbelief.

"Lie him down," snarled Angor. "Let the carnival begin!"

"Enough!" shouted Madoc ap Rhain, his whole body shaking as he glared down at the barbarous captain. "Release my son." His head bowed in defeat. "Name your terms."

"Father, no!" screamed Iwan.

"The terms are simple," Angor called. "You will open your gates and your menfolk will come forth, bearing with them all arms and armor. They will lay their weapons at my feet, my lord, and you will cede to me the lordship of Gwylan Canu."

There was a dreadful silence from the gatehouse; Madoc ap Rhain's gray head was bowed low. His wife turned, resting her hand on his arm.

Branwen bit her lip, torn by her own impossible choice. She realized that even if she were to leap up, sword swinging, and run as fast as her strong legs allowed, she could never cover the ground between her and Iwan before Angor's men caught her and cut her down. She would die in vain. Her death would make no difference. No—as deeply as it went against the grain of her nature, she lay hidden and did nothing save tighten her grip on her sword hilt till her knuckles were white and bloodless.

"So be it," called Madoc.

"No!" Iwan howled, struggling in the grip of the two men. He fought so fiercely against them that he broke free on one side. With wild eyes, he threw himself at Captain Angor—and Branwen understood that he meant to impale himself on the Captain's sword, to die rather than allow his father to surrender the citadel.

Angor pulled the blade back as Iwan lunged at him. Iwan pivoted in the grip of the other soldier and fell heavily to his knees. Angor stepped back, laughing.

"Self-murder, is it, Iwan?" he mocked. "The ultimate sacrifice to save the honor of the House of Puw! No, lad—I'll be the one who decides how and when you die."

"Father—no!" Iwan shouted. "I'm not afraid! I'd rather die."

But he was too late. Madoc ap Rhain had disappeared from the gatehouse, and Branwen could hear the rasp and grate of timber bars being drawn back from the gates.

She was wracked with guilt and despair.

It was her warning that had brought Iwan to this place—and although her intention had been the opposite, her actions had brought this calamity upon the citadel of Gwylan Canu.

What can I do? How can I stop this?

All the while, the vision of Iwan's severed, dripping head darkened her mind. She had seen his death in Blodwedd's foretelling—was she now to see it in reality?

24

BRANWEN COULD HARDLY bring herself to watch as the gates of Gwylan Canu swung slowly inward, creaking and cracking on their hinges. For a moment all was still, then Madoc ap Rhain strode out, his soldiers following in somber silence.

Captain Angor stood over the kneeling Iwan, his sword resting on the back of the subdued boy's neck, a threat to ensure his father's continued compliance.

"Neb ap Mostyn!" Angor called to one of his men. "See that these fine men are disarmed. Have them pile their weapons together and stand in ranks."

The man called Neb ap Mostyn began to organize the men of Gwylan Canu, herding them onto the plateau, while the soldiers of Doeth Palas gathered their swords, spears, axes, and shields and began to pile them in a great heap with much ringing and clanging.

Branwen guessed that Madoc ap Rhain's force consisted of about two hundred and fifty men—easily enough to do battle with Captain Angor's warriors, if not for that sharp blade held at the nape of Iwan's neck. She stared up at the ramparts. A few women were gathered there, watching in deathly silence as their menfolk gave up their weapons and stood in grim, sullen rows while Angor's soldiers guarded them, swords at the ready.

"You have all that you wished for," called Madoc ap Rhain. "Give me back my son!"

Angor wrenched Iwan to his feet. "Take your prize, my lord, and be welcome to it." He shoved Iwan between the shoulders. Iwan stumbled, tripping and falling heavily with a cry, his arms still tied at his back.

Branwen's agony diminished a little—perhaps Iwan would not die here after all! Perhaps there was some hope.

Iwan's father ran to his son and helped him to his feet.

Branwen heard Iwan's voice, shaking with anger and dismay. "You should not have bartered Gwylan Canu for my life!" he cried. "You should have let these dogs do their worst." He turned, spitting at Angor. "Worse than the Saxons, you are, Angor ap Pellyn! May the curses of all the saints come down on you!"

"Keep the boy quiet, my lord," Angor said without

emotion. "You have surrendered your citadel to me on his behalf—do not make that a vain sacrifice."

Madoc ap Rhain put a protective arm around Iwan's shoulders. "Only the weak of heart threaten those who cannot fight back, Angor of Doeth Palas," he said. "You have had your way. What will now become of my people?"

"That you will learn in good time," said Angor. He called to his lieutenant. "Neb ap Mostyn—take a detail into the citadel and make sure that no men lurk there. Search for any weapons that may have been kept back from us. Any man of sword-bearing age that you find beyond the wall—kill him!"

"What of the women and children and old folk, Captain?" Neb replied.

A cruel smile slithered over Angor's face. "On the promontory behind the Great Hall you will find the ground is dug with many deep pits," he said. "In the wars of Madoc ap Rhain's youth, these pits were used to imprison Saxon captives, although I'll guess they are unoccupied now. Have them thrown into the pits. Kill any that resist—be they woman, child, or ancient."

"Yes, Captain." Neb ap Mostyn called for ten men to follow him, and they entered the citadel while the women watched from the ramparts with hollow, frightened eyes.

"One more thing," Angor called after him. "There will be Saxon servants—do them no harm.

They are not for the pits."

Branwen had become so immersed in the distressing and unfathomable events that were unfolding out on the plateau that she was startled when Rhodri came crawling quietly alongside her.

"Do you hear it?" he whispered urgently.

She ducked her head down below the ridge before replying. "Hear what?" she hissed softly.

"Listen! Marching feet!"

Branwen frowned, straining her ears.

Yes! She could hear it now, echoing faintly among the rocks—the steady tread of many feet.

"Are they the rest of Prince Llew's men?" she wondered aloud. "No—surely not. It's too soon for them to have gotten here."

"The sound does not come from the south, Branwen," Rhodri murmured. "Listen more closely. They approach from the east!"

It was hard for Branwen to pinpoint the exact direction of the noise as it bounced from rockface to rockface. But at last, as it grew gradually louder, she knew that she was hearing a force of soldiers coming in along the coastal road—and, as Rhodri had realized, they were coming from the east.

A small figure appeared suddenly among the rocks. It was Blodwedd. She must have circled through the trees and come down into the gulley from their right. She scrambled along the cleft and crawled up toward them.

"Saxons," she hissed. "I saw them from the hilltop. Many Saxon warriors—led by horsemen. One was a great black-bearded man on a tall black stallion. He has gold on his helmet. Pennants fly at his back—a white dragon on a field of red. Those who follow are savage men. Their eyes brim with the lust of slaughter and conquest!"

"Herewulf Ironfist!" said Rhodri. "He's the black-bearded man who leads them—and it is his flag that flies over them." He looked at Blodwedd. "Did you have time to count their numbers?"

"I would guess they be five hundred men strong," she said. "Maybe more."

Branwen remembered the line of Saxon soldiers that she had seen in her vision. All too soon, it seemed, her vivid dream was becoming reality. She closed her eyes, again seeing Iwan's dripping, severed head in her mind.

Here you are at last, Branwen, but too late. . . . The west is lost. All is done. All . . . is . . . done. . . .

She opened her eyes, and determination filled her. If all were truly lost, then she would go down fighting, not skulking among the rocks. "We must go to Angor's aid," she said, drawing her sword. "Ironfist must not come upon him in the open." She narrowed her eyes. No matter what disputes had riven Powys over the years, the great princes of her homeland had always come together to fight their age-old foe. Of course, Captain Angor and Lord Madoc must now join forces against Ironfist.

"Now this madness will end!" she said. "The men of Powys will unite against the Saxons. Angor cannot leave the men of Gwylan Canu unarmed now. He will need every able-bodied warrior if he is to hold the citadel against Ironfist's attack."

Blodwedd's small hand gripped the wrist of Branwen's sword arm. "Do not show yourself yet," she said, looking intently into Branwen's eyes. "One of the horsemen who leads the warriors was no Saxon. He had no beard, and he was dressed in the fashion of the men of Powys. My heart tells me there is more to learn before you act."

"The man you saw was likely a captive," said Rhodri, "a man of Brython, forced to lead Ironfist to the citadel."

"It is of no matter," Branwen hissed. "I will not stand idly by while Gwylan Canu is taken!" She tried in vain to drag her hand free from the owl-girl's deceptively strong grasp.

"Branwen, heed me," murmured Blodwedd. "Watch and wait—all has not yet been revealed."

Branwen grimaced as Blodwedd's fingers tightened about her wrist. She knew Govannon's messenger was duty-bound to keep her from harm at all costs—but surely not if it meant allowing Gwylan Canu to fall to the Saxons? What was the Shining Ones' purpose in bringing her here, if all she did at journey's end was to stand aside while a

Saxon army overran the citadel?

The hurried percussion of hoofbeats sounded—a horse, galloping along the road from the east.

Branwen glared at Blodwedd. She twisted her arm, ripping the owl-girl's fingers away. "I will not reveal myself," she said. "But I must see what is happening."

She lifted her head above the rocks' edge once more. Yes! A rider was coming in fast along the road, and if this was the man Blodwedd had seen riding alongside Ironfist, Blodwedd had been right—he was no Saxon but a warrior of Powys. He was a man of Doeth Palas.

Angor raised a hand in greeting. "Adda ap Avagdu!" he called. "You return in good time. Is all well?"

"All is well, Captain," replied the horseman, bringing his horse up short.

Angor knows him! He must be a scout sent ahead of the warrior troop. But why has he been riding with the Saxons? Has he betrayed his captain?

Hardly had the words of greeting left the horseman's lips than the brazen blare of Saxon war horns sounded, echoing and re-echoing among the precipices.

"Ironfist!" cried Angor, lifting his sword and turning to his men. "General Ironfist is upon us, warriors of Powys!" he called. "How would you greet the great Saxon warlord?"

Captain Angor's men hammered swords on shields as though in defiance of the approaching horde, but Branwen could see consternation among the unarmed men of Gwylan Canu.

Lord Madoc stepped forward, ignoring the swords that pointed toward him. "Angor ap Pellyn!" he shouted. "Give us our weapons, man! You cannot fight Ironfist alone!"

As though spurred on by his lord's words, one of the men of Gwylan Canu broke free of the others and ran toward the mound of spears and swords and shields.

"Bring him down!" snarled Angor.

Neb ap Mostyn hefted a spear in his fist and let it fly.

Branwen stared in utter disbelief as the spear caught the running man in the back. He fell onto his face with a short-cut cry.

A murmur of shock and anger ran through the other men of the citadel. One stepped forward, shouting in protest.

A sword slashed downward and he fell to his knees, his head half severed from his body. He dropped onto his face, and now the other men of Gwylan Canu were hemmed in by a hedge of swords.

Still trying to come to terms with what she had just witnessed, Branwen heard the rumble of marching feet grow louder. She turned her head. Several horsemen had rounded a crag of rock—and at their head was the man from her vision.

Horsa Herewulf Ironfist—lord of Winwaed, commander of the armies of King Oswald of Northumbria—was a huge, hulking man with a bristling black beard and blue eyes as bright and hard as stones. On his head was a round, crested helmet of iron, inlaid with silverwork and gold. A red cloak hung from his shoulders, covering a leather jerkin and a long coat of fine iron mail. At his hip was a sword, and in one fist he clutched a silver-tipped spear.

He rode forward, and behind him came the bearded Saxon warriors, some in chain mail, others in leather trews and brown woolen cloaks with bare feet and helmets of beaten iron. Clouds of dust rose as they marched, and the sunlight glinted like ice on spear tip and helmet.

Ironfist lifted a hand and the marching men came to a halt. The sudden silence was shocking. The brown dust wafted away on the wind. Branwen's thoughts were thrown back to the horde of Saxon warriors who had come down upon Garth Milain, reckless in their battle-fever, war-skilled and deadly. She tasted iron on her tongue and felt a terrible pressure growing in her head as she stared into those brutal bearded faces. So many men—so much hatred.

Herewulf Ironfist rode on alone, slowly, without drawing his sword.

Angor walked forward to meet him, sword in hand.

Ironfist brought his great black stallion to a halt on the road. It stood, pawing the ground and snorting, its dark eyes rolling.

Angor stood for a moment in front of the horse, then dropped to one knee, his head bowed. He turned his sword in his hands and offered the hilt to the Saxon general.

"Greetings, my lord," Angor said. "In the name of Prince Llew of Bras Mynydd, I offer you my allegiance and my fealty." He looked up now. "I give to you a great prize, my lord. The gates of Gwylan Canu are open to you—ride in and take the citadel for your own!"

25

BRANWEN BIT DOWN hard on her lip, tasting blood. Her jaw clenched, and her whole body knotted in horror as she stared at the kneeling captain of Doeth Palas and the Saxon Warlord who loomed over him, haughty and powerful on his huge black stallion.

Herewulf Ironfist leaned out of the saddle and closed his fist around the hilt of Captain Angor's offered sword. He turned, lifting the weapon and brandishing it in the air. A roar came from the Saxons, a bellow of triumph accompanied by the clash of swords on shields and the stamping of feet.

Tears of rage and despair started from Branwen's eyes. This could not be happening. There could not be such treachery in Powys!

And then something came into her mind. Something that Rhiannon had said to her when they had first met, by the silvery pool in the forest outside Doeth Palas. Something that had not meant anything to her at the time.

If you turn from me, child, the enemy will sweep over you like a black tide. There is a festering canker at the heart of this land.

A festering canker at the heart of Powys!

Greetings, my lord. In the name of Prince Llew of Bras Mynydd, I offer you my allegiance and my fealty.

Prince Llew ap Gelert had turned traitor! The richest and most powerful lord in all Powys had gone over to the enemy. How could Powys survive such a betrayal? How could Brython endure such deception and perfidy?

Branwen had set out on this journey with no clear vision of how it might end. Failure and death had been her worst nightmare. In the dark of night she had sometimes seen her own slaughter. In bright sunrise her hopes had risen, and she had imagined herself on a field of battle, bloodied but victorious. But not for one moment had she dreamed of witnessing such a villainous deed as this. To surrender to the age-old enemy—to bend the knee to a Saxon general!

"No," she murmured, her heart drumming in her chest, the blood pounding in her ears. "No, this shall not be!" She lifted her sword and made to stand up—to reveal herself—to put an end to this insanity!

Through the thunder that filled her mind, she was

vaguely aware of Blodwedd's voice, a frantic whisper.

"Rhodri! Stop her! Hold her back."

Hands took hold of her, pulling her down from the ridge, dragging her to the bottom of the cleft. A hand came across her mouth as she struggled to get free. Another wrenched her sword from her fingers.

She fought wildly, but Rhodri's body was across hers, his weight holding her down. Blodwedd's hands gripped viselike on either side of her head.

"Branwen, be calm!" She stared up into Blodwedd's huge golden eyes. "This is not the way," the owl-girl said. "You cannot reveal yourself at this time. Your death will be for nothing if you do! Heed me, Branwen!"

"Branwen, please—listen to her." Rhodri's frantic, breathless voice. "You'll be killed."

Branwen panted, staring up into Blodwedd's face. The red rage began to subside. She became still, her taut muscles relaxing. Through the throbbing of blood in her ears, she could hear the Saxons howling and beating their weapons.

"Get off me," she gasped. "Rhodri, I'm all right—there's no need to hold me down."

Rhodri knelt up. "It's a good thing they're making such a racket down there," he breathed "else they'd surely have heard us!"

Blodwedd's eyes glowed. "You must not throw your life away in futile despair, Branwen," she murmured. "Your life is not your own to do with as you please! Has everything I've told you meant nothing? You are the Warrior-Child! Latest in a great line. Brython needs you to live!"

A frozen anger began to take the place of Branwen's fiery rage. "Did you know of this all along?" she asked Blodwedd. "Did you know *this* was waiting at the end of our road?"

Blodwedd shook her head. "I did not."

"And your master? Did he know?"

Blodwedd's head lowered. "That, I cannot say."

Branwen frowned at her for a moment then turned to Rhodri. "Give me back my sword!"

He looked uneasily at her. "You can't fight them all."

"I don't mean to," she replied, sitting up and holding her hand out. "The sword, Rhodri!"

Reluctantly, he handed it to her. She stood up, sliding the sword into her belt and taking a long, slow breath.

"If we are to turn back this day's evil tide, we will need to know what plans have been laid," she said, and the calmness of her voice surprised her. Her anger was like a stone now, sitting cold and heavy in her chest.

She climbed the slope again. The din of the Saxon warriors had subsided.

Ironfist began to speak, using the language of Brython, albeit with a strong Saxon accent. "I am grateful to you, Captain Angor," the General said.

"You came in good time to save me the hardship of bitter blows and loss in the taking of Gwylan Canu. I had not looked to you for this—the messenger from Prince Llew did not speak of him sending men to aid me in this endeavor."

"We looked to find you already embattled," said Angor. "A messenger was sent to Doeth Palas, telling of your coming." He frowned. "And yet . . . how could that be? How could they have known so soon that a Saxon force was marching on Teg Eingel?" He turned. "Is Dagonet ap Wadu among those captured?" he called to his men.

"Dagonet is not here," said Lord Madoc. "He is with the king in Pengwern. Thus is one brave warrior of Powys saved from your treachery!"

Angor's eyes turned to Iwan. "How did you know, boy?" he shouted. "If it was not Dagonet who told you—who was it?"

Iwan gave a bruised smile. "A power greater than you know," he said. "A power that will see you trodden into the dust ere all is done, traitor!"

"What does he mean?" snarled Ironfist. "What power is this of which he speaks?"

Iwan lifted his head suddenly and stood proud and straight once more. "Do you not know?" he shouted, his voice ringing in the hills. "Do you not hear them? They are awake, they are stirring, they are coming—and they will be the death of you all!"

Angor strode forward and struck Iwan, knocking

him to the ground. But still there was defiance in Iwan's eyes as he looked up at the treacherous captain.

"Do you feel fear, yet, Angor ap Pellyn?" he cried. "The Shining Ones have awoken! Harken! They are close! They will . . ."

A second brutal blow sent him crashing onto his face before he could say any more. His father knelt at Iwan's side, his face livid with anger and his arms protectively around his son's shoulders.

"What does the boy mean?" demanded Ironfist.

"His wits have turned, my lord," said Angor. "He speaks madness. It is of no consequence."

"Then let us go about our business, Captain Angor," said Ironfist. He turned in the saddle, gesturing to his men. Two burly warriors strode forward, carrying between them a heavy, iron-bound wooden chest. At the general's command, they threw it down and opened its heavy lid. Branwen saw the sparkle and glint of coins heaped within—a mountain of coins, more coins than she had ever seen in her life. A king's ransom, she guessed.

"Are your men loyal to you, Captain Angor?" Ironfist asked.

"They are, my lord," Angor replied. "They are hand-picked, and each has pledged to die in my service if need be."

"And what of the others of the court of Prince Llew?" asked Ironfist. "How many know of the treaty that has been agreed between our realms?"

"These men under my command have long known the truth, my lord," said Angor. "And so, too, do some intimates of the prince—but they are all close-mouthed men and trustworthy to our cause. No hint of what is to come has yet been spoken abroad in the citadel, and outside its walls the folk of Bras Mynydd know nothing. The prince deemed it better that way, lest some fools choose defiance."

"Wise thinking," said Ironfist. "Until all is in readiness, I would not have word of our plans come to the ears of the other lords of Powys, nor to those of the king, weak and cowardly though he may be, lurking within the walls of the citadel at Pengwern. I'd not have word sent to the southern kingdoms either. We want no armies arrayed against us before we are secure in Powys."

So that's the scale of their ambition, Branwen thought bitterly, her fists balling and her nails digging into her flesh. *To use Prince Llew's cantref as a base from which to strike King Cynon, and then to eat up the rest of Brython piece by piece!*

Captain Angor spread his arms. "We are yours to command, my lord."

"And the men of Gwylan Canu—how go their hearts in this matter?"

Lord Madoc got to his feet and stepped forward. "Know me, accursed Saxon dog," he spat, his fist hammering his chest. "I am Madoc ap Rhain, lord of Gwylan Canu. I know not what lies you have used

242

to sway Llew ap Gelert to your cause, but hear me now: The men of Gwylan Canu are loyal and true to their king. They will not do your bidding, Herewulf Ironfist—they would die a thousand times first."

Ironfist smiled coldly. "A thousand deaths will not be necessary, my lord," he mocked. "One death for each man will suffice." He lifted his voice to address the gathered warriors of the citadel. "Listen well, men of Powys. Against the forces that gather in Mercia and Northumbria there can be no victory for you. Brython will fall to us—our destiny wills it so! Only a fool goes willingly into a battle that cannot be won. See wisdom, as has the lord of Bras Mynydd. To all who swear allegiance to King Oswald, I will give great riches." He gestured toward the teeming chest. "Find wisdom within yourselves, men of Teg Eingel." His voice rose to a guttural snarl. "For those who defy me, death will be their only release. Choose swiftly! Come!"

Madoc ap Rhain stared into Ironfist's face, his arms spread wide. "Kill us now, Saxon filth—none will take your tainted gold!"

A bleak pride welled up in Branwen as she saw that not one of the men of Gwylan Canu stepped forward. She could see fear and despair in the eyes of many, and anger and hatred in others. But it spoke well of Lord Madoc's leadership that every man chose loyalty to him and the Brython homeland over the offer of the Saxon general.

There was a long, dreadful stillness, broken only by the constant beating of waves on the rocks and the lonely cries of gulls.

"So be it," Ironfist said at last. "Let Lord Madoc and his kin be taken captive and held in the citadel. Their lives may prove useful if it comes to bargaining. The others will be taken east—to captivity or death."

"What would you have me do, my lord?" asked Angor.

"Return with your warriors to Doeth Palas," said Ironfist. "Make it known in the citadel that you have scored a great victory against the Saxons, that Gwylan Canu is secure and Ironfist is sent packing with his tail between his legs. Let no man speak of the things that have passed here, on pain of certain death." He leaned forward in the saddle, a savage smile stretching his lips. "In the privacy of his court, tell the prince that I am well pleased with him. He has shown foresight and wisdom. King Oswald will be generous when the time comes. If all goes well, Llew ap Gelert will one day sit upon the throne of Powys. Tell him that."

"I shall, my lord."

Ironfist sat upright again. "Tell your men to take from the chest what coins they can carry before they depart." He handed Angor's sword back to him, then turned his black stallion and rode back to his men, shouting commands in his own harsh, guttural language. Captain Angor stood, sheathing his sword, staring after the Saxon general.

Branwen tried to imagine what thoughts must be going through his mind. Was it truly the hopelessness of warfare against the Saxons that had made the captain and his prince agree to betray their homeland? Was this treachery fueled by despair? Or had something else spurred Prince Llew to join hands with Ironfist? Even greater wealth, perhaps? This promise of the crown of Powys?

Whatever it was, it left a taste like gall in Branwen's mouth; it soured her stomach and burned her heart. Somehow she would find a way to fight this!

Things began to move quickly. A detachment of Saxon warriors led the men of Gwylan Canu away down the road into the east. At their captain's word, the men of Doeth Palas ran forward, scrabbling for gold and silver in the chest like pigs at a trough. Then Angor bade them mount, and with a final hand raised in farewell to Herewulf Ironfist, he led his army at a trot, back to spread lies in Doeth Palas.

Finally, Madoc ap Rhain and Iwan were taken into the citadel by several Saxon soldiers. The foreign warriors gathered the weapons left by Lord Madoc's men, and then Ironfist and his men poured into Gwylan Canu. The stone-walled bastion of Teg Eingel had been taken without a fight, falling to bloodless treachery.

Branwen saw the gates pulled closed. There was the thud of the great doors as they slammed, the crash and boom as the bars were dropped in place. Saxon warriors appeared on the gatehouse. A banner was quickly unfurled—the white dragon on a field of blood.

And then there was a terrible stillness. Branwen tasted salt tears on her tongue as she made her way down from the ridge.

26

BRANWEN, RHODRI, AND Blodwedd sat among the trees once more as the evening shadows lengthened. They had eaten a bleak meal together, Rhodri and Branwen almost too shocked by the turn of events to put their feelings into words. But no matter how deeply they were hurt by Prince Llew's treachery, they could not remain silent.

"If the prince knew all along that Ironfist was marching on Gwylan Canu, why did he send fifty horsemen to its rescue?" Rhodri asked.

"It was for show, that's all," Branwen replied. "What else could he do? If Iwan had told people that his homeland was in danger and that Prince Llew had done nothing, how would that look? No, he sent Angor here with a troop of warriors who already knew the truth. But not to help Gwylan Canu—simply to ensure that all was going as planned. The moment Iwan rode with them, his fate was sealed!"

Branwen shook her head, still enraged and overwhelmed by what she had witnessed. "In fact, it was Iwan's presence among them that made it so easy for Angor to force Lord Madoc to give up the citadel!" She glared at Blodwedd. "If we had not gone to Iwan, perhaps Gwylan Canu would still be holding out against Ironfist's army! We did no good at all. We only caused harm—and made it easier for Ironfist to take the citadel without even having to fight for it!" She glared at the owl-girl. "Your master has only made things worse!"

Blodwedd had not spoken for some time. She sat huddled on the brink of the hill—staring down at the fires and torches that were igniting in the citadel as the evening deepened. "Lord Govannon did not set your feet on the path that took you to Doeth Palas," she said.

"She's right," said Rhodri sadly. "That was my idea."

"Then we should have been sent a sign or something to show us it was a *bad* idea," said Branwen.

"I don't think it works like that," Rhodri said in a subdued voice.

Blodwedd looked around. "Lord Govannon will show us the way to thwart that Saxon general's ambitions," she said softly, almost as though talking to herself.

"Then share his plans with us," Branwen said bitingly. "All he's done so far is to bring us here too late to do anything other than watch Gwylan Canu fall! What are his plans, Blodwedd? Will he conjure up an army for us, so we can sweep down and assail the citadel? Can he put a battering ram into our hands so we may beat down the gates?" She stood up, anger taking her again. "What will he do for us, Blodwedd? *What?*"

The owl-girl looked up at Branwen with wide, calm eyes.

"What more would you have him do, Branwen?" she asked. "Are you without hope, without thought? His will brought you to this place, at this time, with a purpose. You are the Warrior-Child. Use your skills, use your mind." Her eyes sparked with purpose. "It is for us to find a way!"

"We should try to get word to the king," said Rhodri.

Branwen nodded. "You're right. The king must be told of this. An army must be assembled and Gwylan Canu retaken before Ironfist can bring yet more Saxon warriors here." Branwen had not forgotten the other element of her bleak vision. Not only had she seen Ironfist holding up Iwan's head, and the white dragon flying over the citadel, and Saxon warriors triumphant on the walls—she also had seen a fleet of Saxon ships cleaving the waves, and she knew they were coming.

It was no more than a day's march from Ironfist's great encampment outside Chester to the mouth of the River Dee. If her vision was true, then hundreds more Saxon warriors could already be on the open sea. The next morning could see a whole host of their low, square-sailed ships riding the surf off the coast of Teg Eingel.

"The trouble is, we could spend four days on the journey to Pengwern," Branwen said. "And when we came to King Cynon's court, would we be believed? Will the king accept our word that his most powerful prince has turned traitor? What proof could we offer him?"

"The proof of our own eyes," said Rhodri. "What more could he ask?"

"A great deal more," said Branwen. "You are half Saxon, Rhodri—who would trust you? And for all we know, the prince already has conspirators at the Royal Court. How am I to be trusted if Prince Llew's men are there to give the lie to my every word?" She paused for a moment as the glimmerings of an idea came into her head. "But he would surely trust the word of the lord of Gwylan Canu."

"Doubtless he would," said Rhodri. "Except that Lord Madoc is being held captive behind the walls of his own citadel." He lifted an eyebrow. "Or are you suggesting we three should attack Gwylan Canu and rescue Madoc ap Rhain from under Ironfist's very nose?"

"Not attack, no," said Branwen. "I see no way through that wall. But is it impossible to approach the citadel from the sea?"

"Those who built it must think so," said Rhodri. "Otherwise walls would surround the entire headland. I would say they think themselves quite secure from a seaborne attack." He turned, listening to the drumroll of the surf. "Can't you hear the noise the waves make when they break on the rocks?" He shook his head. "That will be the sound of our bones cracking if we attempt such a deed."

"And that is why no one within will expect such an assault," Branwen insisted. "There are boats drawn up on the beach a little way along the coast. One of those may serve us, if a way onto the rock could be found." She looked eagerly into Rhodri's face. "Couldn't a single boat make secret landfall on a dark night? Couldn't three people enter the citadel unseen? And could they not rescue Madoc and escape with him before the alarm was sounded?"

Rhodri pursed his lips. "What are we, flies and spiders that we may cling to sheer rock?" he said. "The land drops straight into the sea all along the headland."

"We don't know that for sure," Branwen persisted. "We should send Fain to scout the land for us. He can bring back news of any possible landing-place."

Rhodri stared dubiously at her for a moment. "Yes," he said at last. "We should do that."

Branwen stood and walked over to where the horses had been loosely tethered. She peered up into the darkling branches, but saw no sign of the bird. And then, as though Fain knew he was needed, a dark scythe-shaped shadow came flying through the trees.

Branwen held up her hand, and Fain came to rest upon her wrist. She lifted a finger to stroke his feathers.

Blodwedd was standing suddenly behind her. "Ask him to fly down to the citadel to learn whether it can be approached safely from the sea," she said. "I will tell you what tidings he brings."

"Fain—do as Blodwedd says," instructed Branwen, and she lifted her wrist higher. The falcon lurched forward, his wings spreading and curling. "Be swift and sure, my friend!" Branwen called after him. "Bring us back good news!"

"No one has lived here for some time," said Rhodri as they walked among the huddled huts.

Branwen could see that he was right. From afar the little hamlet had looked like any other, but now that they had come down out of the hills and made their way across rough scrubland to the sandy bay, it was clear that the tumbledown huts were derelict.

In many places their daub-and-wattle walls had crumbled away to reveal the broken mesh of wicker-work beneath. Some of the thatched roofs had fallen in, leaving the walls standing like the shards of a hollow tooth. Long-cold firepits and scattered pieces of cracked earthenware were dimly discernable in the growing night.

"What took the people?" Branwen wondered, looking uneasily around herself. "This place has a sad and mournful air to it."

"Disease perhaps?" ventured Rhodri. "Or the village could have been overrun in the old wars, and none ever returned to fish its waters. Who can say?"

Branwen shivered and pulled her cloak around her shoulders. The wind was coming in cool off the sea.

She glanced up to the east. Across this small western bay, Gwylan Canu was a great dark hulk against the sky, cragged and uneven; the roofs of its huts and houses cut sharp shapes against the backdrop of the stars. Taller than all other buildings was the Great Hall, stark and black on its hill. But the citadel twinkled with lights, yellow and red and white, and there were torches lit on the wall, flickering as guards passed in front of them.

"Let's see if the boats are still seaworthy," Branwen said. She looked sideways at Rhodri. "Can you swim?"

"No."

"Neither can I," she said. "Let's hope we find a watertight boat."

Fain's news had been . . . *hopeful*. Speaking through

Blodwedd, he had made it clear that he had found no landing posts or jetties along the headland—in most places the black rock dropped straight into the waves without step or handhold. All along the promontory, the endless pounding of the sea had gnawed and corroded the ancient rocks, leaving cracks and breaches where the water churned white and deadly. In other places the waves had eaten deep into the rock, mining out blowholes and apertures from which the surf spouted.

It was one such chasm that had taken Fain's attention. A deep, sloping tunnel led from the sea up onto the land at the headland's very point, beyond the buildings, even beyond the Great Hall. How easy it would be for a person to climb this borehole to safety above the fury of the breakers, Fain could not tell them. But there was some hope that this perilous way might take them safely into the very heart of Gwylan Canu.

Either they took this chance, or they had to admit defeat—and Branwen was not prepared to do that.

The boats were above the tide line, but as the little group moved from one to the next, they quickly saw that most were falling to pieces. The wooden slatted hulls were long rotted, and the oars were snapped and useless.

"What about this one?" Rhodri asked. He had moved away from Branwen and Blodwedd and was standing by a boat turned upside down in the sand.

Branwen went to look. The boat was narrow and leaf-shaped, not much longer than Branwen was tall. Its hull was made from tough leather, old but thick and durable. So far as Branwen could see in the darkness, the hull had no breaches or tears in it.

"Let's turn it over and see if it's sound," she said. They tipped the vessel onto its back; the timber framework seemed solid enough. It rocked in the sand, revealing two paddles that had been under the boat and looked to have survived the ravages of wind and rain and bad weather.

Branwen saw Rhodri's eyes on her. "We have to make our minds up," he said. "I think it's this one or nothing."

"Then it's this one," Branwen said. She turned to where the owl-girl was standing, her arms wrapped tight around her chest, her forehead creased, her anxious gaze fixed on the sea. "Blodwedd—help us," Branwen called.

Between them, they carried the boat down to the water's edge. As they waded into the surf, dragging the boat with them, Blodwedd hung back, unwilling to set foot in the foaming wash of the incoming tide. Branwen was aware of small, sharp sounds coming from the owl-girl and realized that Blodwedd's teeth were chattering.

Branwen looked back at her. "Come," she said. "What's wrong?"

"I cannot." There was deep terror in Blodwedd's

voice, and her eyes were haunted in her pale face. Pure animal eyes they seemed now—as though Blodwedd's true spirit was staring through them. She shook her head.

Branwen left Rhodri keeping hold of the boat. She splashed back to the shore, remembering the owl-girl's anxious words from earlier in the day. "There is nothing to fear," she said.

"I am Lord Govannon's child," Blodwedd murmured, her voice little more than a fearful whisper. "I dare not leave his realm." Branwen could see that she was shaking from head to foot.

"What do you fear?" asked Branwen, looking into Blodwedd's terrified glowing eyes.

"Beyond the reach of his hand, the sea will drown me," Blodwedd murmured. "My feathers will be waterlogged, dragging me down . . . and down . . . and down. . . . I will fly nevermore . . . never feel the wind . . . cold water in my mouth . . . in my body . . . choking me!" Her voice rose to a wail. "Lord Govannon, forgive me—you ask too much! I cannot! I cannot!"

Before Branwen could act, Blodwedd turned and ran headlong up the beach, the sand kicking high from her heels.

"Blodwedd! Wait!" Branwen chased after her, but the lithe owl-girl sped away into the darkness. Before Branwen had a hope of catching up with her, the slender form had vanished into the night.

Branwen stood in the sand, panting, staring blankly after her. She felt no anger at Blodwedd's flight. Not long ago she would have been relieved to be rid of her, but she didn't feel that either. She felt pity, that was all. Pity for the inhuman creature and for the terror that had caused her to run away from the duty that Govannon of the Wood had laid upon her.

At length, Branwen shook her head and made her way back to where Rhodri was waiting, knee deep in the sea, clinging to the bucking boat.

"Don't put too much blame on her," he said. "At heart, she's an animal still. A bird of the forests—she could not help herself."

"I don't blame her," Branwen said. "But I hope her master is as forgiving. The Shining Ones ask for impossible sacrifices—and make us pay a terrible price if we fail them." She was thinking of her father lying dead and of Garth Milain in flames. If she had not turned her back on Rhiannon of the Spring when the woman in white had first called to her, might those tragedies have been averted?

"Perhaps she hasn't entirely abandoned us," Rhodri said, scanning the shadowed hills, his face hopeful. "She may wait for us with the horses."

"Let us hope so," Branwen said. "Because if she has deserted us, then I fear she will never be an owl again." She glanced at Rhodri. "Although, would that upset you, I wonder?"

Rhodri didn't reply, and instead turned his face away so she could not see his expression.

So, now I know for sure, she thought. *A strange affection, and I don't envy him the pain it will surely cause—whether she returns to us this time or not.*

Without speaking they pushed the boat into deeper water, struggling all the time against the breaking waves. It was a hard, exhausting task. It felt as though the sea were fighting them, working with all its tireless might to prevent them from using the boat. Branwen's muscles ached from the strain of keeping the leaping boat secure. The rush of the undertow around her legs made every step an effort.

Finally she was waist deep; they were out beyond the breakers. She hauled herself up and over the side, gasping and clinging to the light vessel as it rocked and bobbed. A moment later Rhodri came surging up over the other side.

"The paddles—quick!" she panted.

They knelt in the bottom of the boat, gripping the wide-bladed paddles and thrusting them into the water. Branwen bent her back, attacking the sea with the paddle, the muscles in her shoulders and arms knotting as she battled against the tide.

She could hear Rhodri grunting and gasping behind her, but still the surge of the sea drove them back toward the beach. She renewed her efforts, refusing to be beaten, using every fiber and sinew as she plunged the paddle down, then dragged back on it and lifted it again. Down, back, lift—over and over, while the surf spat in her face and her muscles screamed in protest.

At last she felt able to look over her shoulder. Rhodri's face was running with sweat and seawater, his jaw clenched, his lips parted in a snarl of effort and pain. But beyond him, the pale line of the coast had fallen away into the distance.

She let out a gasp of breathless laughter. They had beaten the sea!

Rhodri just looked at her, too spent to speak.

Over to their right, the great, dark bulk of the headland loomed, gray foam lapping greedily at its feet.

"We need to get farther out," Branwen gasped. "Come at it from the seaward end. Yes?"

Rhodri nodded.

They plied the paddles once more. Down, back, lift. Branwen tried to ignore the fatigue that made her arms feel leaden. She did her best to blot out the pain that bunched across her back and bit into her neck.

Gradually they crawled along the headland until they came to the outermost point—a huge, blunt forehead of black rock thrusting out into the sea. The waves broke white, spurting and spewing into the air.

Making landfall looked impossible. They would be dashed to fragments.

"There it is!" came Rhodri's gasping voice. She

glanced back, following the line of his pointing hand. Yes! She saw it. A gaping black hole in the rockface, its lower lip just above the swirl and spit of the sea.

She drove her paddle deep, making for the deadly headland.

The dark cliff reared above them. The noise pounded in Branwen's ears—far louder than the surge of her own blood or the harsh pant of her breath. A wave took the little boat and sent it careering forward. An unseen rock scraped the leather hull, pushing them aside, sending the boat spinning.

Foam spat. The boat heeled over. Water came pouring in, swirling around their feet, cold and deadly. Again the waves lifted and twisted the boat, jerking Branwen's body and jarring the paddle out of her hands.

With a cry she lunged sideways, frantically trying to retrieve it, but the sea sucked it away from her. As she hung over the side of the boat, her arms scrambling at the waves, more water flooded in. She heard Rhodri shout. Another wave slapped down hard on them. The boat tipped, and Branwen was hurled headlong into the thrashing sea.

27

BRANWEN FOUND HERSELF struggling in deep water, fighting to keep her head above the surface, her arms and legs flailing in the turmoil of the sea. She gasped for breath, kicking and clawing, desperate in the wild darkness.

She felt something solid under her foot and pushed herself upward. Her hands grazed over wet rock. Seawater filled her mouth, choking her. The waves pulled at her, trying to drag her off the rock. Coughing and retching, she clung on grimly, using all her failing strength to keep from being dragged to her death.

A wave beat on her back, pushing her forward, pummeling her, spread-eagling her on the rock. But now she was half clear of the water, for a moment at least. She kicked out, heaved herself upward, and hung on, spat at by the angry waves but above the tide line. Foam blinded her, and she lifted her head. The roaring of the sea almost deafened her. "Rhodri!"

A hand took hold of her ankle. She reached down and snatched at the wrist. Surf burst all about them. Branwen looked down into Rhodri's eyes as he struggled to pull himself up the slippery rock.

It was agony for her to keep hold of him; the effort of rowing through the choppy water had all but drained her muscles of strength, and now she had to cling to Rhodri while the tireless sea fought to rip him from her grip. But she would not let him go. She would *not*! She gritted her teeth, forcing her fingers to tighten around his wrist. She twisted around, grabbing his hair with her other hand. Ignoring his cries of pain, she yanked him up.

At last he was at her side, and they clung to each other, gasping and almost weeping with relief.

"A little farther up," Branwen panted. "I don't want to be washed off if a big wave comes."

Side by side, they clambered on hands and knees farther up the rock, struggling on until they were beyond the bluster and boil of the sea.

Branwen wiped her eyes. They were sitting in the mouth of the sloping borehole. Against all the odds, they had made safe landfall on the headland of Gwylan Canu.

But all had not gone as planned.

Their boat was gone. There was no way back.

Rhodri looked at her, his eyes creased in the gloom. "What's that stink?" he asked.

Branwen wrinkled her nose. He was right. There was a foul stench in the air. It was the disgusting smell of rot and putrefaction—the unmistakable reek of a midden.

And then she realized that the slippery, slithery surface beneath her was wet not from the sea, but from the accumulated slime and muck and ooze of discarded waste: castaway filth from the cookpot and the trencher.

"They must use this shaft as a garbage chute," Rhodri gasped. "Ugh! I cannot stand it!" He turned and began to climb up the slope. Trying her best to hold her breath against the appalling fetor, Branwen scrambled up after him.

They came up out of the offal-chute and crouched among the rocks that lay beyond its upper rim. The landscape directly ahead of them was pocked with holes and ridges—a bleak end to the promontory, houseless and deserted—a place where the barren rock dropped stark into the sea.

An arrow's shot away from them, the rocks rose into a long, flattened hill, and upon its high summit stood the Great Hall of the House of Puw.

"Listen," murmured Rhodri, his head close to Branwen's. "Can you hear them?"

She nodded. She could hear well enough: laughter and shouting and the noise of musical instruments and thumping drums. Smoke was pouring from the roof of the Great Hall. A fire was burning in the hearth, and food was being cooked. A grand feast was taking place.

General Ironfist and his warriors were celebrating their easy conquest of Gwylan Canu—carousing on into the night, swigging ale and gorging on roasted meats.

"I have served at feasts like this," Rhodri said. "Ironfist likes to indulge his men when battles have gone well. It will go on all night, I expect. That's the usual way with such debauches."

Branwen narrowed her eyes. "Will all of them be in there?" she asked.

"All save for a few guards on the wall," said Rhodri. "But what do we do now? The plan was to free Lord Madoc and use the boat to take him ashore. But the sea has put paid to that intent. Even if we can rescue him, how do we get out again?"

Branwen looked at him. "We must hope that the Saxons' eyes are blurred with too much ale, my friend," she said. "Our only choice now is to cut our way through whatever gate-guards have been posted— and to have faith that once we are beyond the wall, the old lord can run faster than his girth would suggest."

Cautiously she lifted her head over the rocks and scanned the barren landscape. "I see no one," she said. "No guards here, nor on the hill. You guessed

right, Rhodri—they don't fear attack from the sea."
She smiled grimly, her fingers patting the hilt of her
sword. "We will make them regret that oversight."

"We must find where Lord Madoc is being held,"
Rhodri said. "And we should expect to find guards
watching over him."

"Perhaps," Branwen replied. "But Angor said
something that gives me some hope. When he
ordered his men to search the citadel for weapons, he
spoke of pits dug into the ground beyond the Great
Hall—pits that were used in the old wars to hold
Saxon prisoners."

"Ahhh," breathed Rhodri. "And if good fortune is
with us, you think Ironfist's high-born captives will
have been put there as well? If these pits are beyond
the Great Hall, then surely they must be close by."

"Close by and unguarded, it would seem," said
Branwen. She looked at Rhodri. "Even though his
messenger is gone, Govannon of the Wood may still
be guiding our footsteps to good fortune."

A look of anguish passed over Rhodri's face at
the mention of Blodwedd. Branwen reached a hand
toward him but withdrew it again without making
contact. What comfort could she give him if the owl-
girl truly had fled?

She crept forward, slow and silent as a shadow
among the shadows, ignoring the discomfort and
chill of her wet clothes, refusing to be thwarted by
fatigue. All her attention was focused now on the

ground directly ahead of her. If this cape of bitter rock was indeed riddled with pits, she did not want to stumble into one of them unawares.

She paused, holding her breath. Listening.

"What?" Rhodri murmured, close behind.

She held a hand up. "Hush!"

She listened again. She fancied she had heard a new sound above the steady rumble of wave on rock and the rumor of the revelries taking place atop the hill. The subdued sound of voices.

She crawled forward, turning her head to try and track down the elusive whispering. When she moved between two large rocks, her hand came down on something other than stone. She looked down. It was a coil of rope, knotted at one end and secured to the ground by a great, black iron spike driven into the rock. Branwen saw that the ground in front of her fell sharply away into a wide, black pit. It was from the depths of this pit that the mutterings and whisperings were coming.

She lay flat on her belly, edging closer to the lip of rock.

Voices! Several of them—both male and female.

Branwen lifted her head, looking quickly around. Then she hung out over the black void and called in a low, urgent voice.

"Is Madoc ap Rhain among you?"

She heard gasps and then a sudden silence.

"I am a friend," Branwen called again, trying to be

266

heard without raising her voice. "I seek Lord Madoc. Is he with you?"

"Branwen?" A familiar, astonished voice spoke from the black pit.

"Iwan! Yes, it is me!"

"Look for a rope, Branwen," came Iwan's voice, filled now with hope. "You will find one attached to the rocks."

Branwen fumbled for the rope, feeling its length rough and hard under her fingers. "Yes, it's here. I have it."

"Throw it down to me. Say nothing more. There may be guards."

Branwen knelt and, taking hold of the thick, hairy rope, began to feed it down into the gloom. Suddenly the rope went taut in her hands. It had been grasped from below. She leaned over the hole. The rope thrummed and shuddered as someone began to climb.

A hand came down on her back, pushing her to the ground. She twisted her head in surprise. It was Rhodri, kneeling close behind her. His voice hissed softly. "Stay down. Do not speak."

So saying, he stood up. *"Hael!"* she heard him call out. *"Hael—freon! Liss, freon—cniht betera latteow Herewulf! Liss freon!"*

He was speaking in the Saxon language! She did not know what the words meant, but she recognized their sounds.

A slurred, guttural voice replied out of the night. *"Nama cniht!"*

A Saxon.

Rhodri must have seen him approaching and revealed himself to try and prevent Branwen from being discovered. The rope had become still—whoever had been climbing it had paused.

"Nama Rhodri," called Rhodri, giving Branwen a warning nudge with his foot as he moved away from her and toward the voice. He continued speaking, the tone of his voice conciliatory and submissive.

She heard a harsh gush of words from the Saxon, then a low, dull thud. Rhodri gave a gasp of pain, as though he had been hit. Branwen's instinct was to draw her sword and throw herself on the Saxon—but then she heard a third voice. The Saxon was not alone.

Rhodri spoke again. There was harsh laughter. He must have said something to amuse or appease the men.

Branwen listened as the two Saxons debated. She guessed they were trying to decide what to do with this unexpected interloper.

Rhodri spoke again, his voice servile now, pleading and whining. There was more laughter. Branwen heard scuffling sounds, then Rhodri again—his voice now relieved and thankful. Whatever he had said to them, it had saved his life, by the sound of it.

Rhodri's voice faded.

Branwen lifted herself cautiously up. She could just make out three shapes moving off toward the Great Hall.

Her stomach twisted into knots. To protect her and to save their plans from being revealed, Rhodri had given himself up to the Saxons. She hardly dared think of what terrible fate might await him in the Great Hall. How would Herewulf Ironfist choose to reward a runaway servant who had allowed himself to be recaptured?

28

THE ROPE QUIVERED under Branwen's hand. Whoever was hanging from it had begun to climb again now that the voices had faded.

Finally Iwan's pale face showed at the mouth of the pit. Branwen held out a hand, bracing herself as he snatched at her wrist and hauled himself over the edge of the hole. There was dried blood on his chin and the bruises were livid on forehead and cheek, but there was still an unquenchable light in his brown eyes.

"I'd ask how you got here, Branwen," he murmured. "But as you are aided by the Old Gods, I shall assume you were flown here on wings of air to rescue us and to drive Ironfist into the sea." He saw her wet clothes and the hair plastered to her skull. "Or perhaps you were transformed into a fish and swam here?" he added wryly.

"Not quite," Branwen whispered. "The Old Gods do not make life that easy for their cat's-paws. We came by boat, but the boat is lost."

"We?" Iwan asked. "Is the demon girl with you still?"

"No, she is not. I spoke of Rhodri."

"Ahhh! It was his voice I heard speaking with the Saxons, yes?"

"He must have heard the Saxons coming. He gave himself up to prevent them from finding me." She looked urgently into Iwan's eyes. "We came here to rescue your father so that word could be sent to King Cynon. But I will not leave this place without Rhodri."

Iwan eyed her dubiously. "What hold does that Saxon rogue have over you that you should consider risking everything for him yet again?"

Branwen frowned. "He is only half Saxon," she said. "And is friendship not enough? For good or bad, his life is bound up with mine—I will not abandon him."

"Listen to me, Branwen." Iwan's voice was low and insistent. "My father was not thrown into the pits," he said. "I think he is held captive in the Great Hall—a trophy for the sport of Ironfist and his men. We have no hope of rescuing him and surviving." He looked hard into Branwen's eyes. "I am not a coward," he said. "But I will not die for no reason."

"I know you're not a coward," Branwen replied.

Iwan nodded. "I see that you carry a sword and a knife," he said. "Give me the knife and between us we may be able to get past whatever guards have been posted on the gate and break out of this place before the alarm is sounded. You must have horses—let's get to them and fly away south to Pengwern and the king. We need an army at our backs if we're to snatch Gwylan Canu back from Ironfist's grasp."

"No." Branwen shook her head. "I won't leave Rhodri behind."

"It's pure madness! We cannot free him!"

"I do not care—we must try."

Iwan's eyes narrowed. "Your stubbornness will be the death of us, barbarian princess." He looked at her for a few long moments, his face undecided. Then he let out a hard sigh, as though he knew his fate was sealed. "If you intend to enter the Great Hall with a sword in your fist," he continued slowly, "do me this one favor—give me your knife, as I asked, so that I can at least defend myself for a few brief moments before I am slaughtered at your side."

Branwen stared at him. "Are you mocking me, Iwan?"

"No, I am not." For once his voice sounded entirely sincere and his eyes were on her face, dark and glittering like agate stones. "If you insist on throwing your life away, I will fight beside you. Do you think I would watch you walk to your death and do nothing?"

"A selfless act? Is this the boy who, from the

moment I met him, cared for nothing but his own amusement?" she asked gently.

"Possibly," Iwan said. "Or perhaps it amuses me to care for something other than my own amusement, Branwen. Perhaps I'd have you think as well of me as I do of you."

Branwen sat back on her haunches, perplexed by Iwan's words. She shook her head and decided against asking him exactly what he meant. There was more important business at hand.

"Are there no able men left among the captives?" she asked. "A few fighters to even the odds?"

"None," Iwan said. "The pits are crowded with women and children and the elderly. Some of the women were taken to serve in the Great Hall. But all my father's warriors are gone, taken into the east—to their deaths, I fear." A moment of pain showed in his face. "And they were good men, Branwen. Friends and companions of my childhood. I remember every face—every voice."

Branwen looked thoughtfully at him. "Where are the weapons that were taken from the men of the citadel?" she asked.

"I do not know," said Iwan. "Piled high in the Great Hall, I suspect, or divided among the Saxon dogs. But why do you ask? Even with fifty swords apiece, we two would be no better off."

She looked closely at him. "Are there no brave women in Gwylan Canu?" she asked. "None that will fight for their homeland?"

"There are many—I don't doubt it," Iwan replied.

A plan was beginning to formulate in Branwen's head—an uncertain and perilous plan, but one that offered at least a thread of hope. She turned her head to look up at the Great Hall. "The Saxons are celebrating their victory," she said. "Rhodri told me that such feasts often carry on till dawn—or until all are so drunk that they fall witless to the floor and roll snoring among the rushes."

"I've heard the same," said Iwan.

"And you say that some women of Gwylan Canu were taken to the Great Hall to serve them?"

"I think so."

A grim smile touched Branwen's lips. "Then maybe we shall find a way to take back the citadel after all," she said. "I must speak with the remaining women, to find out whether their hearts are strong enough for the hazard I would lead them to."

"There are many women in the pit below," Iwan said.

"More guards might come if I speak too loudly. I'll descend. You stay here—keep watch. If you see any Saxons, pull the rope up and hide yourself." Branwen gripped the rope and lowered herself over the edge of the pit. She felt for a toehold. There, under her left foot, was a tiny ledge, enough to take her weight while she searched about for another. She found that the wall of the pit was ribbed and cracked, creating meager footholds to help her most of the way down.

Moving slowly and feeling her way carefully, she went hand over hand, down into the darkness.

She looked up and saw Iwan's face against the night sky.

It was good to know he was there—keeping watch.

It was good to have him close by.

The pit was about four times Branwen's height—not so deep that all was pitch-black at the bottom, but deep enough that escape was impossible unless the rope was thrown down. As she came close to the ground, the wall became smoother and her legs swung free, but she felt hands reaching to help her.

She found herself surrounded by women, some close to her own age, others more mature, and a few gray-haired and quite elderly. In the deep shadows, other women sat with children gathered around them, and a few held babes in their arms.

"I am Branwen ap Griffith," she told them.

"The daughter of Griffith ap Winn," she heard one woman murmur. "Yes, child, I have heard your name before." A haggard face came close, and withered hands touched her skin.

"I've come to bring you hope," Branwen replied.

"Hope?" repeated another woman, tall and clear-eyed, carrying a swaddled babe in her arms. "What hope do we have? To be carried east in chains is our only destiny now."

"Or to be left to die of starvation in these pits,"

said another, her round face pale and full of fear. "Or to be the sport of our captors. I have heard that the Saxons delight in torture and cruelty."

"They will throw our babies into the fire!" wailed another. "Our heads will be hacked off and our corpses hurled down into the sea. We are all doomed."

More voices lifted, crying and weeping and calling out to the saints for rescue.

"Be still!" called Branwen. "I have hope for you—for those of you who are willing to follow me. But I can do nothing for you if you despair! Heed me well before you surrender your spirit to the enemy. Who will listen?"

She stared around at the desperate, frightened faces that surrounded her. "Who among you is willing to take her destiny into her own hands? Who among you will fight with me?"

"Do not heed her," said the old woman. "She will lead you to certain death. Our only chance is to bend our knees to the Saxons. Prince Llew has abandoned us. He is a wise leader; he knows it is pointless to struggle against such odds." She pointed a crooked finger toward Branwen. "This child will lead you to your deaths!"

Branwen narrowed her eyes. She could see even in the darkness of the pit that many of the women were in agreement with the old woman. She had hoped to persuade the womenfolk of Gwylan Canu to fight at her side, but few seemed willing to trust her. She did not blame them—the consequences of fighting and failing would be dire indeed.

Then one young woman stepped forward—a bright-eyed girl of maybe fourteen summers, slim and erect. "I will join with you, Branwen ap Griffith," she said.

"Linette, do not be a fool!" cried the woman with the baby. "Carys speaks the truth. We will die if we resist!"

"I fear death," Lynette responded. "But I fear it less than I fear a life of servitude. I will not be dragged away by these dogs if I can fight against them." She turned to Branwen, her eyes burning with resolve. "What would you have me do?"

"And I, too," said another young woman, stepping forward. "Linette is right—a quick but courageous death is better than a life on our knees."

"Yes!" said a third, pushing out of the throng. "I will follow you, Branwen ap Griffith, no matter what the cost!"

And then it was as if a dam had been breached. More and more women stepped forward until Branwen found herself surrounded by a ring of valiant, eager faces. She looked into their bright, undaunted eyes, her heart swelling with pride. So many of these women of Brython were prepared to risk death rather than succumb to the Saxon yoke!

The old woman, Carys, shuffled off to the far side of the pit, muttering dire warnings. Many of the other women followed her, distancing themselves from Branwen and Linette and the others, now about fifteen strong.

"Do any of you have training with weapons?" she asked.

"I have some skill with a bow," said Linette.

"That's good," said Branwen.

"And I have some battle skills," said another, a slight, compact young woman with a mass of black hair and with deep-set dark eyes that looked keenly into Branwen's face. "My name is Dera ap Dagonet—my father is one of Lord Madoc's lieutenants."

"I am Banon—I know something of the hunt," said another.

"And I can spear a moving fish underwater at ten paces," said yet another, a big, powerful young woman with piercing eyes. "I am Aberfa. Lead me to the Saxon dogs, Branwen ap Griffith, and see how well I fight!"

A slow smile spread across Branwen's face. "We *shall* fight, my friends. And with good luck and bold hearts, perhaps we shall show Herewulf Ironfist that there is courage yet in Gwylan Canu."

"What would you have us do?" asked Dera ap Dagonet.

"I'd have you be patient yet a while," said Branwen, staring up at the night sky far above the black mouth of the pit. "Rest until the night is almost done. And then we shall see."

29

BRANWEN LAY SILENTLY on the long slope of the hill, holding her breath and listening intently. Linette and Dera lay on either side of her. Iwan and the other women were a little ways behind. Far, far away to the east, the night sky had a gray hem—the first intimation of the coming day.

Despite being wakeful all through the night, Branwen felt keen-witted and alert. She had given her sword to Iwan, whose task was to stay back and deal with any guards who might come to the Great Hall while the women were busy within.

The din of the nightlong revels had dwindled— Branwen could hear snatches of singing and the occasional shout or peal of laughter from the Hall— but the music and the stamping of feet and the roar of drunken voices had finished.

She stood up, knife in hand, and led the women up to the crest of the hill. They were at the back of the long hall. Branwen turned to her followers, pressing her finger to her lips. Then, quiet as a cloud, she slipped around the side of the Great Hall and ran fleet-footed under the hanging thatch of the high roof.

She could hear the patter of feet behind her as the line of women came snaking along in her wake. She paused, holding a hand up. There was a shape at the far corner of the hall—a man, swaying unsteadily while relieving himself against the wall. Too far away for a slingshot stone to finish him, but close enough for a well-thrown knife.

The man was singing to himself, hardly able to keep upright. Branwen took the blade of her knife between her fingers and drew her arm back. Stretching her left arm out as a guide, she leaned back and then brought the weight and strength of her shoulders into the throw.

The knife hissed through the air. The white blade stabbed deep into the darkness of the man's throat. He dropped like a sack, soundlessly. Branwen pounced after the throw and was on him in an instant. His eyes were wide in the gloom—as though he was surprised to find himself dead.

She pulled the knife out and wiped it on his tunic. She glanced back and saw a new confidence in the faces of her followers. They had seen that a Saxon could be brought down! Gesturing to them to follow, Branwen turned the corner.

Braziers were burning on either side of the open doors of the Great Hall. Branwen crept to the doorway and risked a quick glance inside, craning her neck through the doorway before jerking it back around the corner.

She leaned her head back against the door, her body trembling with suppressed excitement. She could not have hoped for better! In the aftermath of the victory feast, the main chamber of the Great Hall was a scene of excess and overindulgence. The fire was burning low now in the huge stone hearth at the center of the long chamber. Its flames flickered red on charred logs, reflecting on bloated sleeping faces and on bleary eyes, throwing up dancing shadows along the walls, as if the ghosts of the feasters played on while the Saxon warriors snored and wallowed in their debauchery.

Branwen leaned in to take another look. Not all were lost in drunken slumber. A few were wakeful still, swigging from mugs and picking morsels from food bowls. Here and there men squatted or sat, playing at dice and knucklebones, and from this corner and that the occasional snatch of song swelled before subsiding into laughter and calls for more ale.

Branwen saw that the women of Gwylan Canu who had been brought to the hall to serve were mostly gathered together against the wall, their faces gaunt and sleepless, their eyes empty of hope. A few moved unsurely among the Saxon warriors, pouring drink and trying to avoid being struck as they passed. Even as Branwen watched, one young girl—not even her own age—was kicked as she walked past a sprawling man. She fell to her knees, dropping the ewer she carried. It smashed and spilled foaming ale over the trampled rushes. The man snarled an oath and clumsily drew his sword, swiping feebly at the girl as she scrambled to get away. She ran to the others and was held in another woman's arms; meanwhile the drunken Saxon kept swinging his sword and muttering curses, as if he did not realize she was out of his reach.

On the far side of the hall, General Herewulf Ironfist sat in a wide chair spread with animal furs, his legs thrown out, a mug in one fist and the end of an iron chain in the other. His eyes were hooded with drink, and he leaned over the high arm of the chair, speaking to a prisoner who sat helplessly on the floor at his side.

The prisoner was Madoc ap Rhain. His face was bruised and bleeding, his body wound about with chains, his hands wrenched around behind his back.

From the way that Ironfist leaned back and opened his wide red mouth to bellow with laughter, Branwen assumed the Saxon general was taunting his defeated rival, reveling in Lord Madoc's downfall. But Lord Madoc just stared ahead, his face expressionless.

On Ironfist's other side, Branwen caught sight of another bound prisoner, lying on his side. The figure was stripped to the waist, his arms and legs tied, and his back showing the signs of a fresh whipping. It was Rhodri. White-hot anger seethed in Branwen's mind, and rage clenched hard under her ribs—but she could not rush to Rhodri's rescue, as she desperately wanted to do. Not yet. Not until her plans were well and truly laid.

She turned to the women gathered now at her back, nodding and gesturing for them to follow her into the hall. Stepping into the open, Branwen pulled her cloak close around herself to hide her hunting leathers, keeping her knife hand under the swathes of cloth.

They crept along the walls of the Great Hall. A few groggy and fuddled eyes lifted as the women passed the drink-addled Saxons. A slurred voice would call for more ale, or a mug would be raised, but no one seemed to sense the danger creeping in among them. No one drew a sword or called out an alarm.

Branwen made her way cautiously around the chamber toward Ironfist.

He was leaning even farther over the chair's arm now. Spittle flew from his mouth, getting caught in his beard and hanging there thickly as he heaped more abuse on the helpless lord of Gwylan Canu. Now Branwen could hear his harsh taunts.

"My men will wish for sport in the morning, my

lord," he sneered. "Perhaps your son could offer his services in entertainment? Have no fear that he will not have the talent to amuse—I am expert in drawing vivid performances from the most reticent of actors. Have you heard of the blood eagle, my lord? It is a most engaging and imaginative pastime. The performer is laid upon his belly on the ground and the ribs along his spine are cut through and wrenched upward to form wings. And then his lungs are drawn out of his body to lie throbbing upon his back." Ironfist gurgled with laughter. "Alas, the performance never lasts as long as my men would wish. But we have many captives on which to practice. It will while away the time till the remainder of my army arrives."

Revolted, Branwen glanced around. The women had placed themselves at all points along the walls of the hall and were watching, waiting for her to act.

She nodded and stepped up to Ironfist.

He lifted his head and peered at her with glazed eyes. "More ale, woman," he said, holding out the mug. "Be swift, or I'll have you whipped raw to the bone."

"You will not, my lord!" Branwen snarled.

His eyes narrowed, but his wariness came too late.

Branwen smashed the mug out of his hand with a single blow of her fist, then sprang forward, the knife in her hand, grabbing him by the hair and dragging his head back, the blade hard against his throat.

She leaned over him, her mouth close to his ear. "If you value your life, call to your men to throw down their weapons—those few with wits enough to understand you, that is!"

Ironfist breathed hard in her face. His breath was foul with ale, and his bloodshot eyes glared under heavy black brows.

"Who are you, woman of Gwylan Canu, to threaten me?" he snarled.

"I am Branwen ap Griffith," she replied calmly. "And if my name means nothing to you now, you will know me better hereafter, Saxon! Tell your men to disarm or there will be bloodshed here—and yours will be the first throat to feel the pierce of a blade!" She turned to the women. "Pick up their weapons! Arm yourselves. These fools are without their wits, but there will be sober guards on the outer wall."

At her words, the women ran into the body of the hall and began to search among the drunken warriors, taking swords and knives and axes. Seeing what was happening, some of the serving women came forward, stepping among the drunkards to find themselves weapons.

A Saxon who had been playing knucklebones surged to his feet, an ax in his fist, swinging at Dera ap Dagonet's head. She ducked and thrust a new-found sword into his belly. He went crashing to the floor, but others rose unsteadily, their weapons at the ready.

Using all her strength and weight, Branwen heaved Ironfist up out of the chair. Once he was on his feet, she stepped behind him, the knife sliding across his throat, drawing a thin trickle of blood. "Speak to them, General."

"You are a fool, child," grated Ironfist. "Drowsy from our revels, you may take us unawares—but against the forces that are gathering, there can be no hope of victory."

"I've heard that speech before," said Branwen. "I do not need to listen to it again. Have them drop their swords, General."

Ironfist called out something in his own language. Those few warriors who were able to stand on their feet dropped their swords and axes, their drink-sodden faces wrathful but wary as the armed women moved among them, picking up weapons by the armful, binding them hand and foot.

Iwan appeared in the doorway, the sword ready in his fist.

He looked across at Branwen and smiled darkly. Then, seeing his father, he sprang forward with anger and concern on his face.

"Take all the weapons out of here," Branwen called to the women. "Cut down any man who tries to stop you. Show no pity—they would have none for you. Dera ap Dagonet, come here. Watch over Ironfist while I truss him."

The slender young woman came bounding across

the room, her eyes glowing with the wild, feverish light of battle-lust. She stared up at Ironfist, a fierce grin spreading across her face, her bloodied sword pointing up at his chest.

"Do him no harm unless he tries to escape," Branwen said once she had finished tethering the general's hands. "He's more use to us alive than dead." She went to Rhodri and knelt at his side. Gently, she turned him over. His face was battered and bloody, his hair matted with gore.

"You are too brave for your own good, my friend," she whispered, leaning over him, carefully peeling back the sticky hair from his forehead and cheeks. "Look what they did to you!"

Rhodri's eyes opened; they swam for a moment. "Ahhh," he murmured. "A sweet dream to ease my torment. Are you a handmaiden of the gods, sent to bear me to Wotan's hall?"

"Hardly that," said Branwen. "A handmaiden of the gods would look more fair, I think."

"You do yourself injustice." His hand rose and touched her cheek. "I'm alive, then, am I?"

"I think you are, yes." She smiled. "Can you stand?"

"I will try." He smiled weakly. "I hoped to persuade old Ironfist that I came back to him of my own free will, but I think he did not believe me."

"But how did you explain your presence here?"

As Rhodri began to speak, Branwen busied

herself sawing through the ropes that tied him. "I said I found refuge in Gwylan Canu, and that when the warriors were sent out to surrender, I hid myself away among the rocks," he said. "He knocked me about a little while for sport, then had me whipped for running away." With Branwen's support he got to his feet. He rubbed his wrists, which were red and sore with welts from the tight ropes. "I expected you to find Lord Madoc and escape, but not under these circumstances." He stared around the hall. "I under-estimated your ambition, Branwen. What now?"

She turned to see Iwan helping his father to his feet.

Madoc ap Rhain stared at her in astonishment. "You are the child of Griffith ap Winn and Lady Alis," he said. He looked around the hall. "How have you come here—and how have you accomplished such deeds?"

"I have powerful allies, Lord Madoc," said Bran-wen. "But all is not yet won—there will be guards on the wall. We must look to them before Gwylan Canu is in the hands of men of Powys once more." She frowned, seeing how the old man leaned on Iwan's arm. "You are unwell, Lord. Take rest if you can. All shall soon be done. In the meantime, let's bind the hands of this general and take him out to meet his few remaining warriors. And then we shall shut and bar the gates of the hall and leave these drunken sots to their hoggish dreams."

* * *

Branwen stood under the high stone wall of Gwylan
Canu, her knife to Herewulf Ironfist's throat. Iwan
and Rhodri were at her side, and most of the armed
women of the citadel stood at her back. Some few were
missing, led by Lord Madoc to the pits to rescue those
still imprisoned. Two more had remained to gather
rocks from beyond the huts and houses of the citadel,
and then to pile them against the doors of the Great
Hall so that none should escape from within.

"Order your men down off the wall, General,"
Branwen said. She turned her head, looking into the
east, to where the soft light of dawn was suffusing the
sky. "Do you see the light growing? It's a new day—
and your overlordship of Gwylan Canu is already
over."

Ironfist smiled. "A new day and a new hope," he
said. "But not the hope of Powys, girl-child. Do you
feel the east wind?" He gave a harsh laugh. "It blows
ill fortune upon you. Release me and maybe I will
allow you to die swiftly. Continue with this folly and
you will linger to see your body torn to quivering
shreds."

Branwen narrowed her eyes. She had not for a
moment expected to see any trace of fear from him,
but the casual bravura in his words made her uneasy.
He had only six armed men on the wall. All the rest
were captives in the Great Hall. And yet he spoke as
though he was assured of victory.

"Call your men down," Branwen ordered, pressing the knife to his flesh. "I will kill you if I need to."

But before he could speak, the braying of warhorns tore the air. The Saxons on the ramparts ran to the far edge of the wall and stared down, shouting greetings in loud, exultant voices.

Ironfist gave a howl of laughter. "Too late, girl-child!" His voice rose to a commanding roar. "Warriors of King Oswald, get to the gates. Open them to our most welcome brothers!"

"No!" Branwen yelled. "Make no move! I'll cut his throat!"

"Do as I order!" bellowed Ironfist. "And then avenge my death!"

The men on the walls drew their swords and came pounding down the stone stairs of the gatehouse. Iwan and the women rushed forward to meet them.

Branwen stared for a moment into Ironfist's defiant eyes. The general was unarmed. His hands were bound. She could not bring herself to slit his throat when he could not defend herself. She pulled her knife away.

"Rhodri, watch over him. See he does no harm!"

Rhodri nodded grimly, grasping Ironfist's tied hands.

Branwen ran forward.

Iwan and some of the women were already fighting, but the Saxons were huge, strong men, and they were beating their way steadily to the gates. Beyond the wall, the war horns brayed continuously, and

Branwen could hear also the commotion of men shouting and of swords being hammered on shields.

She threw herself into the battle, leaping in front of the warrior closest to the gates. He was a great scarred beast with a yellow beard and eyes like blue diamonds. He swung a two-handed war-ax at her. She ducked, feeling the air sing as the sharp iron swept a hair's-breadth over her head.

She lunged forward and stabbed her knife upward. Its blade was deflected by the man's chain-mail jerkin, and she found herself falling to her knees with the momentum of her wasted blow. He roared, lifting his ax high and bringing it down. Branwen curled up, rolling in against the brute's legs, knocking him off-balance. He staggered, his face red with wrath, and his open mouth sprayed spittle.

She turned onto her back on the ground, with her head between his feet. Taking her knife in both hands, she thrust upward. Blood sprayed down on her as the man tottered sideways and fell. She leaped on his back, plunging her knife into his neck.

A hard blow sent her reeling. Another warrior had come up behind her, but he had struck first with his shield rather than his sword—otherwise it would have been the last of her. Groggily, she crawled away, picking up the dead man's fallen ax. Twisting her torso and opening her shoulders, she threw the ax behind her. She saw the curved blade strike the man full in the face. She looked away as he fell.

But another man sprang over her and ran to the

bar that held the gates closed.

"Stop him!" she shouted, staggering to her feet despite the ringing in her head.

An arrow cut the air. It struck the man in the shoulder. Dera ap Dagonet ran forward, swinging her sword and shouting. But the man grasped the bar with both hands, leaning down on it, too consumed with battle-lust to heed his wound.

Branwen could hear a tumult from outside, the sound of men hammering on the gates.

A shrill voice called out. "Ships! Saxon ships!"

Branwen gasped. The voice came from one of the women on the hill of the Great Hall. She was staring and pointing into the east. The buildings of Gwylan Canu blocked Branwen's view out over the sea, but the woman's terrified alarm was clear enough. Her hellish vision was coming true. Ironfist's fleet had arrived.

Even as she despaired over this news, Branwen heard the crashing thud of the gate bar being pulled aside. She turned back in time to see the doors swing open and a whole host of Saxon warriors come pouring in.

Ironfist had been right—the sea's wind had indeed brought ill fortune to her. Now all that she could hope for was to die valiantly and take with her as many of these Saxon dogs as possible.

30

"FALL BACK!" BRANWEN cried. "Fall back to the hill!"

Her instinct had been to hurl herself at the Saxon warriors as they came flooding through the open gates of Gwylan Canu with bloodthirsty whooping and howling. But when she saw how the women she had urged to fight were being driven back, she knew she had to do what she could to get them out of immediate danger. Then she could rally them in a good defensive position.

A sword swung and Linette fell. Branwen started to run to her aid, but feet were already trampling over her. There was nothing to be done. The words from her vision hammered in her mind.

Too late! Too late!

She saw Dera ap Dagonet running toward her,

blood streaming from a cut on her forehead. "We cannot hold them!" she gasped. Resignation filled her sable eyes, as though she knew she was going to die—but there was no fear in them. No fear at all.

"We must keep them from rescuing Ironfist!" shouted Branwen. "If we have him, we may still be able to negotiate for his release."

"But you heard him—he is willing to die!" exclaimed Dera.

"Let's hope his men are less willing to let him be slaughtered!" growled Branwen. "Go! Gather the others! We will make a last stand on the hill if need be."

Branwen ran to where Rhodri was still standing with the Saxon general.

Ironfist had an exultant, savage smile on his face. "Kill me or don't kill me, girl-child!" he spat in her face. "It will make no difference now. My army will sweep over you like the tide! Before the sun rises, every man, woman, and child who is not Saxon-born will perish here—and their deaths will be upon your head!"

Branwen refused to give him the satisfaction of a response. "Bring him," she said curtly to Rhodri. She strode rapidly past the huts and houses of Gwylan Canu, making for the hill of the Great Hall.

She would make a last stand there, with her back to the Great Hall of the House of Puw. Or maybe there was the chance that some lieutenant of Ironfist's army would be prepared to barter the lives of the women and children of Gwylan Canu for the life of his general. Even if *she* had to die in that place, it would offer her some solace to know that the women who had followed her to this ruin might survive.

She ran up the long slope. A spear grazed her shoulder and glanced off the stony ground. She turned. The Saxons were streaming up through the buildings. She saw another of the women fall with an ax in her back. Ironfist was dragging back despite Rhodri's efforts to force him up the hill. With a hissed curse, Branwen ran down to them, snatching hold of Ironfist's arm and pulling him forward.

They came at last to the doors of the Great Hall, piled high with stones and rocks. The timberwork rang to the sound of hammering fists and Branwen could hear the oaths and shouts of the imprisoned men within.

Let them howl! These men at least will not join the battle—not till all is lost!

Branwen turned at the top of the hill, staring out over the sea. As she looked into the east, all hope left her. Six ships rode the foam, and a seventh was already beached upon the sand. She stood frozen in despair, watching the ships. They looked strangely elegant as they rose and fell on the waves, their low, wide hulls leaf-shaped with high prow and stern, their single masts holding white sails billowing with the sea-scented east wind.

Each ship swarmed with Saxon warriors—there

were five, ten times the number that had taken Gwylan Canu.

A second ship made landfall, and the warriors poured from its sides in a dark flood. Branwen felt the chill of death come over her, almost as though Saxon iron was already piercing her heart. But why should she be surprised? She had always known in her heart that this "great destiny" of hers would end like this—in death. The fates had acted foolishly when they had picked as their tool the girl-child of Griffith ap Winn and Lady Alis.

Their mistake would doom all of Brython.

"Branwen?"

She turned at the voice. It was Iwan. He looked keenly into her face.

"No!" he said sharply, as if he could read her thoughts. "No! You won't give up! I won't let you!" He gestured to the women gathered on the hill—the ten or so who had survived the initial Saxon onslaught. "They are yours to command!" he said. "You cannot abandon them." His eyes blazed. "You cannot abandon *me*!"

She saw Rhodri looking at her—and beyond him, the eyes of the warrior women were turned to her, waiting for some word.

"Take your sword back," Iwan said, holding the hilt out to her. "There are plenty of others for me." In that he was right—all around her feet were scattered the weapons taken from the hall.

She closed her fingers around her sword hilt, and at its touch a wild elation poured like fire through her veins. Despair was the ultimate betrayal of life! She would not succumb to it! Her mind boiled. A red mist veiled her eyes. New strength surged in her muscles.

"We fight!" she shouted, lifting the sword and brandishing it at the Saxon warriors that were swarming up the hill. "I am the Emerald Flame of my people! I am the Sword of Destiny! I am the Bright Blade!"

She swept up a shield and leaped down the rocks to meet the oncoming hordes. Striking a running Saxon with her shield, she used the whole weight of her body to crush him to the ground. Branwen looked for an instant into his savage eyes before bringing her sword down into the gap between his chain-mail jerkin and his black beard. Dark blood sprayed up toward her.

A spear thrust at her from the side. She threw herself backward as the iron tip sliced past her stomach. She was on her feet in a moment, digging in her heels and finding her balance—knees flexed, shoulders open, shield up to her eyes, and sword arm bent back, ready for a killing stroke.

Three Saxons came for her. Sword, spear, and ax.

She sidestepped the spear-thrust and chopped down with her sword, snapping the spear in half, then stepped into the spearman and brought the upper rim of her shield hard in under his chin. His head snapped up as he stumbled.

Already, Branwen was turning to meet the swing of the ax. She angled her shield to counter it. The buffet numbed her arm, and she had to throw one leg back to keep from being tossed off her feet. But her shield deflected the ax-blow, and the warrior staggered forward onto her sword point. He roared, and red spittle spattered her face as he reached a clawing hand toward her.

She bent her back, pushing in closer, deepening the thrust of her sword under his ribs. Suddenly his dead weight came down on her, pressing her to the ground. Her sword arm was trapped under him. She fought to get out from beneath his body, but her arm was still caught as she saw a sword plunging toward her face.

She heard a shrill cry. Another sword drove the Saxon blade aside. A slim, dark figure bounded in—Dera ap Dagonet, her face a ferocious mask, blood-smeared and feral. She spun on her heel, sinking her sword into the Saxon's belly.

Branwen heaved and managed to push the dead warrior off. Her eyes met those of her rescuer. There was no time for words. They were surrounded by Saxons. They stood back to back—and it was good to feel Dera's strong shoulders against hers as Branwen fought, striking out with her shield, slashing and thrusting with her sword, constantly shifting her footing as the bearded warriors bore down on her.

Before long, the uneven ground beneath her feet

became slippery with spilled blood. Three bodies lay twisted in front of Branwen; a fourth warrior was on his knees, his hands up to try and staunch the flow of lifeblood from his throat.

But as hard as they fought, Branwen knew they would not be able to survive here, out in the open where the Saxons could come at them from all sides. It would be only a matter of time before they were overwhelmed by sheer force of number.

"We must . . . get to the . . . hilltop . . . ," Branwen gasped.

"I'm with you . . . ," came Dera's voice.

Branwen drove her shield into a Saxon face. "Now!" she howled.

Side by side, they sprang back up the hill, and for a brief moment Branwen had the chance to see how the uneven battle was going.

It did not go well. Rhodri was still with Ironfist, holding a sword at his neck. But he had been driven up against the wall of the Great Hall, and only four warrior women stood between him and the press of Saxons. Iwan had been forced to take a stand up on the rocks that blocked the doors of the hall. He was fighting stalwartly, and several more of the women were gathered there with him.

Branwen saw Aberfa there, swinging a Saxon ax in her powerful arms, sending the blood flying. Banon was with him also, leaping from rock to rock, thrusting down with a spear and then dancing away as her opponent fell back with blood welling from his wounds.

But their courage could never be enough. The daring warriors of Gwylan Canu now numbered ten—against hundreds. And all the while, still more Saxons were surging in through the open gates.

Branwen felt a pang of anguished pride as she saw Lord Madoc appear at the corner of the Great Hall, sword in hand, leading a group of women and old men, armed only with staves and rocks.

They would die. They would all die.

There was only one shred of hope for them—and Branwen knew it existed only if Ironfist was kept back from his men long enough for her to reach him. She knew what she had to do. She had no choice.

Dera had run ahead and was already springing up onto the stones to fight alongside Iwan and the others. Branwen hacked her way along the hill, coming up behind the Saxons who were fighting to rescue their general. She took them by surprise, cutting them down with blow after blow of her sword. She saw with a rush of sudden joy that one of the women holding them back, her gown soaked with blood from a wound in her shoulder, was Linette—alive and fighting still!

Branwen fought her way through the Saxons and came face to face with Ironfist. He glared defiantly at her, no sign now in his flinty eyes of the drunkenness that had earlier blurred his vision.

"Kill me now, girl-child," he hissed. "You'll not get another chance!"

She knew in her heart that he was right. But his death would not prevent the Saxons from swarming over Gwylan Canu and slaughtering all who stood in their way—man, woman, and child.

As she stared into those cold blue eyes, she thought of the warriors she had known in her short life. Bloodthirsty and cruel, many had been—but all of them had a code of honor—every one of them! Could such honor live in a Saxon warlord? Surely it could—surely even such a man as Herewulf Ironfist could be asked to take an oath so deep and strong that he would not dare to break it.

It was a weak hope—a fool's hope, perhaps. But if he accepted her as a leader of these people—as a true warrior ready to sacrifice herself for those who followed her—maybe then she could bring this horror to an end.

"How do I stop this?" Branwen shouted in his face, lifting her voice above the hideous din of the battle. "These people do not deserve to be massacred. If I tell them to stop fighting—if I give myself up to you, to do with me as you wish—will you then spare them?"

"Branwen—no!" gasped Rhodri.

Branwen ignored him. She watched impatiently as Ironfist regarded her warily, a slow grin coming to his lips as he seemed to run this new idea over his palate. "Well?" she demanded. "Do we have an agreement? My life for theirs? Will you give me your word on the name of your greatest gods to honor such a pact?"

"I will," Ironfist replied, his eyes gleaming with a savage light. "By Wotan's fiery spear, I swear it! Your life forfeited for theirs saved!"

"Agreed!" said Branwen. She avoided looking into Rhodri's appalled face as she pushed his sword away from Ironfist's neck. She stepped behind the Saxon general and slashed through the ropes that bound his wrists.

He turned, his eyes burning into her face. Wordlessly, she offered him her sword, letting her shield fall to the ground at her feet.

Ironfist took the sword from her.

"Keep your oath. Call off your armies," Branwen said, hearing her own voice through the dense white fog in her mind. "Bring this slaughter to an end." She felt a profound sense of calm and peace. A curious emptiness grew and grew inside her chest, as though her heart, her lungs, her very spirit were being absorbed and lost in an expanding void.

Ironfist's guttural laughter brought her tranquility to a sudden and brutal end.

"Foolish child," he hissed, lifting the sword and running its cold edge along her neck. She felt warm blood trickling. "Did you truly believe I would honor such a pact?" He laughed. "Know this, girl-child. You will die now at my hand, and before the sun has risen on this day of triumph, every man, woman, and child of Gwylan Canu will die with you."

Branwen looked into his eyes, furious with herself for having believed this Saxon might have shown some sense of honor. In truth, there was nothing in his eyes but lust and brutality and murder.

She had gambled her life and she had failed. There was nothing more to be done.

31

"NO!" RHODRI'S VOICE rang in her head, cutting through the white mists that blurred her brain.

She felt the sword jarred from her neck and heard Ironfist spit a curse as he turned savagely. She saw Rhodri's terrified, courageous face beyond the great general's shoulder. She saw Ironfist lift his sword arm and crash down his sword across Rhodri's weapon, breaking the blade and jolting the hilt out of her friend's fingers.

She saw Ironfist's other fist pound downward, striking Rhodri in the face, driving him to his knees.

All this happened in the space of a single breath—and still in a daze, she could do nothing. The other young women fighting close by had not even seen what was happening—they were too busy battling to save their own lives.

Branwen saw the sword arm lift again. Rhodri cringed from the deadly blow.

No! She could not let him be killed.

Gasping with the effort, she flung herself on Ironfist's back, one arm hooking around his throat, the other reaching to grip the wrist of his sword arm.

He spun, roaring in anger, and tried to dislodge her, fighting to free his arm. But the desperation that had jerked her out of her stupor had also given her new strength. Her arm tightened on his throat, and he began to choke and cough as he stumbled. Ironfist wasn't so easily bested, however. He dug in with his heels and threw himself backward, crushing her against the wall of the Great Hall. He surged forward then pushed back again, beating the breath out of her lungs. Two, three times he drove her into the wall, until the pain made her lose her grip on his wrist and she was no longer able to keep the pressure against his windpipe.

His hand groped over his shoulder for her face, fingers stretching to find her eyes and gouge them out. She jerked her head back, but he caught her hair and brought her head down so her face smashed into the chain mail that covered his shoulder. She tasted blood. His elbow came into her stomach, and he twisted as she fell to her knees, spitting red, her mind reeling.

The hand caught her hair again, yanking her head up. She knelt as he raised his sword.

Forgive me. Forgive me. I've led you all to your deaths.

A sudden sound shivered the air.

A howling, braying, whooping noise—skirling and swirling, rising above the sounds of battle.

Ironfist paused and turned, his face confounded by the strange noise coming from beyond the wall of Gwylan Canu. He stared off toward the distant mountains, glowing now, touched by the first light of the new day's sun.

And then the wind came.

It came down from the mountains, screaming like a thousand lost souls, shivering through the crags, bending tall trees as if they were mere meadow grass before its rushing breath. It came down from the high places of the Clwydian Range, with ice on its lips, driving all before it. It came rushing down through the ancient forests, ripping boughs from trunks, sending branches whirling, filling the air with leaves and twigs and flying debris.

The wind raced out over the bare rock and the long beaches, and it burst upon the Saxon hordes like a hammer, whipping their feet out from under them, tearing the swords and shields from their hands, tossing them through the air, piling them up against the outer wall of the citadel like stalks of wheat at the harvest.

As Branwen watched in silent awe, the wind fell upon the beached ships, ripping their sails to shreds, cracking their masts, splintering their timbers, throwing the terrified Saxons into the seething sea.

Roaring, it came surging over the wall of Gwylan Canu, dislodging stones, tearing the gates from their hinges, howling through hut and home and pen and paddock, ripping the thatch from the roofs, lifting wickerwork hurdles and throwing them like leaves across the sky in front of Branwen's stunned eyes. It blasted up the hill, rolling the Saxons before it, their heads cracking on stone, their swords and spears and axes skimming the ground, their cries drowned out in its wild halloo. Branwen's body tensed for the impact as the wind swept toward her.

Ironfist staggered back, holding his arm up to shield his face as the wind beat its way up to the very doors of the Great Hall.

Branwen felt its force hit her like an avalanche. It lifted her, plastering her helplessly against the wall of the hall, holding her there, her clothes glued to her body, her hair pulled back hard on her scalp, her skin lashed and pricked and scourged. It bellowed in her ears, its ear-splitting pandemonium heaping and piling in her head until she had to open her mouth in a soundless scream from the pain and the fury of it.

And then a sudden, stunning silence fell—the wind was gone, and the noise and the mayhem with it. Branwen could breathe again. She alone was still standing. She saw Rhodri close by, rising unsteadily to his feet. Iwan and the fighting women were picking themselves up around her, their faces stupefied, their eyes uncomprehending.

Ironfist was sprawled against the wall of the Great Hall, panting for breath, the sword gone from his hand—blown away by the wind.

Then, as though the wind had been no more than a prelude, there came a new sound and a new wonder. From her vantage point on the hill, Branwen could see shapes—strange shapes, dark and sinister—moving down from the southern foothills with a rolling gait.

Branwen gasped as the great forms came swarming down the beach—they were *trees*! Enormous trees, walking on gnarled and angular roots, their heavy leaf-laden heads tossing from side to side as they jerked and lurched toward the sea.

And running among the spindly and crooked roots she saw wolves and stags, bears and wild boar, howling and bellowing and roaring and snorting as they came surging through the sand. It seemed to Branwen that all the beasts of the mountains had been summoned to drive the Saxon army back into the sea.

Some Saxon warriors tried to stand against the ravaging animals, but they were brought down by teeth and claws and stamping hooves, overrun by tusks and stabbing antlers and chomping jaws. Other soldiers simply fled in terror, floundering helplessly in the surf, trying vainly to get back to their ships.

But the wind had smashed the beached ships to shards, and those still on the open sea were being tossed like eggshells on the surge of the waves.

Then a different sound caught Branwen's attention—the crack and crumble of tumbling stonework. She stared beyond the wind-ravaged huts of Gwylan Canu and saw that the wall of the citadel was falling inward, thrust down by the living trees. The gatehouse crashed in ruin as the unwieldy creatures climbed and clambered awkwardly among the fallen stones. Animals came leaping and bounding and crawling and running among them, falling on the warriors of Ironfist's army as they scattered in horror.

Flying like a dark cloud above the moving trees, Branwen saw flocks of birds—crows and eagles and hawks and falcons, buzzards and goshawks and harriers and kites—sweeping down on the Saxons, claws stretching, beaks open, eyes bright with a predatory light. All were led by a great, wide-winged eagle owl along with another bird—a bird she knew well.

"Fain!" she shouted, although she knew he would not be able to hear her voice in all the tumult. *"Fain!"*

"And Blodwedd," said Rhodri's awed voice at her side. "Surely that owl is Blodwedd!"

"Yes—perhaps it is," Branwen gasped. "Rhodri—oh, *look*—Rhodri!" Her voice trembled. *"Look!* He has come!"

A new form came striding through the wreckage of the gatehouse—a tall, brown-skinned figure, as tall as the trees. He was manlike but in no way human, clad in a simple green tunic that hung down to his massive thighs, the mossy cloth stretched taut over a great, deep chest. The muscles of his bare arms and legs were huge and knotted, the skin lined with coiling, greenish veins. Solemn eyes flashed like emeralds from beneath bushy brows, and his wide mouth was open to show rows of pointed teeth. Tawny hair tumbled over the towering head, and from the temples there grew massive, branching antlers.

"Govannon of the Wood," breathed Rhodri, taking Branwen's hand. "The Shining Ones have come to our aid."

Branwen saw pure terror now on the faces of the Saxon warriors as they turned from the huge manlike form and ran, tripping over one another, hastening to make their escape.

Branwen gripped Rhodri's hand tightly. "I see it," she murmured, her eyes riveted on Govannon as he strode among the animals like a king.

She heard the clash of weapons close by and tore her eyes away from Govannon of the Wood. She saw that Iwan and the warrior women were still fighting those few Saxons who had survived the windstorm. But this fight did not last long—even those Saxons who had clung onto their weapons had seen the moving trees and the armies of beasts and birds that were

310

falling upon their comrades. For most of them the only thought in their minds was to seek a means of escape, and the final few began to drop their weapons and flee.

"Ironfist!" Branwen hissed, suddenly recalling herself. The Saxon general was gone. He must have realized that his cause was lost and stolen silently away while all eyes were on the marvels that followed the unearthly wind.

She ran to the corner of the Great Hall.

There! She saw him.

A solitary figure, darting among the rocks, ran toward the rear of the headland, a borrowed shield on his arm and a scavenged spear in his hand. Perhaps he hoped to hide there, among the tumble of raw rocks—to hide from the wrath of Govannon until all was done and he had the opportunity to slip away unnoticed.

Branwen had other plans. She would not let him escape so easily. She snatched up a sword and shield.

"Branwen—no!" It was Rhodri's voice. He was at her shoulder. "Let him go!"

"I can't," Branwen hissed. "He has to pay for what he has done!" She stared into his eyes for a moment. "Stay back, Rhodri—you can't help me with this."

So saying, she sprang away after Ironfist, her long legs quickly eating up the distance between them.

"Coward!" she shouted. "Come back and fight me!"

He was at the farthest point of the headland now, standing on the last ridge of wind-blown rock. A single step farther and he would plunge into the pounding sea.

He turned, grinning.

"Would you have single combat with me, child?" he called. "Do you long for death? Do you ache for it?"

Branwen came to a halt, eyeing him carefully. She walked slowly up the slope toward him, her shield up, her sword angled across her back—as Gavan had shown her—her muscles tensed and ready to uncoil.

"Deadain, andgietleas cild!" shouted Ironfist, leaping down at her and thrusting the long spear.

She brought her sword sweeping over her shoulder, aiming for his neck. But he fended it off with his shield and, as he leaped by her, stabbed his spear at her side. She snatched her shield back to cover herself, dancing away from him as he ran past her.

She turned as he came for her again, thrusting the spear at her belly, his eyes burning and his teeth bared. Branwen brought her shield down hard on the shaft of his spear, hoping to break it, but he pulled back and she stumbled forward, only just avoiding the spear point.

She dived headlong, curling up and rolling across the uneven ground as he stabbed at her, missing and missing again. Then she bounced to her feet and brought her sword sweeping in under his shield, hoping to take his legs out from under him.

But Ironfist was too wily a fighter. With a cry, he leaped over her scything blade and came down heavily, his shield pounding on hers, his weight forcing her almost to her knees. She ducked this way and that to avoid his jabs and thrusts.

Her limbs were weary and her muscles ached, but there was no possibility of rest or respite until this fight was over. She surged upward, using all the power of her legs and back to push him off, so that she could bound away and get beyond the reach of his spear, however briefly.

She glanced behind herself—she was on the very edge of a dark cliff that dropped straight down into the hungry sea foam. If she could enrage him so that he threw his spear—and if she could react quickly enough when he did so—then perhaps she could leave him weaponless.

"Do you know me now, Herewulf Ironfist?" she howled, spreading her feet and brandishing her sword. "I am the Savior of Brython! Drop your weapon and kneel to me, Saxon dog—and perhaps I will spare your life!" But Ironfist was not to be taken so easily. Grinning wolfishly, he moved up toward her, his spear reaching out, the point darting from side to side as he sought to find a way past her shield.

But she had planned for this also. She leaped sideways, allowing his spear point to break through the space around her, and then brought her arm down hard into her side, trapping the shaft before Ironfist could withdraw it. Springing down on him, she aimed a deadly blow at his head—but his shield came up under her blade and swept it aside.

Betrayed by her own momentum, she plunged past him. He turned and struck her on the back of her head with his shield. The pain flared in her skull and down her neck as she stumbled forward. But she caught her balance again and turned, angling her shield downward so that his next thrust at her sent his spear point stabbing into the ground.

With a scream of agony and rage, she lifted her foot and brought it down hard on the shaft of his spear. It snapped, but he was hurtling toward her already, his shield up, all his weight behind the charge.

He struck her and took her clean off her feet. She felt dizzy and sick; pain throbbed through her head and jaw as she crashed onto her back. But she'd had wits enough left to keep her own shield up, even as he loomed over her, his face twisting into a malevolent grin as he pounded his shield down on her again and again. Her arm became numb and her whole body shrieked in pain. Her sword arm dropped, and both her weight and his bore down on her bent elbow as she tried to rise.

He stamped down on her wrist, forcing her fingers to fly open, and then kicked her sword away. Agony flared through her wrist as he brought his shield hammering down on it. He was laughing now—sure of her death.

She gasped as lightning flared behind her eyes; the pain was crowding her senses. Using her last shred of strength, she pushed him up just enough to roll away and crawl through the rubble, seeking only to escape the pain and the thunder in her head.

She tottered to her feet, swaying, her eyes half closed.

She saw him snatch up her sword.

She braced herself, her shield up to her eyes, the upper rim angled outward to block the sword and perhaps, if chance allowed, to punch up into his throat.

He came for her, swinging the sword like a scythe.

In the fleeting moment before he would have fallen upon her, a gray shape soared out of the sky, shrieking and clawing, its wings beating and its hooked beak stretched wide open to rip flesh to the bone.

Straight into Ironfist's face the falcon flew, furious and savage, wings flurrying, claws raking. Dizzy with pain, Branwen saw blood spurt and heard Ironfist give a howl of agony as Fain tore at his eyes.

Staggering backward, Ironfist dropped his sword as he brought both hands up to try and protect his face—but his feet stumbled on the rocks, and he lost his balance. For a long moment he hung by his heels on the very edge of the black cliff. Then, with a wavering cry, Ironfist lost his footing and plunged downward.

Branwen staggered to the cliff's edge. Fain was descending in slow circles—but the restless foaming waves had already swallowed up the great general. Branwen stooped forward, her hands on her knees, panting as she looked down at the seething waves far below.

Fain turned and came soaring up. He gave a single cry as he passed her.

She turned, watching as he flew back over the Great Hall.

She stood there for a few moments, gathering her breath, waiting until the pain in her head lessened to a dull throbbing. Then, slowly and painfully, she picked her way back over the rocks.

Branwen and Rhodri stood side by side on the hill of the Great Hall, overlooking the scene of carnage below. Dera ap Dagonet stepped in front of Branwen, her face pale with wonder, her eyes haunted. "What are these things that come to our aid, Branwen—are they known to you?"

"Did I not tell you I had powerful allies?" Branwen replied. "They have been guiding my footsteps, Dera, and it is their path that I walk." She shook her head. "But I had not dared hope for *this*!"

"And can they be controlled?" murmured Dera, staring down the hill to where the forces of Govannon swarmed among the buildings, seeking out and pulling down those few Saxons that remained alive. "I am glad of their help—but I fear them, also."

"I don't think they will harm us," Branwen said. But she shuddered as she watched the animals of Govannon at their dreadful work. It was brutal, that final hunt—and none were spared. Even those Saxon warriors who cast down their weapons and threw up their arms in surrender were killed.

Govannon was standing just inside what remained of the gatehouse, and as the last Saxons were hunted down and destroyed, the animals turned and went back to him, surrounding him, their heads turned toward him as though awaiting some word of command. The trees, too, came to a halt, seeming to know that their task was done. As Branwen watched, their roots dug down into the ground, and they seemed to settle and become still, so that the whole area between the citadel's huddled village and the ruined wall was dotted now with full-grown trees.

The sky cleared of birds as well—save for a solitary slate-gray shape that climbed in the air, heading for the spot where Branwen stood.

She held up her arm and Fain came to rest heavily on her wrist.

"Caw! Caw! Caw!"

Branwen smiled. "My life is yours, Fain, my dearest companion," she said. "What would you have me do, now? I cannot understand your speech."

The falcon turned its head, staring down the hill to where Govannon stood amid a quiet flood of animals.

"Caw!"

She looked and saw that Govannon was gazing up at her.

"I must go to him," she murmured. But even as she spoke, her heart faltered. It felt as though her legs might give way under her at any moment.

"I'll come with you," said Rhodri, his voice trembling. His hand reached for hers and their fingers twined together.

"And I," said Dera. "I would see this marvel up close, though it may be my death!"

Branwen nodded, grateful for their offer.

The thought of approaching the Shining One alone had filled her with unease, but with these two companions at her side, she believed she could muster the courage to stand before Govannon and look up into those daunting green eyes.

Fain spread his wings and went swooping away down the hill.

Her heart crashing in her chest, Branwen followed.

32

THE CONGREGATION OF animals parted to allow Branwen and Rhodri and Dera to pass through. Branwen saw fresh blood on fangs and claws and tusks and antlers as she made her way toward the center of the gathering—to where Govannon of the Wood stood waiting for her.

He was twice her height, a giant creature radiating such power and authority that it was all Branwen could do to gaze up into his noble face. His immense arms reached down so his broad hands were stroking the backs and heads and shoulders of the animals that crowded around him. Branwen saw in the eyes of every beast there a flickering green light that was only a pale reflection of the blazing emerald radiance that filled Govannon's own eyes.

The three young warriors came to a halt a few

paces away from him.

As Govannon looked down at them, Branwen could discern no expression on his face—no more expression than might be found on a tree or a bear or a cloud. But in his profound eyes there were things—lordliness and ancient knowledge and an aching sadness—that wounded her heart.

"So, Warrior-Child," he said, and his voice was deep and sonorous. "We meet on the battlefield. Is this victory honey to your tongue?"

Branwen's mouth was dry, her throat constricted. "No, it is not," she said, trembling slightly. "It is not, and I would have done anything to have prevented this slaughter. The death of Saxons gives me no pleasure, my lord. I did only what I had to do."

"That is good, Warrior-Child," rumbled Govannon's voice. "Dark is the heart that delights in killing. But it was not of your doing that the enemy came into Brython—and without you, great harm would have been done this day."

Branwen narrowed her eyes. "Without me?" she said. "I didn't win this battle, my lord—the victory is yours. Had you not come, I and all who followed me would be dead now."

There was a pause, and Govannon's eyes were thoughtful as he stared down at her. "Do you not know why I was able to come, Warrior-Child?" he said at last. "Do you not know the sacrifice that was made?"

She looked up into his eyes, confused now. "I don't, my lord," she said.

"Do you think that I have the authority to breathe sentience into my trees as I will it?" Govannon asked. "Do you think I have such dominion that I can light wendfire in the eyes of my birds and my beasts without consequence? No, Warrior-Child, I am but a guardian, the steward of the forests. Greater potencies than I must be appeased. A sacrifice must be offered."

"What sacrifice was offered?" asked Dera. "Who gave their life so that you could come to our aid?"

The huge green eyes turned to her. "Death is not the ultimate sacrifice, child," Govannon said gravely. "To live sundered from your true self—to live a half-life of loss and willing surrender—that is *true* sacrifice." His head turned, and the spreading antlers that branched up from his forehead seemed to scrape the sky. "Come forth, my daughter. Take the first step on this new path that you have chosen—and that you must endure now till the end of your days."

From somewhere at Govannon's back, from in among the animals, a small, slender figure emerged and stood in front of them, her head bowed, her eyes hooded.

"Blodwedd!" breathed Rhodri, letting go of Branwen's hand and taking a step forward. "But . . . I saw you . . . ," he stammered. "It *was* you, surely? Leading the birds?"

She lifted her head, and her somber eyes gazed

into his. "Yes, it was me you saw," she murmured. "My lord gifted me one last moment of flight—one final chance to feel the wind beneath my wings—before I renounced myself forever." She looked at Branwen. "I learned much from you, Branwen, in the time we spent together. I learned of duty and loyalty, and I learned of the burden of responsibility and the weight of grief."

"I don't understand," said Branwen. "When the quest was completed, you were to be given back your true form. You were to become an owl again."

"That is so," said Blodwedd. "But I saw the same vision that was given to you—I saw ships filled with warriors sailing to the place of singing gulls. I knew you would not be able to stand against such numbers. I knew you would be lost, so I went to my lord and I begged him to come to your aid. And I offered myself in your place—offered my life. It was forfeit anyway—I fled your side in fear, Branwen. I failed in my duty to you. I would willingly have taken death as my punishment."

"Death is not the ultimate sacrifice . . . ," Rhodri murmured, as though understanding now what Govannon had meant. He looked at Branwen. "She gave herself up to save us. She will be human now for the rest of her life."

"No," Branwen said in dismay. "It's worse than that—she will be an owl trapped forever in a human form." She looked up at Govannon. "Can this be

322

undone?" she asked. "Can I do anything to change her fate?"

"The bargain has been made," Govannon replied sadly. "It cannot be unmade."

"I did this of my own free will, Branwen," said Blodwedd. "Do not weep for me. I am reconciled to my exile. I will roam the forests and know that my loss had purpose. It will be enough."

Filled with pity and gratitude, Branwen reached out her hands to the forlorn owl-girl. "I would rather you stay with us," she said. "Will you do that?"

Blodwedd slid her slim fingers into Branwen's, her eyes glowing. "Gladly," she said softly. "Gladly."

"But what new purpose do you have?" asked Dera. "For I see that yours is no easy destiny, Branwen ap Griffith, and that great deeds await you."

"I must go to Pengwern—to the court of King Cynon," Branwen replied. "He must be told of Prince Llew's treachery. An army must be gathered, one strong enough to lay siege to Doeth Palas and bring Llew ap Gelert down."

"No, Warrior-Child, that is not your path," said Govannon. "Let others go to the king." He turned, pointing up to the mountains. "Thither wends your path, Warrior-Child, up into the cold peaks, into the high places of the land. You must seek Merion of the Stones." He turned to look down at Branwen again, his eyes smoldering. "My part in the great tale is done for now, Warrior-Child," he said. "My sister shall show you the next task that awaits." He raised a hand. "Farewell, Emerald Flame of Brython. I leave you now."

"But how am I to find Merion of the Stones?" Branwen asked.

"Fain will be your guide," replied Govannon.

So saying, the great lord of the forests turned and strode away. As he went, the animals followed after him. The birds that had rested on stone and thatch and on the ground all around him rose into the air and flew southward, back into the forested foothills of the Clwydian Mountains. Only the trees remained, their roots sunk deep into the ground, their leaves stirring in the gentle sea breeze.

Branwen stood high among the ruins of the gatehouse of Gwylan Canu and watched the last few animals melt away into the forested hills. As they went, it was as though she was waking from a feverish dream. But she knew this could be no dream—her head still throbbed with pain, and her hands and arms and face were sticky with the blood of Saxons.

She was about to turn and climb down again when she heard the distant rhythm of galloping horses coming along the winding road from the west. Puzzled, she stared along the coast. At that moment five horses came speeding around a bend, saddled and bridled, but with no riders and with their reins flying.

Branwen jumped down and ran to the road. She recognized the leading horse.

"Stalwyn!" she cried, throwing her arms up.

Stalwyn came to a clattering halt in front of her. He rose up, neighing loudly and beating the air with his hooves.

Iwan came running to her side as the other four horses all came to a stamping, whinnying halt on the road.

"What does this mean?" Iwan gasped, staring at the horses. "These are steeds of Doeth Palas—why have they come riderless to this place?"

Branwen laughed as she caught Stalwyn's reins and pressed her face into his sweating neck, breathing him in.

"He was my horse. He came back to me," she said gleefully. "Don't you see? He must have thrown his rider and bolted! He knew I needed him!" She thumped the great stallion's flanks. "Good boy—great friend!" she said. "And you brought companions!"

Stalwyn snorted and seemed to nod his head; his eyes were bright and knowing.

"Why so many?" Branwen mused. "I have need of but two."

"Three, at least," said Iwan. He gave a sweet, tuneful whistle between his teeth, and one of the other horses—a dun mare with a creamy coat and a mane, tail, and muzzle of black—came trotting obediently forward to nuzzle his shoulder. "Welcome back, my beauty," he said, stroking the mare's nose. "This is Gwennol Dhu. She also must have known I would have need of her." He smiled at Branwen. "She has a wise head on her and is surefooted among the mountains."

"But your journey lies south, along the road to Pengwern," Branwen said, confused. "There are no mountains in your way."

Iwan gave her a crooked smile and for a moment she was reminded starkly of the teasing lad from the Great Hall of Doeth Palas. "Oh, but I am not going to the king," he said. "My father can undertake that errand. There are brave men of Gwylan Canu—elderly but hale—who can accompany him. No, I have decided on an altogether more amusing journey." He cocked his head and his eyes sparkled. "I'm going with you, barbarian princess. Don't you remember what I said to you when you bound me and escaped with the half Saxon?"

She gazed at him, remembering it very well. "You said you thought I would have an interesting life," she said quietly. "You said you wished you could have shared it with me."

"And now I shall." He lowered his head and gave her a sideways look. "If you will have me as a companion." He turned his head and glanced over to where Rhodri and Blodwedd were standing. Rhodri seemed to be watching them carefully. "The half Saxon is a good fellow, I am sure, but he has spent most of his life as a captive servant, Branwen. He has no learning, no culture. On this strange journey of yours, I think you could do with a man of wit and intelligence—and thus I offer my services."

The bantering tone left his voice, and his eyes fixed on hers. "I want to be with you, Branwen, at your side—no matter what. Will you let me ride with you?"

Before Branwen could answer, she heard the patter of running feet.

Dera came up to her, a determined light in her eyes. "I have spoken with the women of Gwylan Canu," she said briskly. "I have told them I wish to journey with you, wherever you may go. I wish to share your adventures and your destiny, Branwen. And Linette and Aberfa and Banon wish it also." Branwen opened her mouth to speak, but Dera gave her no time. "You will meet with many perils and dangers on your path, Branwen—we can help you. We fight well. We are unafraid. You alone cannot sweep Brython clean of Saxons. A princess needs followers—let us be the first of your warrior band!"

Branwen let out an astonished breath. She did not know what to say. But the words spoken to her by Rhiannon of the Spring came into her mind.

All of Brython will be your home, and you will gather to you a band of warriors who shall keep the enemy at bay for many long years.

"It seems that Stalwyn was wise to bring companions," said Iwan with a wry smile. "Even if we ride double, five horses will be only just enough."

Rhodri strode up. "Are we departing soon, Branwen?" he asked. "Blodwedd says we should not leave it too long before we take the path to Merion of the Stones. She fears that any delay may be costly."

Branwen turned to him, a smile widening on her face. "We are leaving very soon, my friend," she said. "But not we three alone."

Rhodri gave her a confused look, but before she could explain, a single shrill, compelling cry exploded from the air.

"*Caw!*"

She looked up to see Fain hanging in the sky, borne up by the sea wind, his wings spread wide, his black eye on her.

He, too, was eager to be going.

Branwen turned, gazing up into the mountains, and as she stood staring out at those distant peaks, in her head rang the words of the old song. The song of the Shining Ones. The song of the Old Gods.

> *I sing of Rhiannon of the Spring*
> *The ageless water goddess, earth mother,*
>   *storm-calmer*
> *Of Govannon of the Wood*
> *He of the twelve points*
> *Stag-man of the deep forest, wise and*
>   *deadly*
> *Of Merion of the Stones*
> *Mountain crone, cave dweller, oracle, and*
>   *deceiver*

And of Caradoc of the North Wind
Wild and free and dangerous and full of
    treachery

It was time to take the path to Merion of the Stones. It was time for the Shining Ones to reveal to her the next stage on the long road to her destiny.

The Bright Blade! The Emerald Flame of her people! The Savior of Brython!

She was Branwen ap Griffith—the Warrior Princess.

Branwen's adventure continues in

The Emerald Flame

— WARRIOR PRINCESS BOOK THREE —

1

A PROFOUND DARKNESS had fallen among the close-packed oaks, and it felt to Branwen ap Griffith as though she and her small band of riders were wading through a flood tide of shadows, thick as black water.

They were climbing the forested flanks of a great hunchbacked mountain in the deep dark of a starless night. Heavy clouds blotted out the sky. The going was hard as the five horses picked their way slowly through the rising trees.

Branwen leaned forward, her thoughts racing; a fire burned so brightly in her mind that she felt she would never need sleep again. Between the new moon and the old, her life had changed beyond all recognition.

My brother killed—my dear, gallant Geraint— slaughtered by Saxon raiders. And before the ashes of his funeral pyre were cold, I was sent from my home to escape from danger. And all the while I was thinking I might never see my parents again. Over the mountains they sent me, to the safety of the cantref of Prince Llew ap Gelert. Safety? Ha! A poor refuge that turned out to be. And what was to happen to me after that? A long journey south to marry that loathsome boy Hywel, although I met him only once, almost ten years ago. Well, at least my destiny spared me that ending.

It would have been a miserable fate for a girl who had spent her first fifteen years riding the hills of her homeland, free as an eagle, untamed as the landscape that she loved.

But Branwen never went south. Rhiannon of the Spring saw to that. One of the Old Gods—the Shining Ones—Rhiannon told Branwen of the path that lay ahead.

"You are Destiny's Sword. The Bright Blade! The Emerald Flame of your people!"

Branwen sighed now to think of the way she had fought against that destiny. It was only when Rhiannon had warned her that Garth Milain, her beloved home, was in danger that Branwen had acted.

Although I rode hard and arrived in the garth in time to warn my mother and father, I was still too late to save them from all harm. The Saxons were thrown back, but Father died in the battle. And if that wasn't hard enough to bear, I had to leave my home and my mother that same night to follow this pitiless destiny again.

Rhiannon's words rang in her ears.

"All of Brython will be your home, and you will gather to you a band of warriors who shall keep the enemy at bay for many long years."

And what a strange group of wanderers they were!

Riding directly behind her was the shrewd and crafty-tongued Iwan ap Madoc. She had first encountered Iwan at the court of Prince Llew. He had annoyed her and fascinated her in equal amounts in that first meeting—and he still did.

Ahead of her, only half visible in the darkness, Branwen could make out the shapes of Blodwedd and Rhodri, riding tandem on one horse. Even if there were enough horses to go around, Branwen suspected Blodwedd would wish to ride with Rhodri.

She shook her head. Theirs was a strange affinity— the half-Saxon runaway and the half-human owl-girl. *Half* human? Blodwedd was nothing more than an owl wrapped in a human shape . . . save for her eyes. They were huge and golden and had no whites whatsoever. No one looking into those eerie eyes would have any doubts that Blodwedd was not human.

Govannon of the Wood, another Shining One, had sent Blodwedd. Govannon, the huge man-god of ancient times, with his sad green eyes and the twelve-point antlers that soared majestically from his temples.

Branwen had detested and mistrusted the owl-girl

at the start, but Blodwedd had proven herself faithful and true.

Iwan's voice made her turn.

"Are you managing to keep awake, Branwen?" he asked. "I'm told a spur of hawthorn in the britches is a fine way to stay alert on a long ride."

She looked back at him sitting upright in the saddle, his light-brown hair falling over his lean, compelling face. His eyes met hers and he gave her a crooked smile.

"I'll be fine, thank you," she said. "This is not such a night that I will have trouble with drowsing."

"No." His eyes were bright and wakeful. "I imagine not."

She gazed back beyond him to where the rest of her band rode, two to a horse. They were four young woman of Gwylan Canu—fiery Dera riding with lithe little Linette, and flame-haired Banon riding with heavyset Aberfa, who had dark, brooding eyes.

In the dying embers of the day just passed, this wayfaring band had won a great victory. The Saxon warlord Herewulf Ironfist had sought to conquer the seagirt citadel of Gwylan Canu, guardian outpost of the coastal road that led into the very heartland of Powys.

But speed and stealth had not been the only weapons in Ironfist's arsenal. He had deep and dreadful treachery to help him. Prince Llew ap Gelert—the richest and most powerful of the nobles of Powys,

4

second only to King Cynon himself—had turned traitor!

Branwen still did not know the reason for this terrible betrayal. It was almost beyond belief that a lord of Powys would side with the ancient enemies of Brython. For two hundred years the people of Brython had battled wave after wave of Saxon incursions, and they had always thrown the butchering invaders back. Why, then, did Prince Llew go against his homeland? As a result, never had Powys been closer to defeat than in the battle they had just fought. If not for supernatural aid this night, all would have been lost.

Govannon himself had joined in the battle, beating down upon the Saxons with an army of birds and beasts, even awakening the trees of the forests to help sweep them into the sea.

And upon a rocky promontory, Branwen had done her part—fighting furiously with Ironfist himself. Almost bested by him, she had been saved at the last moment by the beak and claws of her faithful companion Fain the falcon, who had flown into Ironfist's face and sent him plunging over the cliff and into the raging sea.

Then had come the momentous meeting with Govannon. He had towered above her, wild and dangerous and yet strangely benevolent, and told her what she needed to do next—what new effort her great destiny required of her. He had pointed the way up the mountains. *"Thither wends your path,*

*Warrior-Child, up into the cold peaks, into the high places
of the land. You must seek Merion of the Stones."*

Faithful, kindhearted Rhodri had insisted on
coming with her, of course. And Blodwedd, too. But
it had been Iwan's insistence on journeying alongside
her that had filled Branwen with a heady mix of joy
and confusion.

*"Don't you remember what I said to you when you bound
me and escaped with the half Saxon?"* he had asked, his
eyes shining.

*"You said you thought I would have an interesting life.
You said you wished you could have shared it with me."*

"And now I shall. If you will have me as a companion."

She had no control over her destiny. It was harsh
and relentless, and people had died on the way.

*But these people shan't die. I won't let that happen. I am
Branwen ap Griffith. The Emerald Flame of my People. I
will keep them safe from harm.*

But the responsibility weighed heavily on her.
What perils was she leading them into on these high
mountains?

She knew virtually nothing of Merion of the
Stones. In a mystic glade that had been shown to
her in a vision, she had seen a devotee dressed as
Merion—bent-backed, stumbling, clutching a stick,
masked as an ugly, wrinkled old woman.

But Branwen had learned not to trust appear-
ances. The forms that the Shining Ones took when
they interacted with humans were not their true
ones. What would Merion want of her? So far the

requirements of the Old Gods had all been for the good of Brython. Surely the most vital task now was to unmask the traitor Prince Llew ap Gelert, and to bring him down before he could do any more harm.

To that end, riders had already been sent from Gwylan Canu, racing pell-mell down the long road to Pengwern—to the court of King Cynon—with urgent warnings from Iwan's trustworthy father.

Hopefully, that would be enough to thwart Prince Llew's grim ambitions. But even with Llew's duplicity laid bare, there was still a great Saxon army on the border of Powys, poised to strike at Branwen's homeland.

And here Branwen was—a thousand lifetimes away from the world she had once known—treading again the veiled path of her destiny . . . riding through the impenetrable night with seven souls in her care.

"Ware!" It was Blodwedd's scratchy voice, its low pitch at odds with her small, slender body. An owl's voice in a human throat.

Branwen snapped out of her thoughts, alert in an instant. "What is it?"

Blodwedd had by far the keenest eyesight of them all. That was why she had taken the lead through the forest once the night had grown too dark even for Fain's sharp eyes. The falcon was at rest now, perched upon Branwen's shoulder, his claws gripping her chain-mail shirt.

"I am not sure," called Blodwedd.

Branwen urged Stalwyn on with a touch of her heels to his flanks. She came up alongside Rhodri and Blodwedd. The owl-girl's golden eyes shone in her pale, round face.

"I smell something not of the forest," Blodwedd said, arching her back, lifting her head to sniff, her long thin hands resting on Rhodri's broad shoulders, the nails white and curved.

Branwen heard a metallic slither. Dera ap Dagonet, daughter of a captain of Gwylan Canu, had drawn her sword.

"No beast shall come on us unawares," she growled, peering into the fathomless dark that lurked under the trees.

"It is no beast," said Blodwedd. "It is worse than beast."

Her head snapped around toward a noise beyond Branwen's hearing and she let out a feral hiss.

Branwen drew her own sword. There were shapes in the forest. Large, fast-moving shapes, blacker than the night.

Moments later, with a rush and a rumble of hooves, a band of armed men came bursting into view, their swords glowing a dull gray, iron helmets on their heads, and their faces hidden behind iron war-masks.

2

THE ATTACKERS CAME crashing into Branwen's band, horses neighing and kicking, shields raised, swords slashing. In the forest gloom and in the utter chaos of the assault, Branwen could not make out how many horsemen had fallen upon them. *Five at least*, she thought, *maybe more*.

She saw a blade slice down torward Iwan. He managed to draw his own sword and deflect the full blow—but the flat of the blade still struck Iwan savagely on the side of the head. The last Branwen saw of him was as he tumbled from the saddle.

A scream of alarm came involuntarily from her throat. "Iwan! No!"

She was given no more time to fear for him. The largest of the attacking horsemen came for her, his face hidden behind a ferocious war-mask, his sword raised high.

The attacker's horse butted up against hers, forcing it to stumble sideways so that she struggled to keep in the saddle. Fain rose from her shoulder, wings spreading, screeching raucously. Fighting for balance, Branwen managed to bring her shield up high, the top edge angled outward to fend off her attacker's blow.

His sword struck her shield like a thunderbolt, and had she not been holding it at an angle, the hungry iron would have split it in two. As it was, the force of the blow numbed her arm and shoulder and sent her rocking back in the saddle.

She had never fought on horseback before. She was used to feeling solid ground under her feet to be able to maneuver—step forward, step back, circle the enemy, come at him from the side. She felt awkward and vulnerable in the saddle—and like an easy target in the darkness of the forest.

The man's sword arm rose again, this time swinging in a low arc, clearly intending to slip the blade in under the curve of her shield and strike at her belly. The natural defensive move would be to smash down on the encroaching blade with her shield, driving its tempered edge into Stalwyn's neck.

No!

Instead, she threw herself forward, lunging half out of the saddle, beating her shield hard into the attacker's chest, her own sword jabbing for his neck. She felt the hilt of his sword strike against her side, hurting her, taking the breath out of her—but her sudden move forward had caused his blade to sweep past her, gouging the empty air where she *had* been only a moment before.

She followed up, using her shield as a ram, pressing in on him with all her weight. She felt him slip sideways from his horse as she pushed him. But even as he was falling, his sword arm hooked around her waist and she was dragged down with him.

For a few moments she was too winded, dizzy, and hurt by the heavy fall to do anything other than gasp and flounder in the forest bracken, menaced on every side by the pounding hooves of the frightened horses, dimly able to hear the shouts of the battle around her. Then she realized she was on top of her attacker, lying across his chest. One good thrust of her sword and it would be over. But she was not given the chance. He heaved up under her, throwing her off in a tangle of arms and legs. Branwen only just had the presence of mind to keep hold of her sword and shield as she came smashing to the ground, tasting earth and blood in her open mouth. The horses backed away, neighing and whinnying.

She turned onto her back, her thoughts scattered. The gloom of the night-shrouded forest swam in front of her eyes and it seemed that the earth beneath her rocked and pitched like a tormented sea. Then a deeper darkness loomed over her—a black pillar topped by a grimacing metal face.

A sword came scything down. She twisted away and the blade bit deep into the forest floor. She kicked out, catching her attacker's knee, making him roar with pain and stagger backward. A moment later, Fain was in his face, pecking and clawing, his gray wings whirring.

But the iron mask protected the man from the falcon's attack, and soon it was Fain who had to withdraw, speeding upward and away from the man's whirling blade.

Ignoring the pain that jangled in every part of her body, Branwen sprang up, moving in on the man cautiously, balancing on the balls of her feet, her shield up to her eyes, her sword arm bent back, ready to unleash a killing blow.

There was no time to take in the mayhem that was erupting around her in the deep shadows, no time to organize and encourage her embattled followers. But she quickly scanned the scene around her, catching a momentary glimpse of the fighting taking place among the trees.

So far as Branwen could tell, there were four other men involved in the confused skirmish. One was large and broad-shouldered. Banon and Aberfa were on foot, attacking him on horseback while he rained ringing blows down on their shields. Rhodri and Blodwedd were also unhorsed—Rhodri lying on the ground with Blodwedd standing over him and holding off another mounted swordsman with a length of broken branch. A little farther off, the fighting between Dera and Linette and the third man was partly obscured by trees and branches, and Branwen could not see who was getting the upper hand.

There was something odd about the last horseman—he was small and slight. Even in the gloom that much was obvious. No more than a boy! And he was holding back from the fighting. His helmet had been knocked off and he looked terrified as he tried to control his bucking and rearing steed. And he was unarmed.

Why would a band of warriors bring a weaponless child with them?

Who were these horsemen? Where did they come from?